THE RED SHOE
ADVENTURE CLUB

J.D. Delzer

Alban Lake Publishing

The Red Shoe Adventure Club
J.D. Delzer

Story copyrights owned by J.D. Delzer
Cover art by Alexandra Mihai

First Printing
December 2019

Alban Lake Publishing
P.O. Box 141
Colo, Iowa 50056-0141 USA
e-mail: albanlake@yahoo.com

Visit www.albanlakepublishing.com for online science fiction, fantasy, horror, scifaiku, and more. Stop by our online book-store at www.irbstore.co for novels, mag-azines, anthologies, and collections. Support the small, independent press and your First Amendment rights.

Introduction

Rachel Arlen is not based on a real person, and in my research, I have yet to find a situation where a student or teenager went missing in Friday Harbor. Despite that, I understand the importance of missing persons throughout the country, and the seriousness of such incidents. As I wrote this novel, a boy from St. Joseph, Minnesota named Jacob Wetterling was finally found, over 27 years after he went missing on October 22nd, 1989. Only after many years of worry and many months of porch lights being left on to help him find his way home did the guilty finally reveal Jacob's true story. As Jacob went missing when I was young, the story of his abduction was something children of my age had to think about all the time, even when playing hockey in the street, walking home from school, or while canvassing the neighborhood when dressed for Halloween or while involved with other childhood games. Tragically, Jacob's body was found buried in a cornfield, about thirty miles from where he was last seen, and his life ended the very day he vanished. Just like the number 11 jersey he had worn on the soccer field, Jacob was only eleven years old.

As this story was submitted for publication, another young person named Jayme Closs went missing after her parents were murdered. Fifteen weeks later she escaped her captor with her life, and all across the country people who knew her story and had followed her on the news breathed with a sense of relief. While it is no small feat that Closs was able to escape and return to what remained of her family, the trail forward since that day has surely been difficult. Reality continues to challenge fiction, and events like these aren't always relegated to the published press. But the story you're about to read isn't about imposing morals or pressing judgement.

Across the country, stories like Jacob's and Jayme's continue. Tragically, many of those children who are either kidnapped or go missing never make it back home. Those that do make it home are rarely the same again, and often go on to write their own stories, filled with heroism and dangers that should never be forgotten. Stories like theirs should be told, but never honored or immortalized; surely their lives would be far better if they were never kidnapped at all. Those who live to be survivors undergo a dramatic change and are never the same afterwards. Perhaps stories like theirs should not have to happen in the real world. All lives are precious, and all life is important. Everybody should make it home at the end of the day.

This story is dedicated to the children who make it home every day. I also dedicate this story to those who were taken, declared missing, and able to return home to tell their stories. Finally, I dedicate this story to those families who still keep the porch lights on for their missing loved ones. Thank you for reading.

Saturday July 4th, 2009
Friday Harbor Herald

Tonight's festivities will be held at Saturday Square across from the Bridgewater Marina. Ferry service will be suspended from 5 p.m. until midnight. Westbound passengers may depart upon the Seath for Sidney, B.C. at that time should any passengers require travel after an evening of fireworks, frankfurters, and firecracker cotton candy. Eastbound passengers, take note that the Chelan will not depart for Anacortes, Wash. until the following morning at 5:30 a.m. July 5th.

The Friday Harbor Festival begins at 1 pm with a parade lead by the Friday Harbor Marching Sailors, followed by the Main Street Craft Fair and our annual blueberry pie eating contest. All entries for the baking contest must be received by 12 noon. If you wish to participate in the triathlon, your application must be received by 10 a.m. No fee is necessary.

Be sure to attend the annual presentation of "Pig War Picnic" presented by volunteers from the local Kiwanis club. The curtain drops at 3:00 PM at the grounds of the San Juan Historical Museum. All are welcome. Donations of food and gently used clothing are encouraged. Proceeds will benefit the local chapter and are greatly appreciated.

Lastly, please don't forget about our sixth annual writing contest, open to all writers, containing an essay about your favorite moment of this year's celebration. Winners selected will be categorized by age. All stories, poems, or essays that showcase our town festival and the season are welcome. Contest entries must be 5,000 words or less for fiction or essay and poems amounting to less than 40 lines. All entries must be submitted by July 15th. Please include your name, age, and a short bio separate from the entry. Make certain that your entry shows your patriotism! Any subject related to the Fourth of July, themes related to patriotism, freedom, and stories of American courage are just a small sampling of the theme's winners have used in past contests. Please note this contest is closed to Friday Harbor Herald staff members and their families. All rules, judging criteria, and age categories can be found on the newspaper website. Submit your contest entry today and get the most out of your July 4th Celebration!

It was her voice I heard first, rousing me from my bed that July evening well past midnight and long after the fog chased away the pyromaniacs with their sparklers and firecrackers. Fireworks were illegal on San Juan Island, especially after July 5th, but that never stopped anyone from burning the stock they purchased at the firework stands in Sidney. The customs people hated the practice, though nobody ever seemed to notice the illegal importation of fireworks across the channel from Canada into the United States. But then, nobody who rode the ferry ever went there with the intent to smuggle fireworks into the country. We were all American citizens who called Friday Harbor home.

Friday Harbor was filled with dreamers who ended up here, for one reason or another, and hoped to make the most of their surroundings. Some dreamt of the occult. Some sang to the moon. Whoever this person was, she clearly belonged to the latter group. Her voice was soft, innocent, soprano. Mrs. Erickson would surely love to have her in our twenty-member choir at the high school. I was second soprano in those days; this voice outshined mine and I couldn't just go back to sleep without finding out who owned it.

The air outside was thick with fog, as was often the case after a night of fireworks. This fog was different, almost creating a private space meant just for me. All the waters were so calm, it looked as if the dock was floating above the sky, not the water. While I could normally see the lights of Vancouver to the north at night and the peak of Mount Baker to the east in the daytime, that night I couldn't see past the end of the 140' dock that ran from our property southeast of town into the waters of the Strait of Juan De Fuca.

Leaving on my night time attire, consisting of black fleece shorts and a loose tank top, I threw on a pair of sandals and headed outside. I quietly closed the screen door behind me so not to wake Tim or my father. While my first instinct might have been to bring a flashlight, I slowly advanced toward the source of the voice at the end of our dock. I made certain to be gentle.

She sang a song that I had never heard before. There were no lyrics but the melody was serene and smooth. The waters were flat and the winds were calm. It was as if her voice were somehow setting the scene for my arrival. Everything was peaceful and private. Her song might have spread beyond the fog, but at that moment, only I could hear her.

She sat on the dock, damp from the fog. She was apparently basking in the moist air of the evening. Her brown blouse, looking like it had been salvaged from the *Black Pearl* or the *Queen Anne's Revenge*, dripped of seawater and was thick enough to maintain her modesty. Her long hair, held in place with two long shells, was red, brown, or a combination of both. In the darkness I couldn't be sure. What I was sure of, however, were the blue scales that covered her body from the waist down a tapered fishtail to broad, twin flukes. The scales matched her eyes. There was no mistaking her for any of my fellow classmates, for none of them had a fish tail like hers.

My mind began to wander. How long had mermaids lived off of San Juan Island? No, more basic than that. Mermaids exist? They're not just fairy tales anymore. Like any other young girl with wild dreams, I had grown up wanting to believe and now, sitting halfway down the dock that extended into the channel, sat a mermaid. A mermaid that was more real than any movie, theme park, or anything else I could ever imagine.

The soprano siren's song drew me closer, even as she blissfully fumbled with a net of some kind that had tangled around her flukes. Was she hurt? Although I knew I might frighten her and cause her to swim away, it was time to act.

"Are you okay?"

She hesitated, but only for a moment. The corners of her mouth began to smile, as if she were expecting me. "I wondered if I'd wake someone."

I had startled her but she didn't try to flee. Perhaps she couldn't escape so quickly. If anything, she seemed to welcome the assistance. Maybe if I ignored the fact that she was a mermaid, I could help her without gushing like a giddy schoolgirl. I took a deep breath and did my best to pretend she was just another student from my school. "What happened?"

"Caught in a fishing net. I so wish that Mr. Bridgewater would clean up after himself."

"Mr. Bridgewater, the marina manager?" I knew the man, just as everyone in town did. Friday Harbor was a town of around 2,100 depending on what time of year it was. Some folks lived here seasonally, while others, like my family, were full-timers. Mr. Bridgewater was a fisherman, a widower, my boss, and a bit of a drunk, but otherwise harmless.

"You're stuck?" I asked.

She gave a nod and pulled on the strings of the fishing net. "I really did it this time."

"Should I get a scissors?" The tool kit was inside but I didn't dare leave.

Her bob of hair shook slightly. "He won't be able to use the net again if you cut it."

"You're stuck, yes? Besides, if he left it lying around, it's not his anymore."

She looked up suddenly, a curious glint in her eye. Even the side of her face was lovely. "Do you think so?"

"Absolutely! He's got hundreds of these. He won't miss one little net."

"It's larger than you think." The mermaid smiled. "And it sure has slowed me down. I can unwrap everything but all the lines are knotted."

I came to the end of the dock, standing with my back to the house. "If that's all it is, maybe I can help?"

She looked me over at last. "I love your shoes."

I couldn't help but laugh. "What would a mermaid know about shoes?"

"They're a lovely shade of red."

For as long as I could remember, I'd always bought red shoes. There was something about Converse that just stuck with me. "They stand out in the closet, I suppose."

Her eyes drifted behind me. "You have beautiful blond hair."

I shrugged. "Didn't have time to comb."

"Don't be so modest. Your hair reminds me of waterfalls. Have you ever seen a waterfall?"

"Sure, but there aren't any waterfalls on this island."

"North of here, beyond the big city, there's a creek that curves up to a park," she said as she continued to work the fishing net from her flukes. "I can only reach it when the spring thaw comes, but your hair reminds me of the falling water."

I kneeled at her side. She had a musk like a freshly fallen rain. Her fins were sparkling in the dim light. I almost forgot she was looking at me.

"How good are you with knots?"

"Okay, I guess." I giggled at myself. "Sorry, this must be strange for you."

"For me?" She paused to laugh, turning to gaze toward the

shore. "This isn't the first time I've had to untangle myself. You have a lovely house."

"It's okay," I said. "I've always wanted a pool table, but there's no room."

She looked to the stars, a glowing glimmer in her eyes. "I've always wanted to be an acrobat. You know what an acrobat is?"

"Sure," I said. She never hesitated to pose these questions to me, as if she was so amazed that I knew what she was talking about. "They're fearless, flying between the swings like that." I paused to glance at her tailfin. Even though we both seemed to fascinate each other, I soon found myself doing the same thing. Her scales were so foreign to me; they were simply mesmerizing. "Where did you get the idea to be an acrobat?"

"When the large ships come by, sometimes they drop flyers for the various shows on board. One dropped a flyer for an acrobatics show. It's one of my most treasured possessions."

"I wouldn't have guessed a brochure like that could survive underwater."

"Anything can last forever if someone takes care of it." She tugged on the net and winced as the net became taut around itself. There must've been a place that was tightening on her flukes. I wondered if there were blood vessels inside that might be constricting.

"Hang on, you're making it worse." I took hold of the net. "May I?"

She nodded and leaned back, as if granting me access to a secret cove.

"Wouldn't this tailfin of yours make becoming an acrobat difficult?" I began to unravel the net as best I could, loosening the knot before unwrapping the tips of her flukes.

With a dreamy sigh, she gazed off into the channel. "My father always said I should follow my dreams."

"Even if they bring you on shore? Most of my friends have only seen mermaids in films, and very few of them would ever admit to meeting one."

"Just because you haven't seen us doesn't mean we're not here," she replied with a confident smirk. "We watch you all the time. Humans are entertaining creatures."

I nodded. "I can see how we might be, though I might be dreaming."

"You're not. I promise."

"Sure, and the promise of a mermaid is worth, what, exactly?"

"A wish."

I looked up suddenly. "Mermaids don't grant wishes. Genies do."

"We don't carry around bottles, and we don't grant wishes with magic, but I want to repay you for helping me. Do you play the piano?"

"Yes, but my mother plays it better than I do." I hesitated a moment. "How do you know it's called a piano?"

She giggled quietly before glancing toward the bench at the end of the dock. "I often sit just below that bench and listen. You haven't played in some time."

"I've been busy." I released another knot and began unwrapping the rest of the net. "What if my wish isn't to become a better piano player?"

"The outcome of a wish should be your choice, of course," she said with a solemn smile. "Would you play the piano again sometime? For me?"

"Is that what I have to do for a wish or are you changing the subject?"

"No," she smiled with a giggle. "Granting wishes is a complicated process, and we'll have to work together if that wish is ever to be granted. But I'll promise you, if I say I'll grant a wish, I mean it. Anything is possible."

"Perhaps." It was hard not to agree when I knew what I was sitting next to. "Tell you what. I'll play if you'll come to visit again." I carefully removed the rest of the net, which now hung loose beneath her and down into the water. "How does that feel?"

"That feels much better, thank you very much." She inspected her fins, confident that all was well. "What's your name?"

"Jessica. And yours?"

"Cheryn."

"I know a girl at school named Sharon."

"You're pronouncing it wrong. There's a harder C on the front and a softer N at the end." She held up her hand and drew an imaginary C in the air. "Spelled like that, and then—" she drew a Y in the air next to it. "Do they teach you letters at your school?"

"Of course they do," I replied. "I was an A student in tenth grade English. How long have you lived under my dock?"

"Here?" She smirked. "The water is far too shallow here. But I have a grotto across the channel that's very cozy. I'll tell you a secret, though. The best view of the passing ships is from that bench right there." Cheryn pointed to the end of the dock. "Haven't you ever thought so?"

J.D. Delzer

I would never admit how many hours I had wasted watching the cruise ships sail by, but I nodded, inclined to agree.

"Speaking of my grotto, it's very late and I should head home." Cheryn gazed out beyond the channel towards Shaw Island. "You wouldn't mind if I continued to come here, then?"

"What about being seen? Aren't you afraid of humans? Of us?" Suddenly I began to wonder why she found me so harmless.

"You seem nice enough," Cheryn said with a shrug. "As long as I'm not tangled up in anything, I'm pretty hard to catch. You've never noticed me before."

"What about my neighbors? About Mr. Bridgewater?"

"He's not very observant, and never checks his nets."

"Cheryn—" I trailed off, realizing that I was about to sound like my mother.

"These waters are my home, Jessica. If I'm going to live here, I have to be able to enjoy myself. I'm really more of a night owl, besides, and I'm certainly not going to hang around town with so many people around." She moved closer to the water so that her tail dangled into the water before turning to me. "Speaking of which, what did you think of the fireworks tonight?"

The question struck me as odd. "They're always kinda loud."

"I thought they were beautiful. The view from the other side of the channel is perfect, though there are many lights. Can't they turn off the street lights during the fireworks?"

The suggestion didn't seem unreasonable. "I'll have to ask Mayor Glendale next year."

Cheryn folded the net carefully so that it wouldn't tangle upon itself. "Here, you keep this. Don't give it back to Mr. Bridgewater, okay?"

"But, it's his," I began.

She shook her head. "It's yours. We have a rule back home. If it sinks, it's ours. Consider this a gift from me to you, okay?"

"Didn't you say something about granting a wish?"

"Oh," Cheryn waved her hand to channel the thought away. "Those take a while to conjure up. Don't worry, we'll make it happen soon. You think about that wish in the meantime, and I'll get back to you again. The next time it gets foggy like this, come look for me."

"When will that be?"

With a little hop, Cheryn quietly slid into the water. "Just watch for me."

I watched her, mesmerized by her subtle movements. She moved out beyond the edge of the dock, moving so gently that she didn't even leave a wake.

She then turned back to me. "It was nice to have met you, Jessica."

"You too, Cheryn."

With a little hop, she vanished beneath the water and disappeared within the fog.

Sunday July 5th, 2009
Friday Harbor Herald

BREAKING NEWS. Police are asking for assistance from the public in the disappearance of a young woman, sixteen years of age, known to have dark blonde hair and standing about five-foot-six inches tall. Rachel Arlen was last seen near the Tilt-A-Whirl in Saturday Square at approximately 5:47 p.m. July 4 and is presumed missing. No foul play is suspected.

According to local sources, search parties are being organized at the Hungry Clam Restaurant, located across from the ferry assembly area. Police are asking search crews to avoid Saturday Square while they conduct their own investigation into the incident. In cooperation with the investigation, the Castaway Carnival will open at 3:00 p.m. today. Any information about the case is requested to be delivered either in person or by phone to the Friday Harbor Police Station, 170 Spring St.

Visitors and citizens of Friday Harbor and the surrounding islands are reminded that fireworks are illegal on San Juan Island after today. Yesterday's carnival will be open through Monday. Enjoy your Sunday!

Attention contestants from yesterday's baking contest: Please come and pick up your entries. The staff at the Friday Harbor Herald appreciate every participant who took the time to enter but cannot keep all entries due to a lack of space in the break room freezer. Sunday office hours are from 12 Noon to 5 p.m. and unclaimed entries will be donated to St. Francis Catholic Church by 5:00 p.m. Act fast if you want your entries returned.

I was biking home from church when Naomi flagged me down from the front porch of her bungalow on 2nd Street. Of course, I would've stopped anyway, but Naomi always felt like she had to get my attention.

"Come over here, Jessica." Her dark brown hair and hazel eyes stood out in just about any crowd, yet Naomi always found a way to blend in. "I've got to show you something!"

"What's so exciting?" I pulled up my bike and left it on the steps before following her inside. She led me straight past the living room, around the kitchen and up the stairs to her bedroom in the attic. Both windows on either end of the house were open, letting the sea breeze touch the many built-in bookshelves of her blue-walled room which could be seen between several movie posters of *Harry Potter*, a *Mockingjay* logo and the *Divergent* series.

"I won third prize for the blueberry muffins I entered in the bake sale." She held up the large yellow ribbon with gold lettering. "You were right, they loved them."

I punched her playfully in the shoulder. "Told you they would, all you need is confidence; I keep telling you that, Naomi."

"I know, it's just—" Naomi always shook her shoulders when she was nervous. "It's the first time I've ever participated in the contest, and so many of those muffins didn't turn out right."

"Collateral damage," I said. "Do you have any left?"

Ten minutes later, the two of us were sitting on her front porch with a glass of milk and a muffin each. Some of the boys from our school's track team were running down the street. One of them paused to talk, a boy I knew from the school choir.

"Hey, Jess! Naomi!"

I waved, though Naomi smiled nervously, almost hiding behind the American Flag that hung from the pole attached to the support beam.

"How'd the triathlon go, John?"

John, a tenor who would've been attractive if he wasn't such a goofball, trotted up to the porch, all sweaty and with wet, dirty brown hair. "Placed in fifteenth, but I really only entered for the workout. You should've come!"

"I got enough of a workout carrying water for the marching band," I replied. "But fifteenth is fantastic."

"Naomi? Didn't I see your name in the baking contest?" John asked.

She nodded nervously. "Third place."

"Congratulations!" He offered a high five, holding up his hand.

Naomi only smiled.

"Okay!" He put his hand down. "Say, are you still having a campfire tonight?"

I nodded. "Every Sunday from June to September, unless it rains. If you want to come, you have to bring a story."

"And marshmallows," Naomi said.

"Done!" John replied.

"I've got mine all set," Naomi said. "It's about my great uncle Chataln, who was a hunter for the Lummi."

"I can't wait!" John said.

"But you'll have to shower first," I said.

"I'll bring the marshmallows," John said. "Is nine good?"

"Perfect," I replied.

"See you then!" He ran off to re-join his classmates.

Naomi turned to me abruptly. "Why did you invite him?'

"The more the merrier." I rose to my feet. "Dad's expecting me for lunch. Can I bring him a muffin?"

"Of course, take a few. I made so many..." Naomi trailed off.

"I have to tell you something first." I looked out onto the empty street. "Can I tell you something?"

Naomi smirked. "You always tell me everything. What's so different this time?"

I felt like I had to whisper. "You'll never believe who I met last night."

Inside the house, the phone rang. Naomi rose. "I'd better get that. I'll be over later."

Realizing the time wasn't right, I headed home. Maybe she was right. But how do I tell my best friend I have met a mermaid, knowing we're not little kids anymore? It was hard to keep secrets in a town this small.

"Jessica! There you are!"

I arrived home to find Dad working in the backyard. His

truck was there, along with a tool that was large enough to be towed that I had never seen before.

"Where you been, Dad? I didn't see you before church."

"The pastor will understand when I show him my new log splitter." He did his best Vanna White impression as he walked around the orange monster. "What'cha think?"

"I think it's a big hydraulic tree splitter," I replied. "Won't a tool like this destroy the forest? And where'd you get it?"

"Drove to La Conner this morning," he said as he began to disconnect it from the truck. "And for the record, I got it used. You said you wanted to have campfires all summer, right? I thought this would make getting firewood easier, and we don't have to keep it here, I can always rent it out to customers from the store."

He had a point. I had been using my money from the juice stand to buy a bundle of firewood a week. Cost only five bucks for a bundle of a dozen split logs, enough for two to four fires at a time. I didn't think it was that expensive. Then again, with a few logs of this size, I would have enough lumber for the whole summer. For a used log splitter, it was unusually clean.

"I can just buy bundles of wood each week," I said.

"You want to waste your money on firewood? The fellow I bought it from gave me all this hardwood to try it out. I don't want you spending all your money from that job. Plus, it'll be a chance for us to do something together. We'll get Timmy out here—"

"Dad, he's too little to be playing with power tools."

"Invite Naomi over, play some poker—"

"Dad!"

"And we'll have a barbecue, it'll be fun! What'cha say?"

Ever since Mom moved to Seattle three years ago, Dad's been working overtime to engage with me and Tim. While it had been clear to me that Tim was too immersed in the Nintendo to ever recognize a real adventure when he saw it, Dad was the type to never give up and never give in until the last nail was driven. Frankly, it had become a little annoying. But lunch was lunch.

"What should I pull from the freezer?" I asked with a sigh.

I swear he actually jumped. "Great! I'll fire up the barbecue."

"Dad?"

"Whatever looks good, sweetie, something that'll go good with the leftover potato salad from yesterday."

"All right." I parked my bike near the garage and headed inside.

As the smell of burgers and hot dogs flowed in from the outside, I sat on my bed and tried to figure out where I lost control of the afternoon. Dad had a habit of taking things too far sometimes. Like yesterday when he bought a whole package of fireworks for the festivities, but because it was so foggy, we never fired them off. Or the first night I had a campfire. He wouldn't shut up about his many summers at Boy Scout jamborees where they set bonfires so large that the Air Force had to enlist planes to put them out. Or the time he went to Seattle and taught Kurt Cobain how to play guitar.

Maybe my father's stories weren't true. But I guess he did inspire my love for adventure.

I looked up at the posters on my wood panelled walls. Where Naomi had movie posters of the most epic film series and special effects masterpieces, I had only one that had been a gift from her. An advance teaser for the movie *Aquamarine*, a film that came out when I was nine. Naomi had gotten for it me last November for my birthday. She bought it because I once said that I didn't hate Ariel. I've never even seen the film though I have the DVD on my book shelf. I've since removed it from the cellophane, but as of yet, the film was unwatched.

To be fair, I was never a *Disney* princess. *Barbies* and doll houses were politely returned. Mom never could get me to play traditional girl games. I guess I loved to explore too much. A hike along the west side of the island through the nature preserve was more interesting than the latest boy band single. The more I think about it, the more I realized that I have never taken much stock in impossible things, though I have always appreciated a good story.

Yet, I cannot deny that I met Cheryn last night. I still have her cargo net, carefully folded and placed upon my dresser. Maybe I can use it to hang my old plushies from the ceiling and bring them out of the closet for some fresh air. I certainly couldn't go up to Mr. Bridgewater and return it to him. What would I say when he asked where I got it?

"Jessica!" Dad's voice sailed through the open window from the backyard. "Naomi's here! Bring out that Kool Aid I made from the fridge!"

I pulled a purple flannel out of the closet and smoothed out the turquoise comforter atop the grey sheets. Perhaps it was time to open my mind to the impossible.

Lunch proved to be better than I expected, and Dad didn't ruin it by trying to be too interesting. Best of all, we fired up the log splitter afterwards. It was so loud that I could hardly hear a word he said, drowning out his crazy stories about his camp-outs. By three in the afternoon, there was a pile of firewood piled up under the overhang beside the tool shed, stacked four feet high, all of it Washington birch.

He screamed loudly from the other side of the machine, but was drowned out.

"What?" I called back.

"Do—we—have—enough?"

"Yes!"

He was clad in a leather apron, wearing safety goggles, noise-cancelling headphones and thick gloves. Honestly, the machine wasn't all that loud. But because he couldn't hear himself, he felt like he had to yell every single word.

Now that the machine was idle and the engine was silenced, he removed the headphones. "Wow! That's better. Quite a piece of work, huh?"

"It's great," I feigned a smile. "How much did you pay for this?"

"Oh, don't worry about what I paid," he paused to pull the sawdust-roached gloves from his hands. "Anything else we need to do before tonight?"

"Where do you expect to keep this thing? It won't fit in the tool shed."

He smiled with a chuckle. "The garage, it'll fit back in the corner where your mother used to park."

"And if she comes to pick up her things from her office?" I asked.

His smile faded. "We'll move it, I suppose."

Naomi came over from behind the tool shed, having finished her handiwork with the wood pile. "Are we done? Or do you need any more free labor from me?"

"We're done," I said.

"Great." Naomi tossed her gloves on the ground at my feet. "Can we go onto the water? It's a beautiful day."

"Can we take the canoe out?" I asked Dad.

"You know you can go out just about whenever you want," he said with a nod. "Don't go too far, okay? I'll take care of this. Go have fun."

Inside of twenty minutes, Naomi and I each donned a life

jacket and were adrift in our fifteen-foot canoe. The waters within the bay between our three-bedroom house on Barnacle Point and Brown Island were perfect for canoeing, as the currents were light so long as we avoided the main channel and avoided the large cruise ships. There had been shipwrecks in the bay before, but not in my lifetime. As long as we stayed in this area, Dad was usually okay with us being out.

"How come you didn't go to the fireworks last night?" Naomi asked once the house was out of sight and we were able to see Saturday Square in the distance.

"Tired," I replied. It was an accurate statement if there ever was one. "A whole day of walking with the parade, pushing my way through the crowds, taking Tim through the carnival—" I shook my head. "After all that, I had my fill of the festivities."

"At least the guy from the Tilt-A-Whirl was cute," Naomi said.

"You should've gone with John. He seems to be following you a lot lately."

"John?" Naomi splashed the water with her paddle. "As if. He'd never have gotten an article in the *Herald* if his mother wasn't the editor."

"I like his articles, especially the one he wrote last week about Miss Hathaway's consignment store; it never occurred to me where she gets her merchandise."

"You've seen *Antique Roadshow*; her store is just a garage sale on steroids."

I shrugged as I steered the canoe into a gradual left turn. "Sometimes she finds some nice flannel shirts."

We paddled around in silence for a moment or two. A lot of boats were in the harbor today. The carnival was still set up in Saturday Square, including the Tilt-A-Whirl, the midway, the miniature roller coaster and a Ferris wheel. Two food trucks had also parked nearby and seemed to go wherever the carnival went. One sold wood fired pizzas, while the other sold typical fair food. Needless to say, the place was hopping. If I was in their business, I'd hate to have to pay the ferry fee, even after everything packed tightly to fit on board.

"Should we go over there later?" Naomi asked. "They're only here through tomorrow."

"I've got to work extra hard this week to avoid working last weekend," I replied. "I've never been one for the crowds."

"Since you brought it up, did you read the paper this morning?"

"No, why?"

"They were talking about a missing girl. Rachel?"

"The only Rachel I know is Rachel White." I hesitated. "Or maybe Rachel Arlen, you don't suppose they were talking about her?"

"Maybe." Naomi swished the paddle through the water. "Sounds pretty serious."

I nodded. "Yeah. Surprising Dad let us go canoeing." Maybe he hasn't read the paper yet either. Otherwise, we'd never get to have any fun.

"We should sign up for the search parties."

"You can," I replied. "But I sure hope it's nothing serious."

"Say, were you trying to tell me something earlier? Was it about the newspaper article?"

"No," I replied. "It's not about that."

"What were you going to say?"

We were too close to the marina. "We should go further out." I turned the canoe towards the left so we pointed almost due east toward the main channel.

"Jessica, is everything okay? This isn't about your parents, is it?"

"No, it's not about my parents."

"I mean, I know it's been a few years and all."

"It's okay," I replied. "It's nothing."

"Didn't you say you met somebody?"

As we passed by the marina's boat house, Mr. Bridgewater, standing there in his overalls, his yellow-plaid shirt, his boots and his Panama hat, raised a hand and gave a wave.

I waved back.

"Jess?" Naomi asked.

"Later," I replied.

After having soup and leftover hot dogs for supper, we humored Dad with a game but not poker. Instead, we played *The Game of Life*, Tim's favorite board game. He won, like always. My nine-year old brother may be largely immersed within the electronic games, but *Life* couldn't be played alone. I keep thinking there's irony to that statement. At least playing a board game with him was less painful than activities little brothers might cast upon the world.

As the sun began to set, I could hear *Big Brother* emerging from the family room TV and spilling into the backyard as I stuffed an empty pizza box into the fire pit. Dad sure loved that show. Guess it gave him something to focus on. It must've been more interesting to see a bunch of strangers living together than face the situation he was going through.

I piled the logs against one another, using the trick that Dad had showed me many years ago. Truth be told, he had learned a lot in Boy Scouts growing up, and if I had the patience to have stayed in Girl Scouts as long as he had I might've learned the same tricks. I suppose it didn't help that there were only seven of us in our local troop. Some of them only stayed in so they could order cookies for their parents.

"Is it ready?" Naomi asked as she returned from the house with the newspaper.

I snatched it from her. "I haven't even lit a match yet, of course not."

"Well, they're going to be here soon." She picked out the folding chair with the black armrests. "At least it's not foggy tonight."

"Or buggy, like last week," I said as I began weaving pages of newspaper through the hardwood logs. "Tonight should be a good night."

"I still can't believe you let John come."

"You know you like him," I said.

"It's not that I don't, I just don't need you encouraging it."

I chuckled as I lit a match and touched the flame to the pizza box. "Okay, but I'm not trying to force anybody on anyone. He tells a good story."

"What if he hates my story?"

"Don't worry, your story is special to you," I replied. "He's not going to make fun of your family history."

"It's not that I'm ashamed," Naomi said. "I just don't know if—"

"Naomi, you're always hiding behind books," I said. "Haven't I always told you to live in the moment?"

"Sure, but in books the girl always gets the guy."

"Not in the books I read." I stood up to check on the fire, which had spread to the newspaper and the logs. Something caught my eye, however. A face I had seen. Last night, a face that I had seen in the fog, that belonged to a person who had sat upon my very dock.

Cheryn?

Quickly, I reached for the page of the newspaper and stamped out the fire with my shoes.

"Whoa!" Naomi stood up suddenly. "Did you find a spider?"

I took the bottle of water from my red chair and poured some onto the singed corners of the newspaper image. Once I was certain it wouldn't re-ignite in my hands, I picked it up and turned it around so I could confirm my suspicions.

"What do you see?" Naomi asked.

The image was below the headline. BREAKING NEWS. TEEN GOES MISSING IN FRIDAY HARBOR. Though the article had identified the missing teen as Rachel Arlen and not the girl I thought I knew, I swore the face belonged to Cheryn. There was no mistake. The eyes were the same, and though the hairstyle was different, the brow line was similar. Suddenly I wondered if this Rachel and Cheryn could have been sisters, their resemblance was so unremarkable. Could such a thing be possible?

"Jessica, you look like you've seen a ghost," Naomi said.

"Perhaps I have," I replied as I folded the newspaper clipping. "Naomi, remember that movie poster you gave me a few years ago?"

"Sure. Did you ever watch the film?"

I shook my head. "I think I should. See, I met one last night."

"What?"

"Last night, out there on the dock," I said. "She looked just like this missing girl."

"That's impossible," Naomi said. "You mean to tell me, you met a mermaid?"

"They look alike," I held up the folded paper. "Rachel and Cheryn, I don't believe it."

"And she told you her name, too? Did your dad spike the Kool Aid or what?"

"It's true," I said as I sat down in my red chair. "You don't have to believe me."

Naomi paced her way back toward her chair. "I believed you when you said you saw a dolphin swimming in the western channel. The time you watched an eagle catch a salmon in his beak. And when you saw the blue butterfly perched on a wildflower near the nature preserve's visitor center."

"I've wanted a camera for years now," I replied. "Especially after the camera on my phone quit working; maybe after enough shifts at the juice bar this summer I'll be able to afford one. Then I can start proving my stories to you."

"But a mermaid?" Naomi sat down, shaking her head. "That's awful *Disney* of you."

"Naomi..." I trailed off and stood up as I heard laughter. John was here, and he wasn't alone. A soccer ball rolled into the backyard from between the garage and the house, and soon another boy was there to stop it from rolling down to the shore.

He was short but spry, and I thought I recognized his round wire-rimmed glasses and black hair from the photography club at school. The surplus Korean Army jacket was definitely familiar.

"Hi there, Jessica," The boy kicked the ball back toward John who had caught up. "I haven't seen you since Mr. Glaston's science class!"

"No, not since you transferred out of it," I said. "Martin, right?"

"That's me."

"You said the more the merrier," John said. "Martin said he has the perfect story."

"Oh? I'll bet Jessica tells a better one," Naomi said.

I couldn't shush her fast enough. "Don't!"

"No spoiler alerts," John said with a wink. "Unless you have some kind of protocol for these campfires?"

"No," I slowly returned to my chair. "Not that I've made any."

"This is a cool backyard," Martin said as he kicked the ball up against the wood pile before walking out onto the dock. "Does the tide ever flood your backyard?"

"No, I've never seen it flood here," I replied. My attention suddenly drew to the air beneath the bench at the end of the dock. Did I see a ripple in the tide?

"Have you ever caught anything out here? You know, halibut, blackmouth, salmon?" Martin mimed the casting of a fishing rod before pretending to set the hook.

"This is all wildlife preserve," I replied. "All we fish with around here is marshmallows, so long as you brought them."

"Of course." John held up a plastic bag from the Safeway. "Not to mention graham crackers and Hershey's."

"Good, at least you passed the initiation," I said as I took the bag and brought the goods over to the picnic table. "Take a seat wherever you like, but the red chair's mine."

"And I already called the black chair," Naomi said.

"This'll do." John flipped a slice of the log we left uncut from this afternoon and brushed it off before putting his denim down. "I tell better stories if I'm able to lean forward."

"Are you volunteering to go first?" Naomi asked.

"What about the s'mores?" Martin asked.

John shook his head. "Let the coals form first." He motioned to the blue chair across the fire from him. Martin took it, pulling a can of Mountain Dew from his jacket pocket and cracking it open.

"For your consideration," John began. "I present the story of

The Lost Spatula."

Naomi drew aback. "The lost spatula?"

John nodded, reaching into the pockets of his windbreaker. "Indeed. The events of this tale occurred many years ago, on this very island. Some people claimed to have found it, but they were proven wrong."

"Why not?" Martin asked.

"Because," John said as he cast his hand across the fire, causing the logs to spark as he threw what might have been sunflower casings into the coals. "The spatulas that turned up weren't bloody enough."

I leaned in. "This is going to be a good one."

For years, the butcher on First Street had ran a good business. Every day he got a carcass from a nearby ranch or shipped in from the mainland, though the cut varied between pigs, cattle, or venison depending on the time of year and what his supplier had on hand. Sausage was his specialty, they said. No part of the animal was ever wasted, and the neighborhood dogs made regular stops throughout the day for the scraps.

One Saturday, the butcher didn't open his shop. He worked without any apprentice, and performed the small shop by himself, leaving many to wonder about the sudden closure. Even though his usual hours were from ten to five, that particular Saturday the blinds on the windows remained drawn. For the next week, nobody went inside, nor did the blinds rise. It was as if he had suddenly gone away. Deliveries of meat continued but were refused, for nobody answered the door to accept them.

After seven days of bringing carcasses to the loading dock without answer, the delivery man decided that he couldn't simply walk away anymore. Where had the butcher gone? Had there been an accident?

He enlisted the police officer, who contacted the local locksmith and forced open the shop. Inside, everything appeared normal, save for a layer of dust upon the meat counter. Behind that, in the kitchen area, a small spider was spinning a web atop the grinder.

Nothing had been disturbed in this part of the shop. The many knives, the hooks for carrying flanks of meat, the clipboard that listed the daily deliveries and the refrigerator that contained week old cutlets were all prepped and ready for sale but had been forgotten and ignored. Save for the same layer of dust, everything was clean and sanitary, just as it would have been following the end of the day.

Only one thing was missing. Beside the quiet and cool flat top, where sausages were cooked for customers waiting at the walk-up lunch counter, one tool was gone. An outline in the dust suggested the spatula had been there only a day or so before. Surely it hadn't just walked away? Why, of all things to be disturbed in a humble meat shop, would one insignificant spatula have someone failed to have been put away with the others?

The police began to question the citizens of the city. In the course of a weekend, every citizen had been interviewed. Had they seen the butcher? Did he skip town? Could he have left a forwarding address? Did anyone hear anything?

Finally, they brought in the police dog to investigate the shop. The bloodhound sniffed the kitchen, but his handler worried that the dog might have been having trouble with the perpetual smell of meat that permeated the space. Without any clear luck in the kitchen, the handler brought the dog into the front shop. Again, false positives. Hoping to explore every option, the officer directed the dog down the narrow back stairway into the basement.

Why nobody had gone before, nobody could say. Neither the police officer who filed the initial report or the other deputies couldn't say why.

There, among the discarded bones and rolls of butcher paper, the dog suddenly turned on the handler and ran up the stairs and down the block. What had caused the dog to flee so suddenly? For lying there in a mass of blood and bile, there, in a pile of aprons and carcasses—

"Nah, I'm not going to tell you, it's too gruesome," John shook his hand and leaned back on the log. "Sorry."

"What?" Martin was livid. "Are you kidding? You're telling a story that would gross out Tim Burton and you're not going to finish?"

"It's too, too rated R," John said. "After all, there are ladies present."

"Dammit, I want to know what happened to the butcher!" Naomi threw her pop can into the fire. "What's the matter with you?"

"I agree," I said. "Stories gotta have an end."

"Okay, so at least tell us where the spatula ended up," Martin said. "Tell us that much."

John sighed and leaned forward again. "Very well."

There, amongst the most foul-smelling refuse to ever defile the butcher's shop, was the spatula. It stuck within the top of the mountain of flesh like a lightning rod, glowing with the electricity from a shattered fluorescent bulb. Coated with the flesh and bile of its former owner, it reeked with a scent that radiated death.

Nobody ever discovered how, or who, or why. Rather than waste more time on an investigation, the police shuttered the shop and removed the equipment from the kitchen. They then hired a bulldozer and levelled the building, basement and all, without any fanfare or press release. Upon the site, they laid down a concrete pad and a heavy brick square, and named it after the best day of the week, Saturday, hoping that the fun times above would help the citizens forget the atrocities that occurred below.

"The end," John said, standing and taking a bow.

Naomi and I clapped politely, though Martin just shook his head.

"You left out the best parts, man. Motive," Martin said as he slapped his hands together. "Motivation." He slapped his hands again. "Incentive." Once more. "Not to mention the identity of the murderer!"

"I think the spider did it," I said with a cock of my head.

"Yeah," Naomi agreed. "I didn't notice any other characters."

John chuckled to himself. "Maybe. Nobody knows the real story, for sure."

"That's gotta be the lamest horror story ever told," Martin rested his feet on the fire pit. "Can we at least break out the s'mores now?"

"Of course," I said, getting up. "Allow me."

"Maybe you can tell a better one?" John asked Martin.

Martin nodded. "I know my local legends. You're damn right I can."

After a very inventive tale about vampires, werewolves, the Grimace and the Hamburgler, a stunned Naomi was the first of us to comment on Martin's story. To call it a masterpiece would be a sarcastic insult.

"That was not a better one," Naomi said. "There isn't even a McDonald's on San Juan Island. And what was the point of the dog?"

"He was drooling over the Hamburgler's head," Martin replied defensively. "He would've eaten him if you'd let me finish."

John crossed his arms and shook his head. "That's Mayor McCheese. Don't you know anything? I told you to bring a good story, not just make up something stupid on the spot."

"What's your rule, Jess?" Naomi asked. "One good story per participant, right? Are there demerits for stories that are terrible?"

"There's nothing official yet," I began.

"Maybe there should be," John said.

"I don't know," I trailed off as I glanced at Martin, who suddenly appeared very sullen.

"I liked it," a quiet voice said.

We all jumped. The voice came from behind me.

"What was that?" John asked.

The comment had to have been made by Cheryn. I looked past John as everyone turned towards the dock. Nobody was sitting on the bench, on top, or even below. If anyone had been nearby, they were gone in an instant and were very sly. Cheryn would have been under the dock, beyond my view, blocked by John. Clearly, she had been listening to our stories for some time.

"Did you two say anything?" John looked between Naomi and me. "I heard a girl's voice. Didn't you hear it?"

Naomi narrowed her eyes and gave me a knowing glare. Maybe she was starting to believe me.

"I think I've had my fill of horror stories," Martin said. "Maybe you could indulge us with a better story?"

I could sense the sarcasm in his voice, but I agreed, it was best to move on. "You'll have a better story next week, Martin." I cracked my knuckles. "It's interesting that you mentioned local legends. For your consideration, I present the *Tale of The Island Visitor.*"

San Juan Island was charted by Spanish conquistadors in the 1790s, led by Francisco de Eliza who had also fought during the American Revolution at the siege of Pensacola. Although the explorer did not spend much time on these islands named for St. John the Baptist, his crew charted the isle as he himself spent most of the expedition amid ship and preparing his charts for the Straits of Georgia. At that point in history, the area had been unknown to the Europeans.

During one fateful mission believed to have occurred in late April, the explorer went with a crew of cartographers and landed on this very island. His flagship, the San Carlos, *worked to chart the remaining islands of the archipelago, comprised of Shaw, Orcas, Blakely, Decatur, and Stuart. Of those islands, San Juan was chosen specifically by Eliza to study. Why he chose to chart this island personally remains a mystery.*

Two nights into the charting of the island and its natural splendors, his team made camp near this very location, here upon Barnacle Point. Their charting was complete for the day's toils, and the men enjoyed a meal of freshly caught salmon from the nearby waters.

Near the end of their feast, one of the men complained that something was amiss. Eliza wrote in his journal that the man reported being watched and that their camp did not feel secure. There was good precedent to be concerned, for Eliza had met with the local Nooksack tribes before landing. While their initial meetings had gone well, the tribe had suspicions about the Spanish establishing colonies on the Nooksack's native lands. While they had been welcomed with open arms, there was distrust among the local tribes. Thus, the men were certain that every move had gone observed.

However, this man who raised the alarm believed it was not the Nooksack warriors who were watching them. These eyes, he reported, had come from the sea. Were there yet other tribes who feared the approach of the Conquistadors? Or were there other explorers, already present, who the Nooksack had failed to mention?

Soon all the men in Eliza's team were on guard. Beyond the channel, near the water line, eyes were on them. Eliza himself fired a shot from his pistol, a warning shot, and the water suddenly rose up in formation, sending a tidal wave towards the beach.

The camp was washed away with the wave, and the Spaniards found themselves under attack from an unseen foe. Their attackers, however, were nowhere to be seen. Had there been a trace of their presence before, now there was none. To mount a counterattack would be foolish.

Eliza left the island immediately and pleaded with the Nooksack leaders for an explanation. They gave no rational answer for the men's encounter. Instead, they gave Eliza this short, cryptic message.

"Beware the water spirits."

"That's it? Beware the water sprits?" Martin asked.

"There's one out there right now," John said. "I believe it."

"Oh really?" Martin asked.

Naomi held her hands up in his direction, twitching her fingers. "They're after you!"

"Knock it off."

Martin was anything but amused. However, the sudden approach of a small wave against the beach set him off. Martin had jumped up and was up to the house's back deck within a fraction of a second.

John, Naomi and I couldn't stop laughing.

"Are you kidding me? How'd you do that?" He glared at me but was holding onto the railing of the deck for dear life. "Jessica?"

"Do what?" I asked, trying to contain my giggling. "I can't control the waves."

"You big wuss," John went over to the deck. "You're embarrassing yourself."

"Nobody told me this campfire thing was all about scaring each other," Martin said.

"It's not," I said. "It's more of an adventure club. Stories of adventure. They don't have to make you scared."

"A club?" Martin asked. "Sounds like some twisted after-school special."

"It doesn't have to be, if you take it seriously," Naomi replied.

"Agreed. Maybe I just like horror stories," John said. "Now are you going to chill out or what?"

"I'm liking or what," Martin said.

"Oh please," John muttered.

"Can I tell my story already?" Naomi asked.

"Is there more to the story?" John asked me.

I shrugged. "Basically, Francisco de Eliza returned to complete his survey. Martin," I turned to him. "You know your local legends better than I do."

He nodded. "An expedition a year later by a British man named George Vancouver rearranged a lot of the names. But a few hundred years later after Fort Camosun was constructed, the harbor and settlement named after him began to grow, when most of the official names reverted back to Eliza's original records and the locals adopted his vision."

"You said that Eliza wanted to investigate this island personally?" John asked. "Do you think there was something special here that interested him?"

"It's hard to say," Martin said. "Our island is one of the larger ones. They searched for anything that might be valuable. Gold, of course, but also anything that they could grow or trade for financial gain; the Spaniards had done wonderful with the discovery of the Aztec, after all. Down there, they discovered chocolate. After that, they wanted to discover marshmallow."

"Marshmallow?" Naomi scoffed. "Come on."

"Or graham crackers, whatever," Martin replied with a smirk.

"I'm sure Mr. Banes would be pleased to know someone paid attention during his unit on local history," John said.

"Sure," Marin replied. "So fess up, Jess. What's up with these water spirits?"

I chuckled quietly. "Felt like it needed something extra."

"Did it?" Martin grumbled to himself.

"I liked it," John gave me a nod.

"Can I tell my story now?" Naomi asked. "Or are we finished?"

"No," Martin said before heading back to the campfire. "Let's hear it."

"Agreed," John said as he added a pair of logs to the fire. "Even if it is scary."

"It won't be," Naomi replied.

Naomi went on to tell a rich story of her family's heritage. My father broke us up after that, when Martin's mother called and said he needed to come home at once. Sounded like she was worried about him after seeing the news report on Channel Seven. At any rate, our first official meeting was over. Maybe the story about the missing student was serious after all. If Rachel Arlen remained missing, there was a chance this could have be our last meeting, even though none of us realized it at the time.

Monday July 6th, 2009
Friday Harbor Herald

On Sunday, searchers begun to fan out across the woods north of Friday Harbor along Point Caution, the farm fields near the Trumpeter B&B Ranch, and Pear Point in search of the missing teen, Rachel Arlen. Arlen, 16, has not been seen since the evening of Saturday, July 4th. Upon completing their initial investigation Sunday, a police spokesman reported that there are no current leads, nor any suspicion of foul play. Local authorities believe that the longer it takes for Rachel to be located, the more she may be in danger. In accordance, police are asking for volunteers to aid in the search and wish to speak with anyone who may have last seen or spoken with the young woman. Inquires can be made at police headquarters, located at 102 N. 2nd St.

Herald staff and the local sheriff office have issued a statement. "Until either Miss Arlen or the party responsible for this alleged kidnapping is located, tourists and local families should remain on high alert. Friday Harbor citizens are reminded to be 'secure aware' of your properties. Keep close tabs on your family pets, senior citizens, and all family members."

In other news, Dr. Gregory Pruitt has reportedly lost his seven iron in the vicinity of the 14th green at the San Juan Country Club and is offering a free check-up to the person who offers its safe return. Today is Half Price Burger day at Square's, located across the road from the south-eastern corner of Saturday Square. Mention this publication and get half price on a slice of pie.

Please remember to submit your entries for the writing contest by June 15th.

As the earliest rays of dawn penetrated my window, I was awoken by the soft voice I had heard several days ago. Cheryn. There was no mistake. A moment later after I pulled aside the blinds, I confirmed my suspicions. She was sitting on the bench, singing softly to herself.

Quickly, I threw on my sandals and went downstairs, hoping to be quiet so not to wake either Dad or Tim. How would they react if they saw Cheryn? I didn't want to find out. For the moment, she was my local legend.

Continuing my quiet efforts, I gently closed the patio door and walked out to the yard. The fire pit had been blackened from last night's campfire, and the chairs had been left in place, covered with a thin layer of morning dew.

As I approached the edge of the dock, Cheryn's song became brighter and warmer. I hoped her voice wasn't directly affecting me. Perhaps she sensed my approach.

"Good morning." She didn't move from her spot on the bench, nor did she turn.

I walked the length of the dock, pausing at the very end. I was about five feet from her now. Sure, I had gotten very close the other day, but somehow, seeing her sitting on the bench, I suddenly found myself keeping a cautionary distance.

"Morning," I said at last. "You're out of the water again."

"Just because I'm a night owl doesn't mean I don't enjoy the sun. A girl's gotta get a little tan now and then." She patted the vacant half of the bench. "Didn't I tell you this was the best view? Especially this time of the morning."

Hesitantly, I joined her. "This feels so strange."

"Should it?" She smiled and opened her arms wide. "Natural beauty like this should be embraced, not slept through."

"We were telling stories rather late last night," I said.

"Yes, about that. How did you like my contribution to your story?"

I couldn't contain my giggle.

"Oh, good."

"Martin was so spooked, he had to borrow my flashlight

before he'd leave."

"Was he the boy in the uniform?" Cheryn asked. "He is an interesting fellow."

"I think he's somewhat eccentric, but means well enough."

"I suppose you've already told others about us water spirits."

She was right, though I didn't immediately imagine her listening to my whole story. "You were pretty brave to listen in on our campfire. Naomi is my best friend, but even she is sceptical."

"She has such beautiful hair. And a very determined sense of self. Does she have any hobbies?"

"Does she have hobbies?" I asked back. "Well, sure—"

"She's a reader, yes? When I've seen her, she always seems to have a book in her hand."

I nodded. "Naomi loves books. Do you read?"

Cheryn nodded, to my surprise.

"There are a few books I've gotten my hands on, and I keep some of them in my grotto. As you can imagine, they tend to fall apart after a while. It'd be nice of you folks to wrap the binding a little better."

"We design the books to hold up on land," I replied. "Books aren't designed to last underwater."

"Maybe you could work on that sometime," she said as she swayed her fin back and forth. "Those stories were enjoyable yesterday. Was yours really inspired by your town's local history?"

"Most of it," I replied. "Cheryn, I have to ask you something."

She nodded.

"A girl from my school went missing a few days ago. When I saw her photograph in the paper, I thought that she might've been you."

"Me?" Cheryn narrowed her eyes curiously.

"Yes, I recognized you in Rachel's photo. But that's impossible, right?"

"It sounds rather unlikely." Cheryn pushed herself up with her arms and gazed out beyond the channel. "But then, I suppose anything could be possible."

"Yes." My eyes drifted to the sun reflecting upon her blue scales, shimmering in the growing sunlight. "Can I offer you breakfast? A muffin, perhaps?"

"No, thank you." Cheryn leaned back into the bench and gazed towards the sky. "I hope you aren't upset with me for eavesdropping last night. I just love adventures."

"Of course not," I said. "Like I told you the other day, you're welcome to come here whenever you like."

"You're very kind, Jessica." Cheryn turned and offered a warm smile. "Tell Martin that I'm sorry if I scared him."

"Don't be," I replied with a chuckle. "Martin's a good guy, but if you ask me, he needs to be shaken up now and then."

"Who were the other people, then? Naomi?"

I nodded.

"And the other boy?"

"John," I replied.

"They seem like nice people." Cheryn patted her stomach. "Maybe I should find some breakfast after all."

"Can I bring you a blueberry muffin? Naomi made them." I suddenly began to wonder what she eats. Hopefully not just kelp and oysters?

"Sure," Cheryn said. "Have you thought about what you might wish, Jessica?"

"What?" I hadn't, to be honest. If anything, I was still sceptical she could grant one.

She turned to face the water before I could answer. "I see a ship approaching."

"Oh?"

Sure enough, a ship was coming into view from beyond Brown Island as it traversed the channel eastward. It was the eastbound ferry, the *Chelan*, embarking for Lopez Island.

I heard a soft splash, and before I knew it, Cheryn had already returned to the water. Oddly enough, I hadn't even felt that she left the bench. Since I was now sitting alone, I went back to the house and collected a muffin from the bag Naomi gave me. I sliced it almost in half and put a small pad of butter inside it. Then, I went back out to the end of the dock to see the ferry had moved beyond the open view of the channel past Barnacle Point.

Though it felt strange, I placed the muffin on the dock by the water. I was spinning on my heel when I heard the softest splash.

"Thank you."

Again, I didn't see her. She was good.

"You're welcome." I didn't need to know where she was, or if she had been above water for even the slightest moment. All I knew is that it was too early for breakfast, and I needed at least another hour of sleep.

~ ❀ ~

On my way to the juice bar for work around ten that morning, John stopped me. "Running away from more of those water spirits, then?"

"What do you mean?" I slowed down and spun in a circle before coming to a stop on my bike in front of his house. "You don't really think they're real?"

"They sure seemed real enough to me. How'd you trigger the wave?"

I smiled, hoping to show him it was just a silly joke. "Really, it must've been a passing boat or something."

"Well, however you did it, it sure gave Martin a start. Good work."

"I had nothing to do with it."

"If you say so." John wrinkled his nose, something I had come to recognize as a tell. Dad had one too. He always wrinkled his nose when he had a good poker hand.

"So when's the next meeting of the Red Shoe Adventure Club?"

"The what?"

He motioned towards my red Converses. "Every Sunday, right?"

"Sure, but—"

"I think we should make a more official thing. Something to look forward to, something just for us." He paused as a pickup with an Iowa licence plate drove by. "Especially during the summer months when we have to put up with all the extra tourist traffic."

"I have to get to work," I said. "But that's a nice idea, John."

"For your consideration, Miss Summers?"

"Sure," I nodded. "I'll write up a charter tonight, okay?"

"I look forward to reading it."

Twenty minutes into my shift at the juice bar, I was making a smoothie for a customer when a student I didn't immediately recognize from my high school came in wearing a diving cap, a tuxedo, dress shoes and a placard. Red hair poked out from the diving cap here and there. To be honest, she looked a little like a penguin, even with her hair sticking out. She blew a conch shell, obviously trying to create a diversion.

"Attention, attention! Let it be known that a sister has come home!"

"They found the missing girl?" my older customer asked.

The young woman firmly put her hand up. "All questions must be in writing. Good people, I wish to announce that one of our ranks has been invited into the fantastic sisterhood of mermaids, centaurs and fairies."

The customers in line groaned and went back to their phones.

Melissa, my blonde co-worker, leaned over the counter. "Take your silly fantasies outside, you're disrupting our business."

"But this is a celebration, not a disruption!"

"It's Kelsey, right?" I came out from around the counter to the woman. She was a grade ahead of me, yet in my opinion, a few grades behind mentally. "Every time someone goes missing in this town, your society—"

"The Society for Interesting Re-integration of Endangered Non-humanoid Species, or S.I.R.E.N.S. for short," Kelsey said.

"Whatever," I replied. "Every time someone goes missing in the national news you go around town and say that they swam away as a mermaid, or became a centaur, a fairy—"

"You can't deny it if you can't prove it!" Kelsey protested.

"Have you seen a fairy?"

"They're small!"

"Centaurs?"

"Hoof prints in the dirt, yeah—"

"Where?" I drilled her. "In the valley west of the airport? On the beach? Nesting with the camel in Roche Harbor?"

"Don't make fun of poor Myrtle," Kelsey said.

I stood beside the exit. "Look, it's not fair to Rachel to pretend she became a mythical creature and flew away, it's rude. What would her family think?"

"Mermaids don't fly, silly, they swim away."

"Just go." I pointed at the door.

"Can I leave a flyer for our ascension ceremony? It's at dusk Wednesday." Kelsey held up a flyer that resembled her placard. It showed a mermaid sitting on a centaur while two fairies flew above them, along with their group name and contact information.

I sighed, snatching the paper. "I'll discuss it with Mr. Bridgewater."

"That's all I ask, Jessica. If nobody comes, then nobody comes. If one person comes, then we'll have accomplished—"

"Okay, okay," I shooed her outside. "Your disrupting my customers. Point taken."

Melissa poured the smoothie I was working on into a cup and gave it to the elderly woman. "Sorry for the delay, ma'am."

"Does this happen often in Friday Harbor? I mean, it's a charming town, but is this some kind of local acting group? Or did a girl really go missing?"

"No, madam," I replied. "The news stories are real, and a girl is missing, but don't believe what Kelsey says. She's read too many fairy tales. Thanks for coming to visit us today."

"Thank you," she said as she exited.

"What's all the noise?" My supervisor, Leia, came out from the back room. As she was Mr. Bridgewater's aunt, she mostly made sure things operated smoothly while Mr. Bridgewater managed the marina, leaving most of the responsibility to the younger workers, stepping in only when she had to. She was an older woman with silver hair who made sandwiches to order, even though all the ingredients arrived pre-sliced. Since most of the employees were minors, by law we couldn't use a deli slicer or an oven, though blenders were okay. "What was that all about, Jess? Some kind of solicitor?"

"I took care of it, Miss Jackson."

"Good," she replied. "Gary wants you kids to be responsible. The less I have to do to keep this place going, the better."

I realized I would never tell any Leia, Melissa or Mr. Bridgewater about Cheryn. I knew I had met a mermaid but if I could hardly tell my best friend, I certainly couldn't tell my co-workers or the tourists. But Kelsey's idea was ludicrous. I told myself that I wouldn't associate with the SIRENS group if I could avoid it, if not for my own sake than Cheryn's. Her well-being depended on absolute secrecy.

Near the end of my shift, I was making a strawberry lemonade for a customer from San Francisco when Mr. Bridgewater came into the shop. His overalls were oily today.

"Here's your juice, miss." I handed the juice to the woman who had a camera slung around her neck. "Thank you very much and enjoy your visit."

The tourist gave a nod, left a dollar in the tip jar, and headed for the door.

"Jessica," Mr. Bridgewater said. "A word?"

Melissa took over as I headed into the back room with Mr. Bridgewater. "Sir?"

He leaned against the door jamb just out of earshot from the kitchen. "How's the shop running today? Did you enjoy your weekend off?"

"Yes sir, though I spent more time on the water than at the carnival," I replied.

He gave a stern nod. "You'll be pleased to know that the shop made plenty of business all weekend. Our numbers were up more than last year."

"Wonderful! Are the boat rentals up, sir?"

"Yes, they are. Why do you ask?"

I shrugged. "Curious, is all."

"You've got an eye for business, Jessica. I just wish I had your sense of inventory."

"Inventory, sir?"

He nodded and turned to look towards the harbor. "A few of my nets have gone missing, along with two paddles and a canoe."

"Did one of the tourists get lost with a wayward rental?"

"Not sure," he answered. "If it didn't cost so darn much, I'd have sprung for those GPS trackers to be installed last season."

"As for the net, sir, I can't imagine it wandered away on a whim."

A rare smile, showing his gold molar. "I suppose not."

"It'd be nice to know where that stuff ended up."

He nodded. "Along with that girl from the paper."

"Do you know Rachel, sir?"

"Not personally," he shook his head. "She's in your grade, isn't she?"

I nodded. "We're in different classes, and don't see each other much, if ever."

"Girl's been missing two days. Hope it's just a case of miscommunication and she's just gone to her aunt's in Sidney or something."

"Is that right?"

"Yes," he said. "Gwendaline Arlen is a friend of mine. She runs a dance studio. Ballerina, tap, foo-foo stuff, that sort of thing. Awful nice lady. It'd be a real shame if her niece really did go missing."

"Hopefully it's just a misunderstanding."

"In the meantime, did you hear Brian moved to Vancouver?"

"Brian?" I asked. Brian was the manager, second in rank only to Miss Jackson. Along with him and Thomas, they both pretty well took care of things. "When?"

"Family situation. Said he couldn't give me proper two-week notice. But I guess I can't make him stay." He called to Leia. "Didn't you tell them about Brian?"

"Sorry, Gary, I forgot," Leia called.

"Then, Leia will be the manager on days you're working the marina, sir?" I asked.

"That's what I wanted to talk to you about. Leia's only in this to make sandwiches, she mainly keeps an eye on things but has told me many times she's not interested in being a boss. Since the day it opened, I've always let this place operate as a chance for you kids to learn how to make a living."

It was true, Mr. Bridgewater and Miss Jackson mainly let the younger workers be responsible for their own stations. Very rarely did she have to pick up for us.

"Thomas is a fine co-manager but I'll need someone else to pick up Brian's shifts," Mr. Bridgewater said. "This your second season, are you up for it?"

I was struck silent. All I could do is nod.

"Hoped you'd be okay with that. You'll like having that raise too, I suspect. Twelve dollars per hour instead of eight."

A soft mumble was my only reply.

"Good. All you need to worry about is ensuring the fresh fruit inventory is correct at the end of the day. Leia and I'll worry about the till. No free drinks for your friends."

"Never, sir."

"Good," he said with a smile. "Your responsibilities start today. Congratulations, manager."

I quietly smiled. "Thank you."

"Anything else happen today?"

I thought about the flyer that Kelsey had brought, but decided it was something I could handle and left it obscured by the newspaper upon the desk. Luckily, something else came up.

Melissa appeared in the doorway. "Mr. Bridgewater? Officer Roberts is here."

"I'll lock up tonight, and tomorrow I leave it to you." Mr. Bridgewater patted me on the shoulder. "Keep up the good work." He then turned and went into the main shop. "Officer, what can I do for you?"

I took the newspaper and the flyer with me when I clocked out a few minutes later.

~  ~

"Bridgewater's a suspect?" I asked. "Why?"

Naomi had come over that evening, after my shift ended at four. "The police have been investigating Rachel's disappearance. My mother doesn't think Mr. Bridgewater could have been involved. He would've been at the marina all day."

"Officer Roberts spoke with Mr. Bridgewater, but I didn't hear them. He made me assistant manager and then went back to the marina afterwards."

"Wait, he made you manager?" Naomi asked. "That's great! You got a raise!"

"Co-manager with Thomas," I said. "But if he's a suspect, I wonder what else is going on." I leaned back into the back of the bench overlooking the channel, the same bench Cheryn had sat on that morning. "Maybe I would rather know what's going on than manage the juice bar."

Dad came out onto the dock. "Jess? Got a minute?"

I turned around. "Yeah Dad?"

"Someone here for you. Officer Roberts."

Naomi gave me a glare. "So where were you on the night of July 4th?"

"Funny," I said.

Dad waited in the kitchen as Officer Roberts, a police lieutenant with the Friday Harbor Police with a broad chin and a fit physique, waited in our foyer. "Evening, Miss Summers. I was hoping to catch you after chatting with your boss. Can we talk?"

I showed him into our small living room, which was more of a parlor with a wicker couch, a recliner, a bookshelf and a coffee table. Since the television didn't fit, the space had stayed much the same as it had since Mom last used it as her personal reading room.

He sat on the wicker couch. "May I call you Jessica?"

I nodded and sat across from him in the recliner. "What can I do for you?"

"Are you friends with Rachel Arlen?"

"We don't hang out much, no," I replied. "She's more of a dancer and I'm just a band nerd."

He leaned forward. "You probably know my son, Greg."

"Yeah, he's the tenor sax player."

"Remind me," he said with a raised finger. "What do you play?"

"The flute."

He gave a nod. "Right. Do you mind if I take a few notes?"

"Not at all," I replied.

He reached into his jacket and took out a spiral bound notepad that was about the size of a deck of cards. "Were you at work on Saturday?"

I shook my head. "Took the whole weekend off."

"Wouldn't that be when the juice bar would be the busiest?"

I nodded. "I worked over Memorial Day and Mr. Bridgewater said I could have it off as long as I worked every other weekend. He doesn't like to work us too hard."

Officer Roberts jotted onto the notepad. "The hours are only until five every day, right?"

"Yes, sir."

"How many hours do you work?"

"Twenty hours, over four days each week," I replied.

Officer Roberts drew more notes onto the notepad. "Did you go into town Saturday?"

"Naomi, my brother, and I went to the carnival for a few hours."

He made another note. "Naomi Rovan?"

I nodded.

"Your brother's name is Tim?"

"Yes, sir."

"What time were you at the carnival?"

Since I wasn't entirely sure, I guessed. "Sometime that afternoon, maybe two to five."

"Did you stay for the fireworks?"

I shook my head. "I was home by six. Most of my evening was spent in my room."

"You missed the fireworks?"

I shrugged. "Decided that I'd rather be reading. I've been reading a book called *The Girl of Fire and Thorns*. It's really good."

"Doesn't sound like my kind of reading," Officer Roberts replied as he made another note. "When was the last time you saw Rachel?"

"I guess I saw her photograph in the paper yesterday."

"Yes, but in person?"

As I had told Naomi, I didn't see Rachel much. She lived on the north side of town, spent most of her days at the dance studio, and was in a different homeroom. "Last week of school, I guess. I haven't had a class with her since fifth grade."

"But you know her?"

I nodded. "We hang out in distant circles. Don't see her much beyond school." I hesitated. "Officer, may I ask you a question?"

"I'm here to ask the questions but I'll allow it."

"Do you believe any of Rachel's classmates are responsible for her disappearance?"

"No." He folded the notebook closed. "You strike me as a direct young woman, Jessica. You'd make a good detective someday."

"Thank you."

He rose to his feet. "The biggest part of this job is to piece together the last places Rachel might have been on Saturday.

Who might have saw her last, who might have a reason to be suspect for foul play. It's a small island, but there are many places a person can be hidden."

"Or hide," I said. "If I know anything about Rachel, it's that; she is somewhat shy."

He nodded. "You aren't the first person to say so."

"Has there been anyone unusual standing out among the tourists?" Maybe it was time for me to ask the hard questions. "Anyone who might be worth keeping an eye on?"

"There are always crowds of people in town for the holiday," he said as he walked into the foyer. "But beyond that, I can't say if I've seen anyone suspicious. I'd be compromising my investigation if I did."

"Should I ask around the neighborhood? My circle of friends?"

He nodded. "You might put up a missing poster at the juice bar too. I left one with your boss, but you can download a poster from our department's website."

"I'll do that."

"Thanks very much for your time. Call me if you hear anything I should know." He tossed a business card into our key bowl. "My cell phone's on at all hours."

"I will, officer. Have a nice day."

Outside, Naomi was chatting with Dad, who came inside to chat with the officer as he shooed me onto the porch.

"Well?"

I took her into the backyard and told her about the meeting with the officer, as well as the encounter with SIREN and Kelsey earlier in the day.

"Are they still crazy about that?" Naomi gasped. "Plus, you owe me an explanation about what you were talking about the other day."

I nodded and sat near the fire pit. "Yeah, I do. Listen."

From the foggy meeting to this morning, I described my encounters with Cheryn. How she just showed up, how she didn't seem afraid of me, and how I had received the net for helping her.

"That all sounds incredible," Naomi said at last, "But also sounds too convenient. Why would she just appear like that?"

"There was talk of a wish," I said casually.

"Wish," Naomi narrowed her eyes. "Don't genies—"

I nodded. "Don't really know what I'd wish for, anyway. Maybe I'd wish for my folks getting back together, but—"

"Was she in trouble, or something?" Naomi asked suddenly.

"I thought I read that if you help a mermaid, they can grant wishes?"

"She was stuck in the net," I said. I wasn't convinced that Cheryn was magical, beyond being a mermaid, so I changed subjects. "But wishes aside, she also knew I played the piano."

"Anyone who's been in the bay knows that," Naomi said with a nod. "I'm sure the sound carries over the water well."

"She never seemed jumpy, nor worried. It was like she knew me and wouldn't be afraid."

"Maybe she does know you," Naomi said. "Could Kelsey be right?"

"Of course not," I said as I crossed my legs. "They've been preaching that stuff for years. None of them SIRENS have ever wanted to grow up. Plus, Kelsey's mother runs the Karma Korner on Third Street. If it's counter-cultural centric, they sell it and subscribe to it with a devotion larger than that of the collective audience of the *New York Times*."

Naomi nodded. "Do you think I could meet her? Cheryn?"

It seemed possible. "Sleepover?"

Fog rolled in later that evening, and though it wasn't Sunday, Naomi and I were having a campfire. The sun had since set, and it was probably past my bedtime, but that didn't stop us from staying outside. Perhaps it was the mild weather, or maybe we were waiting for someone.

"You think she'll really come?" Naomi asked. "Or are we wasting our time here?"

I shook my head as I stoked the logs. "She said she's a night owl."

"We could always watch that movie."

"Life isn't like the movies," I replied. "Besides, it's a foggy night. Cheryn said I should look for her on foggy nights."

"Let's talk about that," Naomi stood up and paced in a circle.

"About what?"

"How life isn't like the movies." She crossed her arms and turned towards the dock. "Every summer, we talk about going to summer camp, or looking at colleges—"

"We're going into eleventh grade," I said. "It's a little early to worry about college."

"Not that early," Naomi glared at me. "We have to get off of this island someday."

I stoked the logs again. "There aren't any colleges on the

island."

"Yes, but Jessica, would you come back here after you get a degree? Would you want to keep putting up with the tourists? How many jobs can there be here?"

"Why all the sudden interest in college and our future?" I looked up.

She gave a sarcastic wave. "Dad lost his job today."

"What?"

"The management at Jaquim Labs suddenly sent home the Ichthyological division. I didn't think they were in any financial trouble."

"The whole division?"

She nodded.

"Naomi, why didn't you say anything before?"

She shook her head. "I couldn't figure out how to face it, and tried to do my best to leave the news at home. I mean, Mr. Bridgewater made you assistant manager today, and—"

"Yeah, but your dad losing his job is a pretty big thing." I rose to my feet. "That's awful. Sometimes it's better just to say it. You of all people know that."

"I know." She made her way back to her chair.

"How's your mom handling this?"

She sniffled. "Okay, I guess."

"Your family's been through worse," I said. "I'm sure there's a good reason why they got laid off. If anything, I'll bet it's temporary."

"I hope you're right."

We sat in silence for a while. There didn't seem to be any hope of Cheryn coming to our campfire, and if I put another log on the fire we'd be out here until midnight.

"Should we put that movie in?" I asked.

"Okay."

For some reason, I regretted not watching that film sooner. Quite the adventure.

Naomi prodded me sometime after we had both gone to bed. She was sleeping on a cot on the floor and I was sleeping in my bed.

"Jess? You hear that?"

A nearly full moon was illuminating the night, and though there was probably fog outside, it had lifted enough to show the stars. But, eerily floating over the lapping of the tide against the shoreline, I heard Cheryn's soft soprano.

"We should go outside."

"Is it her?" Naomi asked.

I nodded. "But you have to be quiet. I don't want to wake the boys."

"You sound like your mother," Naomi giggled.

Outside, Naomi and I walked on the cool grass as the song continued. Now that we were outside, the evening felt almost magical. The fog obscured the channel and Brown Island, but the water beyond the dock was open and was perfectly calm, mirroring the moon above in a perfect exchange. If not for the bench, I wouldn't have been able to tell where the water ended and the sky began.

I quietly closed the door to the house and crept down to the yard, but the song had stopped.

"Didn't I hear something?" Naomi asked. "Where is she?"

I slowly walked onto the dock and kneeled before leaning over and looking beneath the wooden deck boards. Nothing. I had been certain I heard her.

"Well?" Naomi asked. "Are you messing with me or what?"

"I'm not," I said before sitting up. "I know what I heard."

"And so do I," Naomi said. "So where is she?"

I went all the way to the end of the dock.

"Jessica?" Naomi gave me a stern gaze. "Well?"

"I don't know," I confessed. "Maybe I did dream it all."

"You're so predictable," Cheryn said.

The sudden sound of her voice was enough to make me lose my balance. Naomi must have seen her first, because her gasp was so loud the crickets were distracted. When I turned, Cheryn had surfaced just behind the bench.

"Mind if I come up?"

I shook my head. "What if I say no?"

Cheryn chuckled quietly. "Just a moment." She gave a flick and quietly emerged from the water, pulling herself out with the bench. With a quick flip, she used her remaining momentum to slide onto the seat. The entire motion was both quiet and graceful.

Naomi glared at me. "Is she for real?"

Cheryn turned and looked at us both. "You must be Naomi. Hello."

"Um, hi," Naomi said, staring back at me. "Are you kidding me?"

"I could tell a joke if you like," Cheryn said. "Let's see." She held her hands in thought while her tail curled out in front of her. "Okay! A mermaid walked into a bar—No, that would never work, I can't start it like that."

"What if she walked on her hands?" Naomi asked as she started walking down the dock.

"I like that!" Cheryn nodded to herself. "That's perfect. But..." she trailed off, putting her finger to her chin. "No, that still wouldn't work."

"How does the rest of the joke go?" I asked.

"Anyway, she finds a seahorse, an anemone, and a flounder. The flounder asks all kinds of questions, and soon the anemone says 'hey, buddy, why all the questions?' and then the flounder says, 'it's because I'm investigating a crime, I'm a flatfish.'"

It was a horrible joke but we both couldn't contain our giggles.

"I got my laugh," Cheryn said with a shrug. "How is it? Don't quit your day job?"

"What is your day job?" Naomi asked.

"Picking up coins I find in the channel," Cheryn said. "Or just whatever."

"There's not much money in that," I said.

"No, but then I suppose I don't need much," Cheryn replied, turning towards Naomi. "It's nice to meet you, Naomi. I'm Cheryn." She actually offered a handshake.

Naomi looked her over, beside herself. "This, I mean, I can't—"

"You going to keep me hanging here?" Cheryn asked with wide eyes.

Naomi quickly took Cheryn's hand. "Your skin is so soft!"

"I use moisturizer," the mermaid replied.

Oh please. "Of all the fish in the sea, I find a comedian."

Cheryn smiled politely. "Actually, I'm glad you brought Naomi, Jessica." She pointed out beyond Brown Island, though we could scarcely see the distant shore in the fog. "Do either of you know the research facility across the bay?"

"The one north of town," I said. "Naomi knows it better than I do."

"It's on Point Caution," Naomi said. "My father just got laid off from that place."

"You mean, he lost his day job?" Cheryn sighed. "I'm sorry to hear that. I think they've been doing something odd to the water here."

"What do you mean?" I asked.

"I'm not sure how to describe it. The water tastes different."

"Can you try to describe it?"

Cheryn thought a moment. "I'm not sure I can. I mean, the water doesn't really taste like anything but there's something, just, different about it. Since a few days ago."

"Before I met you?" I asked.

"Maybe," Cheryn said. "It's possible I only noticed it today."

"Are you feeling okay?" I asked. "Nothing in the water is making you sick?"

Cheryn shook her head. "Aside from acting sillier, I feel okay."

"I want to know what they're doing over there. Find out why my father got laid off," Naomi said.

It wasn't like Naomi to be ambitious. "We can't just go over there," I said. "It's not a public facility. If you want in, you have to be a registered researcher."

"I wonder if that has anything to do with the lost girl," Cheryn said.

Naomi looked at me. "Does she know about Rachel?"

"Is that her name? Once in a while a newspaper ends up in the water. Yesterday I found a flyer for a missing girl," Cheryn said. "She looks like a beautiful young woman."

"Cheryn, she looks exactly like you," I said. "It's like you're twins."

"Don't be silly," Cheryn moved her tail up and down. "We're nothing alike."

I headed for the house. "I'll prove it."

Naomi and Cheryn were talking quietly when I returned with a police flyer that I printed out from Officer Robert's webpage. I showed it to Cheryn.

"Huh." The mermaid held it up in the moonlight. "How about that. Just like a mirror, though she styles her hair differently."

"There's no way you both could be sisters, is there?" I asked.

"It's hard to say without any color in this image," Cheryn said as she narrowed her eyes and scanned the grainy image again. "What shade is her hair?"

"I can get my yearbook," I said.

"That's black and white too," Naomi said. "She's a darker blonde."

"Wait, it's listed here," Cheryn said before reading from the flyer. "The missing teen is described as sixteen years old, with blue eyes and blonde hair. Five-five."

"Five feet five inches tall," I corrected. "That's what the marks mean."

"Oh, yes," Cheryn continued. "Was last seen by the Tilt-A-Whirl." She lowered the flyer. "What's a Tilt-A-Whirl?"

"It's an amusement park ride," I answered. "Rotating cars go around in a circle while moving up and down."

"Have you ridden on it?"

"The Tilt-A-Whirl can be a tame ride, but I always get dizzy on it," Naomi said. "I guess you both couldn't be sisters if your hair's that shade of red."

"My mother called my hair merlot," Cheryn said. "That's a grape used for wine, right?"

"We're not old enough to drink," Naomi said. "How old are you?"

"Maybe eighteen?" Cheryn asked herself. "I'm not sure, beyond the seasons it's difficult to keep track of the tides."

"We need to figure out how you can get a driver's license," Naomi said.

"Sure," I replied. "And a handicap sticker."

Cheryn didn't seem to be interested in driving anyplace. She handed me the flyer. "Unless you both know where this Rachel is, I don't think we'll be able to find out how similar we are."

"If there's a connection at all," I said. "To the research facility, to Rachel, to everything."

"I should probably go. Maybe I'll get funnier if I stay in the water longer," Cheryn said.

Naomi stepped closer to the edge of the dock. "I wouldn't mind being funnier."

Cheryn tapped Naomi's back, winking at me.

"Whoa!" Naomi caught her balance. "Hey!"

"I'd do it, but we should probably go back to sleep," I said. "And I think the dryer would wake the boys."

"Are John and Martin here too?" Cheryn asked.

"No," I said. "Just my brother and father."

Cheryn gave a nod and moved so that her tail was over the water, just to the right edge of the bench. A short hop later, she slipped quietly into the bay and surfaced a moment later. She brushed the wet hair back away from her face and held onto the dock. "Could you both go to this facility tomorrow?"

"It wouldn't hurt to talk to someone there," Naomi said. "I know the guard rather well."

"Perhaps you can keep me posted," Cheryn said. "It'd be fun meeting my double."

"I work in the afternoon," I said.

"We'll go early," Naomi said. "They probably won't let us in anyway."

Cheryn nodded. "Promise me you won't do anything to hurt your father."

"Of course not," Naomi said. "Promise."

The mermaid smiled. "Same time tomorrow?"

"Maybe a little closer to morning," I said with a yawn.

"You'll find me," Cheryn said. She ducked below the water and was gone.

"Nice meeting you," Naomi said before turning to me. "She is a real mermaid!"

"Told you," I replied.

Before I fell asleep again, I wondered why Cheryn hesitated to show herself again. I had decided that her song was no longer for me alone, as Naomi had clearly heard it also. There was a reason behind her inclusion of Naomi, I made certain of that. The mystery I now faced was to discover her reasons for returning to my dock. Something strange was happening in Friday Harbor, and it involved more than just a missing teenager.

The Red Shoe Adventure Club

Tuesday July 7th, 2009
Friday Harbor Herald

Monday, twenty scientists and assistants at Jaquim Labs were sent home from their place of work. The lab campus, adjacent to the University of Washington's Camp Courage located north of Friday Harbor, has reported an electrical incident that temporarily caused a closure of its Ichthyologics division. Jaquim Labs works with researchers from all around the world to maintain the water quality of the Straights of Juan de Fuca as well as an environment ideal for native species, as well as a continued focus on the world's waters.

Ichthyology is the study of fish species, and Jaquim Labs' division specifically studied the patterns of marine life in the region. The Friday Harbor Herald requested an interview with the administrator, Dr. Louise Gardiola. While an official interview was refused, Gardiola's office issued a statement about the situation. "At this time, we have sent the workers of our Ichthyologics division home due to an ongoing crisis within the division's research facilities. There is no need for the public to be concerned. All will be allowed to return to work by Wednesday. We must stress that there are no financial difficulties in the department. Other divisions, such as our plate tectonics, climate studies, hydroponics, hydrogeology and oceanographic cartography divisions should not expect any change in their daily research projects. At this time, we regret to announce that only our scuba training facility is closed until further notice. We hope that the Ichthyologics division will be returning to work soon, though at this time the future is uncertain. Thank you."

The Friday Harbor Herald reminds its readers that the search for Rachel Arlen is ongoing. Search parties continue their efforts on Point Caution, but have now expanded to the surrounding prairie near Star Valley Ranch, the woods near Mulno Cove, and Cattle Point within the national park on the south-eastern cape of the island. Interested parties are encour-aged to visit the Find Rachel Arlen Facebook page if they wish to assist. Inquiries can be directed to Julianna Gregorson, who is leading the search efforts.

Any information as to Rachel's whereabouts should be directed to the Friday Harbor Police or the newsroom offices of the Herald.

Early that morning, Naomi and I biked through town and went straight to the North Washington Marine Research Facility, which had been known as Jaquim Labs after the founder, Dr Keith Jaquim, had founded the facility in the 1970s. The facility is comprised of a series of buildings spread over forty acres as seen from the harbor, the road leading there was nothing more than a guard station and a closed chain link gate flanked by trees on either side. A tourist might've confused the gate as the entrance to a national park if not for the large REGISTERED RESEARCHERS ONLY sign.

As soon as we approached the guard house, a tall guard came out and stopped us.

"I see you, Naomi Rovan," he said. "What's your game today?"

"No games, Mr. Trom. I have an appointment with Dr. Gardiola."

"Do you?" He smirked. "She's not scheduled to be in for another hour."

"Too early," Naomi turned to me. "Great."

"Can I make one?" I asked.

"And you are?"

"Jessica Summers. I'm writing an editorial on water quality for the *Herald*."

He sized me up. "Awful young to be an editor. I didn't know Susan Donaldson was so desperate for articles."

"Mr. Trom, I need to speak with her," Naomi said. "Does she have any free time today? I need to ask why my father lost his job."

"You'll be glad to know he has a job." He pulled out a pair of readers and put them on. "But I should tell you, they pay me to keep unauthorized people from the facility. Generally that includes people who have been laid off."

"Wait, he has a job?" I asked. "What do you mean?"

"Nobody was laid off. Electrical trouble. That's all."

Naomi turned to me with a confused expression. "He said he had been laid off."

Trom shook his head. "Not true. If you're a contributor to the paper, surely you read it?"

Naomi stood her ground. "Then I demand to know exactly what happened. He has a right to know too. Everyone in town does."

"The director issued a statement to the paper."

Naomi wasn't about to give up. "He came home yesterday, very upset and depressed. I'd have a better chance of cheering him up if he received his news from the company, not from the newspaper. Can we hear it from the director herself?"

Mr. Trom muttered quietly. "Let me see what I can do."

Naomi smiled. "Thank you."

The guard went into the house and picked up his phone.

"How did you do that?" I asked.

"Because Jason Trom is a big softie," Naomi replied.

A moment later, Mr. Trom nodded and then hung up the phone before coming outside again. "Turns out Dr. Gardiola is on her way. Lock up your bikes. She said she'd pick you up on her way to the office. But her time is limited."

"I owe you one," Naomi said.

He raised his hand, holding up two fingers. "Two, Miss Rovan. You still owe me from a few months ago when you wanted to surprise your father on his birthday." He then went inside the guard shack and watched the security monitor.

Naomi grinned brightly as we locked up our bikes on a nearby rack.

"Nice work," I said. "I owe you one."

"Don't thank me yet," she replied. "We may not learn anything."

Several moments later, a red BMW drove up to the gate. The driver's window descended.

"Naomi?"

"Hello, Louise," Naomi said.

The doctor gave a wave. "Come on."

After a short ride to the lab complex, the doctor brought us into the lobby where we talked. She was an older Mexican woman with dark hair and glasses. We were given a choice of a hot beverage or a bottle of water if we wanted. Naomi went for the water. I opted for a cup of tea, even though it wasn't cold out.

"Now then. I haven't seen you in a while, Naomi," Louise said as we gathered in a lounge area to the west end of the lobby. "Not since that science project you did. Was that ninth grade?"

Naomi nodded. "My science project about protecting wet-lands."

"And—" She turned to me. "Is it Jessica? I think your father runs the hardware store."

"That's right," I replied. "Nice to meet you."

"Anything I can do for you both?"

Naomi leaned forward in the chair. "I wanted to talk to you about why my father and his co-workers were laid off yester-day."

Louise sighed and leaned back in her seat. "Yes, I thought you might. It's not correct to say he was laid off, though. The staff was sent home while a few electrical upgrades are made to the Ichthyologics lab. The large aquatics environment needs to be updated, along a few other upgrades to the rest of the facility that will disrupt the working conditions."

"The guard said something about an electrical issue?" I asked.

Louise shook her head. "Stories sometime filter down through the employees. No such incident occurred; I assure you. Our decision to send them home was made from a public health standpoint, rather than money, that required they be sent home while everything is checked."

"A public health incident?" Naomi asked. "Why not just say so?"

"Well, in a crisis you act according to safety protocols. Situations change. Parts for filtration units take time to arrive here on the island." She sipped from her coffee. "If anything, I failed to properly communicate the situation to the workers. In fact, I didn't get the full report myself until I was out the door yester-day."

"But why the upgrades?" Naomi asked.

I nodded. "Yeah, wouldn't something like that be scheduled in advance?"

"Usually, yes," Louise said. "This situation is unique, that much is certain."

"Did something happen to require upgrades?" I asked. "Filtration failure, electrical short? Something structural?"

"You're very perceptive," Louise said. "I'm afraid I can't say. It's part of an ongoing research project that I can't reveal the results of until the project is completed."

"Would that project have anything to do with water quality?" Naomi asked.

Louise drew aback. "That's an interesting question."

"I met with—" Naomi hesitated. "A diver commented on a

change in water quality. Said it might be affecting purple sea stars."

"You featured those in your science project, if I recall," Louise said. "Did this diver offer any evidence to support this?"

"He didn't say," Naomi replied.

"Was this recently?"

"Maybe in the last week," Naomi said.

"Ocean water is very stable," Louise said. "Most of the time it takes a few months to notice any drastic shift in clarity and quality. If you like, you can check our webpage and contact one of the student researchers from the university to look into it. Would make for a great summer project if you're interested, and certainly would look good on an upcoming college application."

Naomi gave me a glance. "Sure, I'll do that."

"It's true what they say about the young people these days. Apply yourself, girls, because there needs to be more women like you in science." Louise checked her watch. "I'm afraid that's all I have time for this morning. There's a meeting starting in five minutes. Talk to Brian at the desk and he'll give you a ride back to the gate, okay?" She rose to her feet. "I will send an email out to your father's work group as well. They should be able to go back to work by Thursday. Hopefully that will help to clarify things."

"Thanks very much," Naomi replied. "I appreciate your time."

"I can always find a few minutes for a budding researcher," Louise said. She shook Naomi's hand, and mine, and left for the elevator.

~ ❋ ~

My shift at the juice bar started an hour later, and when I arrived, I saw Kelsey's SIREN poster displayed prominently in the window.

I pulled it down immediately, wadded it into a ball and into the nearest trash bin.

"What'd you do that for?" Hannah, another co-worker, was Melissa's polar opposite. She seemed to believe mermaids were real just as much as I was, only I had more evidence to support that reality.

"I didn't give permission to post it," I said. "What nonsense."

"Since when are you the boss?" Hannah asked.

"Since my nephew promoted her yesterday!" Leia called from the back room.

"Nonsense?" Hannah protested. "It's not nonsense. The

poster is lovely, and might bring people into the store."

"Only to ask what kind of booze we put in the juice," I replied. "Not going to happen."

"You're such a manager," Hannah replied before going back to her work, cutting fruit for the juicer.

"It's my job," I replied.

As I finished work and prepared to bike home after the juice bar closed at 5, John, Martin, and a few other boys from the track team were heading by. It was too early for the track team to be organized for school, and too late to assume they were all running on their own accord. Some of them had hiking gear, while others were just in a hurry.

"John!" I called to him. "What's the commotion?"

"There's been a plane crash!"

I caught up on my bike. "A plane crash? When?"

"Just now," John replied. "Didn't you hear it?"

"No." I must've been in the cooler putting away the rest of the fresh produce. "Where?"

"East of the airport, south of the road that goes to your place. You coming?"

I went along, even though I wasn't a fire fighter. Maybe there was some way to help.

Smoke could be seen before I saw it, and smelled it too. My weekly campfires were nothing compared to this. The damaged craft couldn't have been larger than most planes that land at Valley Field, which mostly consist of 10-passenger cabins or smaller. Even when a plane landed, most of the time the thick trees blocked the noise from the engines. Unless you were standing at the end of the runway, you'd never hear it.

The wreckage was localized to the open field which had been the fairgrounds years ago before everything moved into town and became a more localized event. A tire from the landing gear had ended up twenty yards from the craft, while the fuselage itself was leaning akimbo to the crushed remnants of the landing gear. The engines were engulfed, but the cabin was accessible.

"Where's the fire department?"

Our island's fire department served mainly the airport, though they could reach any emergency, anywhere on the island, in a matter of minutes. Needless to say, they had beat us to the scene. Our group was promptly relegated to the side-lines. The island's only ambulance was also here, though if anyone survived, they'd have to be—ironically—air lifted to Sidney for medical treatment. The clinic on the island was good for minor injuries, flu shots, and the occasional heart attack, but certainly too small to handle an epidemic.

After seeing the disappointment on the boy's faces, it occurred to me that all of them wanted to be the first to save someone, just in case the pilot flew with someone who needed a date worse than triage.

Maybe I wanted that too. So much for that adventure.

John came over to me. "So, what do you think?"

"What do I think?" The question seemed odd. "I think it's a plane crash."

"Fine analysis, Bones," he said with a smirk. "Looks bad."

In the distance the chopping of a helicopter, which had just taken off from the airport, landed in the field. Medics poured out, all of them ducking from the rush of the rotors.

John leaned close and said something in my ear.

"What?"

"Have you seen anything like this before?"

I shook my head. "No."

We watched the scene unfold. John gasped.

I saw it too. A survivor.

"They pulled someone from the wreckage!"

Two EMTs carried a stretcher towards the helicopter. Soon, a second victim was carried. The passengers were wearing neck braces, but otherwise I couldn't see if any treatment had been administered.

"Wait, I think there's one more," John said.

Sure enough, they carried a third stretcher, containing a person who wasn't wearing a neck brace. Perhaps this third passenger was less injured than the others. The first two were loaded into the helicopter, while the third was taken on the ambulance.

"Do you think they're okay?" I asked John.

He shrugged. Perhaps he didn't want to say.

They closed the doors to the helicopter, and cleared the area as it slowly began to ascend. While it took off, the fire department sprayed foam onto the engine. Flames were quenched and soon the smoke began to dissipate.

"I guess that's that," I said.

John shook his head. "Come with me."

"What?" I asked. "Why?"

"Trust me."

I followed him, though I wasn't sure why. He went straight up to the fire chief.

"Chief Erickson, a word?" John tapped him on the back. "Can you tell us anything for the Friday Harbor Herald?"

The chief, a greying but stout man, turned and gave John a smug look. "You're not Art Gedding. Who are you supposed to be?"

"John Donaldson. Junior investigator."

He gave a nod. "Sure, son."

"Can you make a statement for the press release?"

"It's a plane crash, son. Cessna 425, inbound from Seattle. We're assuming mechanical failure, considering the crash occurred on a clear day with light winds and clear skies. With the pilot, there were three passengers. As you saw, two are to be air lifted with serious injuries, while one has minor injuries and is being treated locally."

"Is there anything else, chief? Names?" John asked.

He shook his head. "It just happened, son. The first thing you learn about investigative reporting is that sometimes it takes time for the events to unfold. That's all to say for now."

John offered to shake his hand. "Thanks very much."

Chief Erickson did so. "Aren't you Susan's son?"

"Yes sir."

"Make sure you double check your editorial before showing it to your editor. Just because she's your old lady doesn't mean she'll print anything, ya hear?"

"Yes sir, I will."

John walked as I biked back down the road to my house. "It's nice of you to come down this far, even though you live west of the airport," I said.

"I wanted to know if you had come up with a charter yet for the club."

"No," I shook my head. "Haven't had a chance to yet."

"Maybe I can help you with it." He waved his hands in the air dramatically. "Tell us a story, grand and bold, let be shared with the young and the old. Should it be scary? Fantastic or strange, may it be adventurous, insightful and not spur of the moment, sprung up from the range." He chuckled quietly. "What do you think?"

"Nice poem. But I'm still dancing around the name." I rode around in a circle on my bike. "The Red Shoe Adventure Club."

"What's wrong with it? It's perfect."

Maybe it wasn't so bad. "I could get to like a name like that,"

I said. "Sure."

"Awesome." He clapped his hands in quiet anticipation.

Before dinner, John and I hashed out a charter. For *The Red Shoe Adventure Club*, the rules for stories would be simple.

The Red Shoe Adventure Club. Participants are open to anyone, male or female, as long as they bring a tale of an adventure or event to last between five and twenty minutes in length. Stories must be presented with the phrase 'For your consideration.' All stories must have a beginning and an end. Official meetings require a campfire and requisite snacks. Meetings cannot last longer than midnight.

My father came up with the last one. He originally sprung for eleven, but I negotiated.

John later went home after dinner, and I decided it was time I did something with the fishing net that Cheryn had left me. Using Dad's tools, I used the power drill to make a few pilot holes and hammered the nails into the wall. I was all set to suspend the net around the nails when something fell and hit the floor.

It was a green pearl earring, designed for pierced ears. Could this have belonged to Cheryn? Since she had long hair, I had yet to notice if she wore earrings. I'd have to ask her about it the next time I saw her.

Rain was moving in tonight, and the likelihood of Cheryn coming to the dock would be minimal. Guess I'd have to sing myself to sleep tonight.

Wednesday July 8th 2009
Friday Harbor Herald

At approximately 5:05 p.m. Tuesday a Cessna 425 jet crash-ed just east of the Friday Harbor regional airport on Barnacle Point between Turn Point and Pear Point roads. Emergency crews report there was one death in the accident, believed to be the pilot of the craft. As of press time, the pilot's name had not yet been released.

The Cessna was reportedly carrying two other passengers, one of whom has been reported in serious condition while the other reportedly received light injuries. Neither victim's name has been released. Airport officials believe the crash was caused by pilot error, and the FAA has recovered the flight recorder prior to today's investigation. The accident scene was secured by local officials and air traffic at the airport was restored by 8:00 p.m. that evening.

Teams searching for Rachel Arlen have reported a discovery of a green pearl earring that may or not belong to the missing teen. The earring was discovered near a pile of rocks above the cliffs along Point Caution just east of Jaquim Labs. A searcher who did not wish to be identified claims to have seen a photograph of the missing teen that confirms the earring may belong to Miss Arlen. We regret that this information is un-verified, however, as there is no direct evidence that the missing teen ever wore or owned any such earring.

The staff of the Friday Harbor Herald would like to remind its readers that only information pertinent to the case should be offered. Accordingly, the staff would also like to remind its readers that the writing contest runs through July 15th and to keep sending submissions.

The rain continued through the night and into the morning. I thought I heard Cheryn's voice, but it turned out to be just Tim playing the radio. Dad was kind enough to give me a ride into town when I started work. Perhaps he wanted to keep tabs on me, as he usually went into the store at seven in the morning. The news of Rachel's disappearance must've finally set in.

By nine, I was all set to open the shop but Melissa had yet to arrive. I picked up the office phone and called her cell. She answered on the second ring.

"Melissa? It's Jessica."

"Hey, yeah, I can't come in today," Melissa said.

"Why not?"

"I'm going to Mulno Cove to join a group of searchers who are looking for Rachel."

"Um, you're scheduled to work today," I said.

"Yeah, I know, but I'm in Rachel's class and I'm worried about her."

"So, you're not going to come in?"

"Will that be a problem?"

I sighed. "You know I'll have to write you up about it."

"This is really important to me, Jessica. I know you just got promoted and all, and I don't want to lose my job—"

"Fine, I'll forget it for today, but I want you here all the sooner Friday."

"Thank you!" Click.

I put down the receiver with a groan. "Leia? Can you come in here, please?"

"Yes?" She appeared in the doorway with a wet towel in her hand. "What's up?"

"No Melissa today."

She gave a nod. "We'll just have to step up our game. See if Thomas wants overtime."

"Will do." I grumbled to myself and pulled up the rolodex. Checking Thomas's contact information, I called him up. "Thomas, can you come in early?"

I don't know why I headed to Mulno Cove after work. Maybe because it had been a quiet day in the shop. Maybe because the rain had finally lightened up and I was bored. Maybe because I was genuinely curious.

My bike got stuck in the thick sand at the beach as I approached the group, which was beginning to break up. Guess they all had to be home for supper. Melissa was chatting with a few of her friends in a group in front of me.

"Melissa, good." I gave a tug and pulled my bike out of the sand.

She came over. "Jess! Um—" She brushed aside her face. "Uh, how was work?"

"Quiet. I called Thomas in early, and honestly you weren't missed."

"Good," she sighed with a wince. "I'm so sorry."

"How's the search going?"

"Oh!" She perked up and became excited. "This guy came by to help us. Said a plane crash couldn't keep him away—"

"A plane crash?" I asked. "Was he one of the survivors from the crash yesterday?"

"Yeah, maybe," Melissa said. "A fellow from Seattle named Brooks."

The name wasn't familiar. "Should there be a first name?"

Melissa shook her head. "Only called himself Brooks. Seemed to have a real enthusiasm for the search, though I wasn't sure he was exactly looking for Rachel."

My eyes narrowed. "Why wouldn't he be?"

"Knew an awful lot about fish and marine life," Melissa waved to someone who called to her. "Listen, we're all going to a barbecue at Suzie's, you should come."

"I wasn't here searching all day," I trailed off. "Did you find anything?"

Melissa shook her head. "Nothing. If there was any trail, the rain took care of it."

My eyes drifted across the beach. Logs, sand, kelp and nothing else.

"I should go. See you tomorrow?" Melissa asked.

I shook my head. "It's Tom's shift. But I'll see you Friday, at ten sharp."

She smiled. "I'm sorry, I will. Bye! Thanks!" With that, she ran off.

I sighed to myself before making my way back to the road. A

small part of me was glad that the conversation had gone well, but another part was sad that they didn't find Rachel. The more I thought about it, the more I wondered if there might be any chance she could be found.

I sat up and thought a while that night. While I might have been hoping to hear Cheryn's song on the tides, I also began to wonder how things were working out since the Fourth. Naomi's dad hadn't lost his job, and would be back on the job in a few days. John was writing editorials for the Herald, and Martin-

Actually, I hadn't heard from Martin since I last saw him at the campfire. He must be busy giving swimming lessons at the school.

For some reason, I kept focusing on that pearl earring. Sure, it had to have belonged to Cheryn, but she'd only wear it if she had pierced ears.

When I was ten, Mom took me to Sidney to have mine pierced. I hated every moment of it. I'm not into the girly stuff, and especially anything that might be considered fashionable. Mom insisted, and I got starter earrings and everything. The studs caught on my hair, on my bedsheets, on towels, everything. Six months passed and I took them out. Nowadays, the hole is completely healed. In all fairness, I don't feel like I'm missing anything by not wearing them every given day. Even at work, where most of the time, my hair covers my ears.

The pearl earring was made with a silver base and either steel, titanium or white gold studs. Only a woman with pierced ears could possibly wear it. Cheryn must have pierced ears.

I put the earring onto my dresser. Having neglected to finish hanging the cargo net yesterday, I finished hanging the net by suspending it between the nails along the wall. Then, my stuffed panda, dolphin and rabbit all went inside. Giving the completed display a proper look, I decided it wasn't too girly to stay like this. Mom would certainly be pleased.

One way or another, she must've known I was thinking about her. She called my Skype.

"Hi Mom." I left the video chat off, since there was never a very strong connection.

"Hi dear. How was the Fourth?"

"Fine. Tim had fun at the carnival."

"And you?"

"It was okay."

"Did you have a chance to think about my offer?"

A few weeks ago, when school let out, she offered to invite me for a visit. Officially, Dad and Mom both had joint custody over Tim and I, even though the divorce occurred two years ago. Unofficially, Dad kept custody of us because both Tim and I had our school here and didn't want to leave our friends. Especially Naomi. Without her, I don't know if I would even care about school. Besides, as I've said before, San Juan Island is home. Visiting Mom in Seattle would be fun, but-

"I don't know, Mom."

"How's the job?"

"Mr. Bridgewater made me an assistant manager."

"That's great! Wonderful! You're moving up in the town."

"Or just the juice bar," I replied. "How's Harry?"

My mom suddenly became silent. Guess she didn't want to talk about her boyfriend.

"It's not a secret that you're dating, Mom. I guess I'm okay with it, but you could've waited a while."

"I did," my mother replied. "Jessica, you know I love you and your brother."

"And Dad?"

She hesitated. "Things have become so complicated, dear. Dan and I have agreed—"

"Agreed to try other things, I know," I said. "You explained everything a long time ago."

"Neither of you did anything wrong."

"Me or Dad?" I asked.

"You, Tim," she hesitated. "Or Dan."

"Mom—" I began.

"It's not worth discussing," she replied quickly. "Listen, I promised you this would be temporary. I'll admit it's a long temporary, but for today, it'll have to stay that way. Since you're an assistant manager now, I suppose it will be harder for you to visit."

"Maybe I could find a week in August." It seemed a silly suggestion, but at the same time not that silly at all. Inconvenient, maybe, but not silly.

"Oh, honey, don't try to cheer me up. You're becoming such an independent young woman. Maybe that's all I really needed to talk to you about."

"About growing up?" Suddenly ideas of Martin's after school club rushed into my head. How corny. How vile. How utterly stupid. How did we get on that topic?

"No, no, just glad to hear things are going well. You ever feel the need to talk, or come away for the weekend or anything—"

"I know, Mom, you're just a phone call away," I said. "I'm fine here. There's plenty to keep me busy."

"Okay dear, I have to go but you call if me if you need anything."

"I will."

"Virtual hug, honey. Bye-bye." She closed the connection.

With that, I turned off the computer. I decided I wasn't ready to forgive my mother for breaking up with Dad. Likewise, I suddenly realized that I hadn't told her about Cheryn. But then, could I? I hadn't told Dad about her new boyfriend for the same reason. How do you tell someone you're not crazy, sixteen years old, and still believing in mermaids? The idea of telling my parents about her was just as crazy as asking Mom to move back home.

It wasn't going to happen. I was sure of that. At the same time, I had managed to learn to deal with the absence of her in the house long before. I had learned to do my own laundry, cook my own meals, keep my room and sheets clean all without Dad's help. Yet, I knew he needed someone to lean on, too. Now, with Mom gone, that someone was me and Tim.

I could always contact her when I needed. Suddenly I felt the need to contact Cheryn. If not for any immediate questions I had, I wanted the comfort in knowing that I could.

Thursday July 9th, 2009
Friday Harbor Herald

Police were called to a teen rally Wednesday evening that took place at the baseball fields near Friday Harbor Elementary. A local group, known as the Society for Interesting Re-integration of Endangered Non-humanoid Species, or S.I.R.E.N.S. for short, was holding a rally when the father of missing teen Rachel Arlen, Michael Arlen, arrived and accused the society of defaming his daughter and compromising the investigation into her disappearance.

The leader of the group, Kelsey Marigold, claimed that the teen hadn't gone missing but instead simply chose to "swim away," insinuating that the teen had, according to several interviewed witnesses, become a mermaid. A scuffle later ensued and several S.I.R.E.N.S. supporters, as well as several opposing witnesses, were taken to the local clinic for light injuries. According to police, no arrests were made as the scuffle was comprised largely of pushing, shoving and aggressive name-calling.

"My daughter is missing, and anyone who thinks she simply grew fins and swam away is seriously deluded," said Michael Arlen. He later went on to say "We hope that Rachel will soon be found, alive and well" before admitting a lack of faith in the local educational system.

In other news, FAA officials have announced that Harrison MacGregor was the pilot who perished in Tuesday's plane crash. Flight data recorded a sudden gain in altitude, causing the plane to stall and miss the runway by a half mile before skidding belly first onto the ground and rolling laterally. Accor-ding to the local flight controller, there was believed to have been a heated discussion in the cockpit at the time of the crash. FAA officials have ruled the incident an accident. The two survivors, Dr. Julian Wilton of the Boston Oceanographic Institute and an assistant, Dr. Brooks Bagley, continue to recover. Dr. Wilton remains in critical condition at Regions Hospital in Sidney, B.C., while Dr. Bagley is believed to be in the area conducting research at Jaquim Labs. Citing privacy concerns, Dr. Bagley refused the Herald's requests for an official inter-view, instead claiming to be deeply immersed in his research. When asked again by our staff, Bagley declined to identify the scope of his research project.

That morning I slept in before finally giving into the smell of pancakes and bacon. Something seemed off, though. Usually Dad went into the hardware store early during the week. Who could be downstairs cooking pancakes and bacon?

I threw a flannel over my undershirt and rushed down to the kitchen. Tim was there heating up pancakes in the microwave. As for the bacon—

"It was already cooked," he said before I could ask. "Dad didn't want to wake you."

Tim, who looked just like his father but a third of the height, had surprised the family before on occasion. Like the time he wanted to surprise Mom and Dad by making them breakfast in bed, which didn't work because his plan involved bringing the stove into their room. Or the time he surprised them while they were fighting on the deck, forcing a cease-fire of insults. Or the time he sat and played Nintendo in the living room while they were in a heated discussion behind him, and I had to be the one to break them apart. The following day, Mom decided to move to Seattle.

It was nice to be surprised in a good way for a change.

"Thought for sure you were responsible, munchkin," I said. "Thanks."

"You're welcome," he replied.

We shared breakfast together and then the Nintendo went on. I headed outside after that with my latest Kayak magazine and some orange juice. I'm not sure why I went all the way out to the dock, but I did. If I hadn't, I wouldn't have known that Cheryn was there.

"Psst."

Surprised again, I nearly dropped my juice.

"I'm under the dock. Jessica?"

"Yes, I'm here. Is everything okay, Cheryn?"

"No. There are an awful lot of divers in the bay today."

"Can you come up onto the dock?" I asked.

"I'm not sure I should. Your dock is sheltered, but not that sheltered when everyone is up and awake in the bay."

"What about your grotto?"

"It's hidden fairly well, but not that well. If they find the entrance, there will be no safe place to hide." She held herself tightly. "I have nowhere else to go."

I wasn't sure what she meant. Surely if there was one mermaid in the area, there might just be others. "Aren't there others with you? Friends of yours?"

"No. At least, not now. They've all swam out to sea," Cheryn replied. "They've been gone for some time, and didn't tell me where they were going."

"That doesn't seem very nice," I said. Sounds lonely.

"I don't believe they left to be mean, but thank you for saying so."

"Listen, maybe we can talk about this—" I trailed off and looked toward the house. My view drifted toward the canoe. "Naomi."

"Is she here?" Cheryn asked.

"No, I just got an idea. Just lay low and listen for me, okay?"

"What's this about?" Naomi asked, half awake and sleepy as she leaned her bike against the garage. "Business hours don't start until nine."

"It's like I told you on the phone, something came up," I said as I tossed her a life jacket. "Give me a hand with the canoe."

"You called me out of bed to go for a boat ride?"

"Not exactly. Did you bring that skirt like I asked?"

"Sure." She motioned toward her green backpack. "Why?"

The two of us carried the canoe over to the dock and pulled it into the water.

"Cheryn?" I asked. "Are you here?"

A small pop in the water and she was at the surface, just below the dock. "I'm here."

"You need help with Cheryn?" Naomi asked. "What's going on?"

"What's your idea, Jessica? And what's with the canoe?" Cheryn asked.

"We're going on a boat ride."

Cheryn swam out from under the dock so she was between the bench and the shore. "Great idea. Can we go by the research facility?"

"Of course," I said. "Can you sit on the dock please?"

Cheryn gave a flick of her tail and, using her arms for leverage, pulled herself onto the dock and turned, landing gently afterwards. "What's the plan?"

"How do you do that?" Naomi asked.

"She's a pro," I said. "Where's the skirt?"

"Here," Naomi took off her backpack and unzipped it, removing a carefully folded blue skirt from the inside. "This belongs to my grandmother. Why do you need it?"

"For her," I said with a nod to Cheryn. "She's going to take a ride with us."

Cheryn smiled and clapped her hands quietly. "That's brilliant!"

"More like crazy," Naomi said.

"Can you hold yourself up, Cheryn?" I kneeled next to her. "We have to get that on you."

"This is lovely material," Cheryn said as she reached up to touch the blue linen. "Won't it get wet on me?"

"Jessica, you didn't say it would get wet," Naomi began.

"There're divers all over the bay, Naomi. We have to find a way to hide her, and this was the best idea I could come up with on short notice."

Naomi nodded. "Okay. Guess we have no choice."

I ran over to the canoe and stepped in, carefully moving myself along the dock so that the canoe was next to Cheryn. I was in position. "Okay, give me the skirt."

Naomi handed it to me. "Okay, Cheryn. Tail out."

Cheryn did so.

"Can you sit up?" I asked.

She put her hands onto the dock and pushed herself up, suspending above the wooden planks. "How's this?"

"Good." I put the skirt onto her scales and wrapped it around her lower body, sliding it up onto her waist and securing the clasps. "How's that?"

"Feels a little tight," Cheryn said. "My arms are getting tired."

I quickly adjusted the skirt. "There. Better?"

"Better," Cheryn said before lowering herself to the dock. "How do I look?"

The hobble skirt covered Cheryn from the waist down, though her tailfin could not be fully contained within the wide pleats at the bottom.

"We'll have to do something about that fin," Naomi said. "Do you have a towel?"

"A wet towel," Cheryn said. "I trust you hadn't planned on sinking your canoe."

"There's a beach towel on the deck," I said. "I found the largest one I could."

"I'll get it." Naomi jumped up and ran.

Cheryn casually flicked her tail, getting the bottom of the hobble skirt wet as she dipped it into the water. "How fun is this going to be?"

I gave a nervous smile. "Fun."

"This is a small thing," Cheryn said. "But do you have a sun hat? I tan easy."

"Sure," I said. "But I can't go into the house unless someone holds onto the canoe."

No sooner had I said it, Cheryn hopped into the canoe. She aimed for the center bench, but landed with more momentum than she had anticipated, and pulled me to the ground to stop herself. I landed with a thud in the bottom of the canoe, narrowly missing my head against the side.

"That wasn't very graceful," Cheryn said with a giggle. "Should I sit up here?"

"Let's see what it looks like," I said.

Naomi came back with the large beach towel. "This one?"

"Perfect," I said.

"Cushy!" Cheryn was already sitting on the plush center bench. "Naomi, what do you think? Can you see beneath the skirt?"

"No," she said. "Your scales match the skirt, and even if it is a little see-through it looks good. Very fashionable. I don't think you're a mermaid or anything."

Cheryn smiled and stretched her tail, hitting the chair in the front. "Oops!"

"Yeah, try not to do that," I said.

"Can you get the hat, then?" Cheryn asked.

While Cheryn sat in the canoe and held onto the dock, I collected the oars and life jackets from the lawn. Then I went inside the collect my mother's sun hat from the closet. As I went by the living room, I saw that the Nintendo was on, but not being played. Tim was looking out towards the dock from the window. He hadn't stopped to pause his game.

"What are you up to?" Tim asked.

"Nothing, just going for a canoe ride," I said. I found the large sun hat, a white brimmed cap my mother used to wear on the deck. "We're going to be out for a while. Will you be okay?"

"Who is that in the canoe?"

"Naomi," I replied.

"Who else is in the canoe?"

"I have to go, Tim. Will you be okay? We should back before

lunch."

"Jess, who is that in the canoe?"

I hesitated. There was no hiding her now. "Cheryn."

"Who's Cheryn?"

"A friend. I have to go now, Tim."

"Who's Cheryn?"

"I'll tell you later, okay? I have to go."

"Who's Cheryn!"

It pained me to leave him hanging like that, but it had to be done. I grabbed three pairs of sunglasses from the kitchen counter and exited out the back.

Outside, Naomi was livid. "What took you so long?" She had already donned her life jacket and was holding onto the canoe from the dock.

"Had to make sure Tim was okay."

"And is he?"

I sighed. "Let's go."

"That's your brother, right?" Cheryn looked toward the window and gave a wave. "Hi!"

I put the hat onto Cheryn's head. The white hat matched her blouse and skirt surprisingly well, as if she was a 1920s bouffant on holiday. "Here, and you also have to put on a life jacket."

"Why?"

The question seemed odd. Certainly, she couldn't drown.

"Consistency. Nobody needs to know you're a mermaid. Everyone wears life jackets."

"Naomi, can you help me?" Cheryn asked as she picked it up.

Naomi had to turn around, kneeling on the seat to help Cheryn with the snaps on the life jacket. The purple vest clashed with her outfit, but at least looked honest.

"Are we good?" I asked.

Naomi moved into the front of the canoe and sat. "Good."

I carefully climbed onto the back seat and pushed away from the dock, brought the canoe about, and steered us beyond and into the bay.

"How's that?" Naomi asked.

"Good, thank you," Cheryn said. She then picked up the towel from around her fin and dunked it into the water. "This is going to be so fun!"

"Yeah, fun," I said. All I could think was how bad an idea it would be if she was discovered for what she is. But at least this way she would be safe from any divers. The worst-case scenario meant she'd just dive into the water and swim as fast as she could.

Naomi turned around again and got herself situated. "I'm in."

Cheryn then put the soaked wet towel around her fin carefully so that there was no chance of it being seen by the sun or anyone else. "Did you put on your own jacket, Jessica?"

I hadn't. I put down the oar and put snapped it on. "Done."

"My grandmother might not forgive me for letting you wear that skirt," Naomi said. "But you sure wear it well."

"Thank you," Cheryn said. "Where should we go? The far side of the island?"

"No, the currents are too strong," Naomi said. "Let's go check on the university."

"The research camp?" I said. "Yeah, that's perfect."

Cheryn giggled in spite of herself. "This will be such a treat!"

A few moments later, we were halfway across the bay and cruising along the western shore of Brown Island. I made certain to keep our course away from other boaters and docks in case anyone got too close to get a better look at Cheryn. I made a mental note about the weight of what we were actually doing. Here we were, Naomi and I, in the middle of the bay, with a mermaid in a skirt, in a canoe in full sight of all of Friday Harbor and every tourist in the strait. Any one of them could have a camera phone and post her photo on the National Enquirer website in moments.

"This is another one of those moments where I could really use a camera," I said.

"Those are devices that take photographs, right?" Cheryn asked. "Yes, this is a moment that I'll never forget."

"I'm not going to ask a tourist to take your photo," I replied.

"So let's not talk about that, Jess. How about we talk about why we're doing this?" Naomi asked. "Didn't you say there might be divers in the bay?"

"Yes," Cheryn said. "I saw a few of them in the strait, but I cannot say for certain if they saw me. I hid within a patch of kelp as they swam by."

"How many?" Naomi asked.

"Maybe three divers," Cheryn answered. "There may be more."

"Did you see any markings on them?" I asked. "A name of a company, or a school, anything that might clue into where they came from or were researching?"

"No," Cheryn replied. "At least, I do not believe so. One of them was taking notes on some kind of underwater tablet thing, but I don't think he saw me. Naomi, did you find out anything about your father's job?"

"His whole department was sent home due to an electrical issue," Naomi answered. "The director said that there were repairs and upgrades that needed to be done immediately for both research projects and researchers alike. He was allowed to go back to work today."

"Good, I'm glad for him," Cheryn said. "If only I could be safe in the bay."

"Cheryn, this is going to sound strange, but do you have pierced ears?" I asked.

She turned to me and held back her hair, showing her unblemished ear lobe. "Do humans pierce their skin? How barbaric." She readjusted her hair. "Why do you ask?"

"Yesterday I found a green pearl earring caught up in the fishing net that you gave me, but it could only be worn by someone with pierced ears."

Cheryn sat with her hands in her lap. "Green pearl earring? With the silver base?"

"Yes, but only the one," I said.

Cheryn reached into the shirt pocket of her blouse and held something over the edge of the canoe so I could see. "Did it look like this?"

Sure enough, there was the other earring. "Yes!"

"Good, I hoped I hadn't lost it." Cheryn put the earring back into her pocket. "You'll give it back when we return to your dock?"

"Of course," I replied.

"What's so special about an earring if you don't have pierced ears?" Naomi asked.

"They were a gift for me from Mariana, who was living out of a grotto north of here," Cheryn explained. "She gave them to me before the last snow. I never figured out what I was supposed to do with them."

"Did you stay here all winter?" I asked.

Cheryn shrugged.

"Wasn't it cold?" Naomi asked.

"The currents keep things warm enough," Cheryn replied. "Though some days I could use a coat, or a heater."

"Really? You're crazy to stay here all year," Naomi gasped. "I mean, you wouldn't want to plug a heater in underwater."

"I'll have to find you a wet suit," I said.

"Maybe." Cheryn suddenly changed the subject. "Is that the facility where your father works, Naomi?"

Cheryn had pointed to the two-story glass walled building on Point Caution beyond the research camp, a short distance up the hill.

"Yes, that's the place," Naomi replied. "We shouldn't get too close to their marina."

I adjusted the canoe to turn back toward the southwest, which would bring us closer to downtown Friday Harbor.

"What does your father work on?" Cheryn asked.

"Ichthyology, studying fish and water climate," Naomi replied. "In fact, his department might be to blame for the water tasting better."

"You should thank them for me," Cheryn said. "Can you go there again?"

"Why?" I asked. "What else can we learn about the place?"

"Have you gone inside?" Cheryn asked. "See what kind of changes they're making?"

I put the oar in the water to slow our momentum as the canoe slowly came about, and soon we were pointing north to face Jaquim Labs again.

"Won't we be caught?" I asked.

"Do you see any construction vehicles? Any signs of workers?" Cheryn asked.

"No." Naomi turned to look at me. "Why can't we go ashore?"

"Could you go, Jessica?" Cheryn asked. "Or both of you, if you want. Leave me one of your paddles."

"What if they find you?" I asked. The idea of leaving a mermaid in a canoe so close to the very researchers that were looking for her seemed foolish.

"I'll stay with her," Naomi said. "Jessica, you go. You know where it is?"

"First floor, northeast corner?" I asked.

Naomi nodded. "It has to be on the first floor because of the stasis tanks. Maybe you can peek in through the windows. You won't need a pass or anything, and you shouldn't even have to go inside the building."

"Just go quickly, and then come back," Cheryn said. "It'll mean so much to me."

"This is crazy," I said.

"Please?" Cheryn turned to look at me. "You have no idea how hard it is to stay hidden underwater, Jessica. We mers have to work very hard to stay hidden. I watched you for months before I even had the courage to come to your dock. If I was discovered by researchers, even if a diver caught the slightest glimpse, they would never stop looking for me. They may be looking as we speak. It's my biggest wish to be able to continue to live in these waters."

Wish. I hadn't forgotten she said something about a wish the other day. Guess even mermaids know how to twist arms.

"Okay, okay," I said. I steered the canoe before moving us closer to the dock. "But I'll only be gone fifteen minutes."

"I cannot thank you enough."

~  ~

Once we approached the dock, Cheryn took the oar from me but stayed in the middle. Naomi got out first and held the canoe close to the dock. Then, I climbed out and tossed my life jacket into the front. Finally, Naomi took my spot in the back.

She pulled out her phone. "It's 9:30. You have fifteen minutes, and then we'll circle around here and pick you up. Okay?"

I checked my watch. "Fifteen minutes. I'll be here."

"Be safe," Cheryn pushed the canoe away from the dock. "Thank you."

"If you have time, check the scuba training area," Naomi said. "There should be windows along that north side, just beyond my father's lab."

"Sure," I said. "Why?"

"It's got a large training pool, and might be a good place to hide something suspicious if it can only live in the water. Can you check it out if you have time?"

"Okay, okay," I ran up the dock and onto the shore. I set my cell phone to vibrate after ten minutes and headed up the hill.

Naomi and Cheryn spun out and rowed out into the bay. I was on my own.

There were other researchers around the camp, mostly college age students. Nobody seemed to notice me, even though I knew I was completely out of place. Some of them had identification badges around their necks. I didn't, but hopefully that wouldn't matter.

I continued past a row of cabins and several larger research buildings. Aquatics Center. Breverton Center. Eagle Mess Hall. Wildlife Center. Wolf Camp Barracks. Cougar Camp Barracks. San Jaquim Center for Climatology.

Finally, I crossed the main road that ran the length of the camp and followed it towards the Jaquim Labs complex. The grounds were open and free of hiding places, but there was a path that wound to a maintenance facility on the east side. That would do.

I resisted the urge to run and stayed cool, walking my way down the path and trying not to appear too abnormal. A few researchers were walking by, apparently here to enjoy a mid-morning coffee break out on the small patio area.

There was a hedge and an open green field between the path and the northeast corner of the building, but I hoped that I would be able to see inside. As it was early in the day, the sun would be steady from the east, but there would be no returning here for additional study.

It was now or never.

Behind me, the two researchers, a man and a woman, had their insulated coffee cups in hand and were walking back down the path. The patio area was empty, and now was my chance.

I looked around the area for any cameras, any security officers, anyone who might call me out. The coast seemed clear. With that, I snuck through the hedge and crossed the green.

Holding my hands up to the glass, I looked inside.

There, in the main room of the Ichthyology research area, I first could see a row of workspaces and cubicles. Beyond these areas, which were populated with workers, I could see papers and files among the desks and computers. One workstation had a photograph of Naomi on the desk. That station must have belonged to her dad, but he was away from his cubicle.

Moving onto the next workstation, I was able to see beyond the row of cubicles into the main research area. There were the status tanks, which were like large aquariums. Fish were still in many of them, and there was no evidence of damage or construction equipment. One taller tank was built like a silo, and had kelp running up and down the column of water.

Everything within the Ichthyology lab seemed normal. So why the sudden closure?

Checking my watch, I decided to take up Naomi on her suggestion. I climbed up a retaining wall to look into the next part of the complex.

This was supposed to be the area where they offered SCUBA training. Inside was a large pool that was built several feet above the main floor, along with an elevated platform along the edge. Perhaps the water table was too low to build as deep a pool as they would have liked?

Something was odd about the side of the pool, however.

Large acrylic windows were set up so an observer could look inside. I decided these were there so instructors could check on students. However, the acrylic windows were taped up with masking tape in a large X across the facade. The tank was filled, and seemed to have leaves of kelp floating across the surface. Shop lights were shining into the tank from above, and there seemed to be a few researchers nearby.

I looked again. Was that Louise? Two other men were there also. One of them had a cast on his arm, while the other-

My phone began to shake. I immediately felt exposed, even though the sound couldn't have traveled very far.

Inside, the researchers hadn't noticed me. Of course, the windows weren't open, so they couldn't have heard anything. They were occupied with clipboards and their discussion, occasionally pointing into the tank towards a fine mass of kelp that floated in the corner.

Wait! That wasn't kelp. It was hair! Dark blonde hair. And it had a broad green fluke trailing from below. Was I seeing this right? There were no bubbles coming from the mass, suggesting it couldn't have been a diver. I needed to get a chance to confirm my suspicions—

"Hey there!"

I suddenly bolted for the hedge and began to run. It was time to leave. I didn't stop to see who spotted me, if they spotted me, or who the voice belonged to. I ran and didn't look back until I got to the camp again, before catching myself and jogging toward the dock.

Did they spot me? Or was someone else calling to a co-worker? Didn't matter. I ran past the main road, past the cabins, and ran past a pair of researchers wearing wet suits. I didn't care if they were going to dive, look for Cheryn, or whatever. I didn't stop for anyone.

Out in the bay, Naomi and Cheryn began to circle in. I glanced onto the dock behind me, seeing Mr. Thom on shore in a golf cart. They did spot me!

"Hurry, hurry," I muttered quietly. "Don't call my name."

"Hurry up!" Naomi cried.

Cheryn was paddling furiously, getting Naomi all wet. But they were close enough.

I jumped into the front seat as soon as they were close, and fell backward as the canoe kept moving beneath me. In fact, I fell into Cheryn's lap.

"Are you okay?" she asked.

"Let's go!"

She handed me the oar, and I didn't even bother to put on my life jacket. Naomi kept us going toward the downtown before turning.

"Are they coming?" I asked.

Cheryn turned around. "I don't see anybody."

"Are you sure?"

Naomi turned the canoe about. When I looked onto the camp's dock, there was nobody.

"They had to have been following me," I said. "They had to have been."

"What did you see?" Cheryn asked.

"I hope it was worth getting all wet," Naomi said.

Cheryn giggled. "Sorry."

"Everything in your dad's lab looked normal. The workers are back. But in the training area next door, I think I saw what looked like hair."

"Hair?" Naomi asked.

"What color?" Cheryn asked.

"I think blonde," I replied. "There might have been more. Something green. I couldn't get a good impression of what I thought I saw."

Naomi couldn't hide her gasp.

"Do you suppose?" Cheryn asked. "Was it another like me?"

"I hope not," Naomi said. "But that would explain the sudden release of the lab staff."

"Agreed," I said. "Dr. Gardiola was there."

"The director?" Naomi asked. "Who else?"

"I'm not sure." I shook my head. "There were two other researchers, but I don't know who they were. One had a cast on his left arm and the other wore a neck brace."

"I wonder who they could have been," Naomi said.

"I'm glad you made it away," Cheryn said.

"Me too," I replied.

We didn't talk any further while we passed by a group of boaters. The ferry was coming in and we had to paddle quickly to clear its path. Naomi quickly turned the canoe away from the marina when she spotted Mr. Bridgewater. He must've noticed us, because he gave a wave.

I smiled and waved back.

"What are you doing?" Naomi asked.

"Waving," I said.

Cheryn and Naomi waved too.

"Isn't that Mr. Bridgewater?" Cheryn asked.

"Yes," I replied. "Now I'll have to explain to him who you are too."

"That's not the end of the world, is it?" Cheryn asked.

I sighed. "Not unless I have to tell him what you are."

Cheryn nodded quietly.

Once we were further from downtown and closer to home, the conversation resumed.

"I hope it doesn't sound like we're ashamed of you," I said.

"No, I understand," Cheryn replied. "As a species, we've done a lot to stay hidden. By showing up on your dock, Jessica, I may have started something that cannot be undone."

"But it might not have been your fault," Naomi said. "Especially if they already discovered another one."

"You said you didn't know of any other mermaids in the area?" I asked.

Cheryn shook her head. "As far as I know, they all headed out to the open ocean. Said they'd be gone until the next snow."

As a speed boat came close, we held off on the conversation. Soon, we were free to talk.

"Cheryn, I feel silly asking, but what do you call yourselves?" I asked. "Do you have a name for your species?"

"Mers," she replied. "We used to call ourselves something else, but as you may have noticed, we've adopted your language. We've adopted many parts of human culture, and now we're so used to hearing ourselves called mermaids, mermen, and the like, I guess we've gotten used to that."

"You don't know what you called yourselves anymore?" Naomi asked.

"I've always grown up calling myself a mermaid," Cheryn said. "I know what I am."

"I didn't mean it like that," I said.

"Yes, I know," Cheryn replied. "It's okay. I am what I am, and I'm proud of that."

And you should be, Cheryn. I'm sorry for saying otherwise.

"Jessica, we still have a problem," Naomi said. "If there are still divers out in the bay, she won't be able to go home."

"You're right," I said.

"Didn't you say you wanted a pool table?" Cheryn asked. "Maybe you can find one of these pool tables and I can live in that."

"That's not what a pool table is!" Naomi laughed.

"But there is a pool at the school," I said. "Isn't Martin on the swimming team? Maybe he can get us in."

"What about the swim team practices?" Naomi asked.

"They only compete during the school year," I replied. "I think we could swing it."

"Do you mind chlorine?" Naomi asked Cheryn.

"What's that?"

"We may have a serious problem," I said.

"Let's ask try and figure this out," Naomi said.

When we came close to Barnacle Point, I saw Tim was outside sitting on the dock. It wasn't like him to be outside.

"Is that your brother?" Cheryn asked.

"Yes," I replied. "He's not allowed to be on the dock by himself when nobody's home."

"Hey kiddo!" Naomi called. "You breaking rules?"

We coasted into the dock and caught the side. Tim couldn't stop staring at Cheryn.

"Hello there," Cheryn said. "What's your name?"

"Tim," he replied.

"My name is Cheryn. How old are you, Tim?"

"You're not allowed on the dock," I said. "How long you been out here?"

"Since you left."

Cheryn smiled at my little brother. "How old are you, Tim?"

"Eight and a half," he replied. "I'm going into the third grade."

As we pushed the canoe closer to the shore, Tim got up and followed us, keeping his focus.

"How come you're always inside?" Cheryn asked.

"I'm not allowed to come out."

"Yes, you are," I replied. "Quit talking like that. You're allow-ed to come outside, just not on the dock unless someone else is here. What would happen if you fell in?"

"Can you swim?" Cheryn asked.

"I'm taking lessons," Tim replied. "What about you?"

"Oh yes," Cheryn wrinkled her nose. "You might say I'm an expert."

Naomi and I continued to pull the canoe ashore. We finally reached the beach.

"Could you teach me?"

Oh, here we go.

"Tim, go inside."

He ignored me.

"I'll tell Dad and he'll ground you. No Nintendo for a week."

"Stop bossing me around!" He quickly ran inside. "Dumb big

'ol sister!"

"Little brothers," Naomi chuckled to herself.

"Were you going to find Martin, then?" Cheryn took off her sun hat. "I can stay out of the water as long as I keep my scales and fin moist. Those divers could be anywhere."

"If there's another mermaid being studied at Jaquim Labs, there may not be any safe harbor," I decided. "Cheryn, how long have you ever been out of the water?"

"Not long. In fact, this has been the longest time. Before today, I haven't been out of the water any longer than twenty minutes."

"You sure have a good sense of time," Naomi said.

Cheryn shrugged. "How long are your songs on the piano?"

"It doesn't matter," I said. "Can she keep that skirt for now?"

Naomi nodded. "It's already wet. And I'd like to dry off too."

I had forgotten that Cheryn had drenched Naomi with the oar. If I brought Cheryn inside the house, wouldn't I risk getting everything wet? And that was before getting Tim involved.

"I hate to be a bother," Cheryn said.

"My mother has a wheelchair from when she broke her leg," I said. "Wait here."

Five years ago, Mom had broken her leg while working in the yard. Ordinarily, when one member of a couple gets injured, it strengthens their relationship. Not in my family. I still can't explain how their breakup happened. Either way, we still had the wheelchair in the garage. I had been bothering Dad to bring it back to the hardware store, since there was sure to be someone in town who needed it worse than we did. However, he hasn't had much luck getting rid of anything that was associated with Mom. While most of her personal belongings had been cleared out, some things, like the wheelchair, just weren't worth throwing away. At least now we'd find a use for it.

Cheryn got into the wheelchair easily, but getting her into the house was tougher. It took both Naomi and me to pull her up the steps onto the deck. I forced Tim to go up to his room and pushed Cheryn through the patio door. Once inside, I found a spray bottle and filled it with water, allowing her to keep herself moist.

"This is a lovely room," Cheryn said as she sprayed water onto her fin.

"It's a mess," I said as I pulled out the phone book. "Martin lives with his uncle, right?

"Yes," Naomi said as she collected some drinks from the kitchen. "We're not going to be able to get her anywhere with bikes."

Agreed. There was no riding a bike side-saddle, given what hung below. "Let's worry about the pool first." I picked up the phone and dialled Martin's number.

Cheryn spotted a jar full of jelly beans on the breakfast bar between the kitchen and the living room. She rolled the chair closer and reached up, taking the jar in hand.

"Martin, hey. It's Jess." I turned to see Cheryn had found the candy. "Yeah, this is sudden, but can you come over?" As I listened to his protests, I watched Cheryn pull the jar open and place the lid on her lap. "It's really important. You're on the swim team, aren't you?"

"These are great!" Cheryn said with a handful of jelly beans. "What flavor are the blue ones? Seaberry?"

"Blueberry," Naomi said. "What's a seaberry?"

"They remind me of that muffin I had the other day."

"Just come over as soon as you can, Martin," I said into the phone. "Hurry."

"Is he coming?" Naomi asked.

I put the phone back onto the cradle with a nod. "He'll be here in ten minutes." I then took the jar from Cheryn and put it back onto the counter.

"Hey!" Cheryn moaned. "Augh."

"The rule in this house is that the jar doesn't leave the counter," I said. "That goes for me, Mom, Tim, and even Dad."

"But I can't reach them," Cheryn said.

"And neither can Tim unless he sits on the stool."

"Jess, really," Naomi shook her head.

"Can I sit on the stool?" Cheryn's expression changed to that of a deprived child.

I sighed and collected a small bowl before pouring some jelly beans inside. She brightened up when the bowl was in her hand a moment later.

"Thank you."

"Jessica, how are we going to get her to the school?" Naomi asked. "Someone's bound to see her on that wheelchair."

Yeah, how indeed.

We had bounced off ideas about Operation Obscurity, each more futile than the last, when someone knocked on the front door. Martin had finally arrived.

"Jessica, what's this all about?" he asked when I showed him to the living room. "Hello." Martin dropped his jaw when he spotted Cheryn's tailfin resting on the bottom of the wheelchair.

"Compose yourself, Martin," Naomi said. "Let me introduce you to Cheryn."

"Hello," Cheryn said. "Would you like a jelly bean? They're incredible."

"You're incredible," Martin replied in a monotone voice. "And you're a mermaid."

"Nice powers of observation," Naomi groaned. "Can we focus here?"

"Martin, there are divers all over the bay and we think they might be looking for Cheryn. We need a place to hide her on land, and the only place we can think of is the school swimming pool. It's bigger than a bathtub, it's indoors, it's out of the way, and—"

"And there are lessons every day, but during the week of the Fourth, they don't offer them because Coach takes a week off," Martin replied. "I've been helping Coach Rogers with the classes. Jess, isn't your brother a student?"

I nodded. "Obviously, it'll only be temporary. We need access to the pool."

Martin nodded as well. "It might just work, Jess. Lessons resume Saturday morning, but in the meantime, the pool would be empty."

"This would mean so much to me, Martin. Is there any way you can help?" Cheryn asked.

"We also need a way to get her there. She can't stand on our bikes or anything," Naomi said. "As you might guess, we're having trouble coming up with ideas."

"John has a golf cart," Martin suggested. "You don't need a driver's license to operate them, even on public roads."

"Are you sure?" Naomi asked.

"What's a golf cart?" Cheryn asked with a yawn. "Or for that matter, a golf?"

"That'll be perfect," I said. "I'll call him."

"Jessica?" Cheryn asked. "Can we wait a moment?"

"Yes?"

"If I'm going to be on land for a while, is there any chance I can rest? I've been up all night watching my grotto, and remember, I told you I'm a night owl."

"Can we get you to a pool first?" Naomi asked.

"I'm really tired." She even yawned. "We did a lot this morning."

"Yes, we did." I turned to Martin. "Are you able to hang around today?"

He nodded. "We should hash this out first. How long a stay do you think this will be? As long as there are divers in the bay?"

"Yeah," I said. "Or at least until Saturday. A full search of the bay can't take too long."

"Jessica?" Cheryn asked again. "I can't go home. Not yet."

"I know," I replied. "Come with me."

Cheryn was a quick study with the wheelchair, and I brought her around to the master bathroom, Dad's bathroom. He had left it somewhat unkempt, but once I pulled his dirty clothes and towels into the laundry basket, the bathtub would at least be accessible. Along with the toilet, a tight shower stall, and an open shelving unit for linens, the bathroom had probably not been cleaned in full since Mom moved out.

The question was if it would work for Cheryn, though.

"This room is a lovely blue." She rolled into the room behind me. "I like it."

I had always thought that there was too much blue in this bathroom. But on second glance, I realized there was no reason why Cheryn wouldn't like it. The tile was almost a perfect match for her blue scales.

"I can't guarantee the tub will be comfortable, but if you want to take a nap for now, this will have to do." I rolled her as close as I dared between the counter and the tub. "I can't guarantee it'll stay warm for long."

"You're able to get water into your house, then? To clean yourselves?"

"The first thing you learn about being out in the sun is that the sun makes you sweat," I replied. "Gotta get clean somehow."

She snapped the brake on the wheelchair, and once the wheels were locked, she used the arms of the chair to pull herself up. With a little hop, she moved onto the edge of the tub and slid into the basin. Turning about, she leaned back in the deep end of the pool so her tail was near the faucet. Sitting straight, her tail didn't quite fit into the tub.

"Is that going to be comfortable?" I asked.

She moved slightly, and was able to adjust herself so that she fit better. I wouldn't have thought it possible, but then below the waist, she wasn't human, and didn't move like it either. With a sweeping curl of her tail, she managed to get all of her body in the tub.

"This should work," Cheryn said. "You said something about

water?"

"Let me know if this gets too hot." I turned on the faucet, and water began to pour directly onto her fin.

She began to giggle. "That feels wonderful."

"Too hot?" I asked.

"Can it be cooler?"

I adjusted the lever for the faucet, and it began to cool.

"That's about right."

Once the water level was nearing the top, I slowed the flow and shut it off.

"Jessica? Why did you stop it there?"

"The tub's full."

"But there's air in the room."

"This is as full as it gets," I said. "And if the room floods, Dad will kill me. Okay?"

"Okay," she replied. "I could get used to this."

"Great." I rose and started to exit.

"Say, what's this?" She held up the bar of soap.

"Soap. For cleaning."

Cheryn nodded. "And what about that?" She pointed to the toilet.

Oh joy. Suddenly caring for a mermaid took an interesting turn.

When I returned to the living room, Cheryn was sleeping comfortably. Naomi and Martin were in the living room discussing the events of the week.

As they talked, I found myself in the kitchen cleaning. I don't know why, really. Whenever there were guests in the house, my mother always cleaned. Hopefully it wasn't becoming an unconscious instinct for me.

"How's Cheryn?" Naomi asked.

"Fine," I said. "She's sleeping."

"Naomi told me what you saw in the scuba tank," Martin said. "What does that mean?"

I grabbed a sponge and began cleaning the counter. "I'm not sure. Either they found one of Cheryn's friends, or they are running some other kind of experiment."

"Should I get John in on this?" Martin asked.

"Is he working on the golf course today?" Naomi asked.

I began to clean the sink. All the dirty dishes went into the dishwasher.

"Yes, now that you bring it up. I think he works until two,"

Martin replied.

"Can Cheryn stay here, Jess?" Naomi asked.

I closed the dishwasher. "Yeah, so long as Dad's at work. But I don't know if she wants to stay in the bathtub the entire time." I began to clean out the sink. "I wonder if mermaids get all pruney if they've been in the water too long?"

Naomi giggled, as did Martin. "No, they don't seem to," Naomi said. "Silly."

"I want to get a look at that scuba tank," Martin said. "I agree about what you might have saw, but I need to see it for myself."

"With luck, we might even see something more," Naomi said.

"They might be watching the harbor," I said. "Ask Mr. Bridgewater for a canoe, but don't leave it at the dock by the research camp, if you still want to go."

"We're going," Martin rose. "Jessica, stay here to keep an eye on her."

"If they have another mermaid in there, they might not ever stop looking for Cheryn," Naomi said. "They might be hiring more guards as we speak."

"Don't stay for long," I cautioned. "Remember, don't use the camp dock."

Naomi picked up the binoculars from the windowsill. "Can I borrow this?"

I nodded. "Be careful."

"We will," Martin replied.

Once the kitchen was spotless, I found my stomach rumbling and began to make some lunch. Hamburger mac and cheese may not be the most innovative meal, but it would least keep Tim happy for a while.

Cooking proved to be a welcome distraction, especially since I have to admit I began to grow scared for Naomi and Martin. Ordinarily, I might not have let Naomi go so willingly, but they were right. If even one mermaid showed up in a research lab, soon there wouldn't be any of them in the ocean. How many could there be? And what of the mermen? Would they start a war trying to recover their lost people? I didn't want to see my hometown become overrun, like in those Marvel movies or E.T. or anything.

Martin and Naomi weren't even gone twenty minutes when I thought I saw a patrol boat cruise by in the channel outside. Tim continued to ask who Cheryn was. I refused to say. He gave up after lunch, which I would've shared with Cheryn had she not been in a deep sleep. Maybe she hadn't slept the night before? She was really carefree about all this.

When Dad called around 12:30, the call really surprised me. Mainly he was checking to see that we were taken care of for lunch, but I expected the worst. For all I knew, it might've been Mr. Thom at the lab calling me to take Naomi and Martin out of police custody. Relieved that Dad was just making a welfare check, I convinced him Tim and I were okay and that he didn't need to come home. My anxiety level dropped when I didn't have to figure out how to hide Cheryn from him too. She has told us how good she was at hiding, but then it has to be a lot easier in the strait. Even then, your cover can be blown rather quickly if people think you're there. Nobody can hide from anyone in a bathtub for long, even with bubble bath.

To ease my nervousness, I cleaned the living room, from the hardwood floors to the furniture to the couch. Just when I was about out of distractions, Martin and Naomi came back. Around a quarter to two, they came in through the back door unannounced.

"There you are! Why didn't you call?" I asked.

"We didn't want to risk being overheard." Naomi put the binoculars back on the windowsill. "You're right, Jess. It's another mermaid. We saw her face, and she was in the water without breathing gear."

"Blonde hair, green eyes," Martin said. "I'm sure of it. Who knew, two mermaids living just off of Friday Harbor? No wonder the bay's a nature preserve."

"After I met Cheryn the other day, I wouldn't have believed that either," I said. "Were there more guards? How'd you get in?"

"We never got inside," Naomi said. "But Martin had a great idea to call the guard station and report a sighting of suspicious activity."

"Told them that I thought I saw a shoe in the woods that might belong to Rachel."

"Martin," I shook my head. "That's really awful—"

"But it worked!" Naomi exclaimed. "I mean, we had all the time we needed."

"I'm glad you're both okay," I gave her a pat on the shoulder. "I'll check on Cheryn."

In the other room, I was shocked to discover that Tim had managed to continue bothering Cheryn after all I had done to keep him upstairs. The fewer people she met the fewer people might spread rumors. Guess it was too late now.

"Jessica, there you are. Your brother tells me he's quite the swimmer."

"Tim, I told you to stay upstairs," I replied.

"You didn't tell me you were hiding a mermaid in Dad's bathroom."

"I'm hardly hiding," Cheryn giggled.

"Tim, I need you to promise me something." I kneeled to his level. "Cheryn is a friend, but you can't tell everyone about her."

"She told me," Tim replied. "I'm not supposed to tell Dad."

"Or any of your friends." I put my hand on his shoulder and gripped firm. "Got that?"

"It's a game," Cheryn said. "We made a deal."

"Say goodbye to Cheryn, Tim."

"I don't want to." He didn't even turn away.

"Cheryn has to be going now, and you have to go upstairs again," I said.

Cheryn held out her hand. "I'll have to return to the bay, Tim. But I enjoyed meeting you, and hope we can meet again sometime."

Tim held onto her hand tightly. "Can you stay here?"

Cheryn shook her head. "There are a lot of people looking for me. But I'm confident that with your sister's help, I'll be fine."

Tim nodded. "Okay."

"Go on." I stepped aside so he could run off.

Cheryn sat up in the tub. "Your brother is such a charmer."

"He gets it all from those old video games," I said. "Do you need any lunch?"

"Any blueberry muffins?"

I shook my head. "Sorry."

"How about a sea sprout salad?"

Sea sprout salad? "We might be out of sea sprouts, but I'll come up with something. Need help getting out of the tub?"

"Can I use that bar up there?" She pointed to the shower curtain rod. "It looks like it'd be perfect for a budding acrobat."

I shook my head. "It won't support you."

"Are you sure?"

I nodded with a confident smile. "I've tried."

"Oh, okay." Cheryn held her hands up. "Can you pull?"

I took her hands and pulled. There was no indication that she pushed, but a moment later she was sitting on the edge of the tub and my arms were sore. Once I moved the wheelchair close enough, she was soon back into the seat and rolling herself into the living room.

When we returned, Martin and Naomi were discussing everything we had dealt with all day. Maybe they had a harder time than they had indicated. I went over to the kitchen and began to fix up a small garden salad.

"There must've been three, four boats with divers out and about, they have to be looking for more," Martin said before noticing Cheryn in the room. "Ah, you're awake."

"Did you see what Jessica found?" she asked.

Naomi nodded. "Blond hair, green eyes."

"Scales?" Cheryn asked, lifting her tailfin in anticipation. "Were you able to see her scales? What color?"

Martin shook his head. "Sorry, I couldn't confirm her scales."

"Naomi?"

"Sorry," Naomi replied with a shake of her head. "I could see her shoulders and her head, but the rest of her was wrapped in some kind of kelp or seaweed."

Cheryn sadly leaned back into the wheelchair. "Maybe it wasn't her."

"Who?" Martin asked. "A friend?"

"Obviously," Naomi said.

"How many do you know of?" Martin asked.

"Most of my neighbors are further south," Cheryn replied. "It has been some time since I last saw everyone. You were saying you saw more divers, yes?"

"At least four of them," Naomi said. "Hey, isn't John off work now?"

"Yes," Martin rose and stood by the breakfast bar where the land line was. He then dialled John's cell phone number. "Come on, buddy, pick up."

Mom had always been adamant about having fresh veggies in the house, especially in the summertime, a requirement that had somehow rubbed off on me. On the days I went with Dad to Sidney, I made certain to have fresh foods as well. Thus, I had no trouble fixing up a salad with lettuce, spinach, cucumber, tomatoes, carrots, a little lunch meat and croutons. Okay, the croutons weren't fresh, but I figured it was a necessary addition.

I presented the dish to Cheryn with a fork and a small cup of Ranch dressing.

"What's this for?" She held up the fork. "Some kind of comb?"

"So very Disney," Naomi shook her head in disbelief.

"It's a fork," I replied.

"Oh yes, I remember," Cheryn said. "You see, a few menus have made their way off the cruise liners too," Cheryn said as she picked up the fork to spear a crouton. "They seem to last much better than books and other brochures. They show people holding these fork things."

"Must be the lamination," Naomi said.

Martin hung up the phone. "John's on board. He'll be here soon."

"Excellent. What about the coach?" I asked. "Can you get a key to the school?"

"I'll do my best." Martin leaned forward on his stool. "I'm glad we got a chance to discuss everything. You see, if we're going be pros at hiding mermaids, we first need to learn how to fabricate convincing lies."

"On the contrary," Naomi said. "After fabricating your story the other day, Martin, you should have no trouble telling a lie."

"I'll try not to take that personally." Martin picked up the phone to call the coach.

~ ❀ ~

Twenty minutes later, John pulled up to the house in a golf cart that had the logo for the San Juan Golf and Tennis Club, a sailboat at sunset, across the hood. His father operated the club just south of the airport. John pulled the golf cart up to the deck at the back of the house, where all of us had gathered in the meantime.

"If I don't bring it back in half an hour, my Dad's going to flip," John said as he joined us on the deck.

"Good, we'll keep moving then." Martin came down the back step. "The coach said to stop by his place on the way to the school for a spare key, and he wants it back by Saturday."

"Sounds good," I said.

"So why are we going to the school?" John asked.

Naomi rolled Cheryn over to the step before snapping the brake on the wheelchair.

"Oh." John gave a nod, stopping and catching himself after spotting her tail. "Hello."

"I'm Cheryn." She curtsied in the chair. "It's a pleasure to meet you."

"On the contrary," John said with a nod and a gulp, "The pleasure's all mine."

John didn't seem to react to Cheryn at all. Perhaps he was just trying to remain professional, or focus on the task at hand.

Either way, we needed him.

The boys proceeded to assist Cheryn with the golf cart while I secured a wet beach towel and the sun hat for the ride. Inside of five minutes, I ensured Tim was occupied and the five of us began the trek across town. Cheryn sat in the front of the cart next to John while Martin, Naomi and I followed behind on our bikes. As she had done in the canoe, Cheryn wore the wet towel around her fin and kept her skirt pleated closed. As they rode, she filled in John to the divers.

"That's awful," John said. "You must have lost all sense of privacy."

"If I can hide out for a few days, maybe they'll give up," Cheryn said. "There are only so many places in the bay that I can hide, and divers can enter all of them."

Martin rode up closer to me and the golf cart. "John, you take the girls to the school. I'll stop at the coach's house and bring the key, okay?"

"What did you tell Coach Rogers?" John asked.

"I said I wanted to get a head start and practice on my own. So long as I'm not completely alone, he's okay with it."

"That's brilliant," John replied. "He must trust you."

"You're a swimmer too?" Cheryn asked.

"More of a diver," Martin said. "I'll see you all soon."

"Thank you, Martin."

"See you there."

While we waited for Martin at the entrance to the pool area at Friday Harbor High School, I felt it was time to inform John about what I and the others had witnessed at Jaquim Labs. I also felt rather exposed, as there was a lot of traffic on the road to Roche Harbor that day. I adjusted Cheryn's towel to ensure maximum coverage, as there was also a breeze.

"This feels a little dry," I said as I tucked the towel into the golf cart.

"I'm fine," Cheryn replied. "Will Martin be here soon?"

John nodded and drummed the wheel of the golf cart. "So, there's not one but two mermaids living in the Strait of Juan de Fuca?"

"If that's what I saw, yes," I replied. "All I saw in the tank was hair."

"Martin and I confirmed the sighting, since we both saw a face," Naomi said. "It's incredible what's living nearby, isn't it?"

"And here we thought we had our local legends down pat,"

John replied. "Did you come out to watch the triathlon?"

"Is that the race where everyone swam in the bay?" Cheryn asked. "No, I stayed away."

"Don't be silly, John, why would she go so close to all those humans?" Naomi asked. "Wait a moment. Oh."

Naomi had a good point. Cheryn had reached out to me, but I still didn't know why.

"Cheryn, why did you come to my dock?" I asked. "Really?"

Cheryn gave a shy smile.

"I'm here!" Martin cried, making all of us jump. "Sorry about the wait."

"Good," Cheryn said as she began to scratch at her thigh. "I feel awfully dry."

I knew she was lying about being dry. Was she lying about anything else?

"I can imagine." Martin rushed up to the entrance and used the key. "Give me a moment to deactivate the security system."

"How long do you expect the divers to be in the bay?" John asked. "Jess?"

I was distracted all of a sudden. There were a lot of cars on the road, and it felt like they were slowing down on purpose.

"Maybe a day or two?" I asked. "What do you think, Naomi?"

"I still think it's illegal to drive golf carts on public roads without a license."

My eyes narrowed. "I meant about the divers?"

"Oh, right," Naomi replied. "I'd say the divers give up after no more than two days. There's a lot of water, and lots of places where mermaids could hide, and I can't expect they'd want to check them all."

"Agreed," Cheryn said. "They'd have to be very determined."

"Of course, there's another possibility," Naomi said.

"What's that?" Cheryn asked.

"They could be looking for Rachel too."

"Of course," John said. "She's still missing, isn't she?"

Martin came back and held the door open. "Come on!"

John carried Cheryn inside, and we followed. Inside, the pool area had a diving well that was twenty feet deep. A small jet spa was near the corner on the far side of the diving well. In the middle of the room was an Olympic size swimming pool. Towards the west wall, there were two entrances to locker rooms. In between each were five rows of bleachers for use during competitions. The San Juan Islanders wore their purple and gold with pride.

"This is wonderful!" Cheryn was almost giddy as she held onto John's shoulders tightly.

"You know, pool regulations say all swimmers must hit the showers first—" Martin began.

John helped Cheryn to the water, where she went straight in without removing any of her clothing. She took to the water well.

"I don't think it'll be a problem," Naomi said. "Unless that skirt gets caught in the filter."

"Martin, does the school have any swimsuits?" I asked. "Girl swimsuits?"

Cheryn surfaced a moment later. "This water tastes funny."

"That's the chlorine," I said. "It might take some getting used to."

"Uniforms are almost always kept by the students," Martin replied. "We'd be hard pressed to find any spare uniforms here, plus I think they're normally a one piece."

"What's a one piece?" Cheryn asked.

The four of us hesitated a moment. There's a conversation I hadn't planned on.

John rose to his feet. "I should get the golf cart back to the course before Dad notices."

"Will you come back here afterward, John?" Cheryn asked.

John looked to Naomi and me. "Sure?"

"Who else would be coming by the pool, Martin?" I asked.

"Only the maintenance man, but he won't be in until Saturday morning."

"Can we leave her here?" I asked. "Alone?"

"That sounds awful lonely," Cheryn said.

"I don't know if I like that suggestion," Naomi said, shaking her head. "Someone's bound to notice a few things."

We all glanced at Cheryn, who was holding onto the edge of the pool and swishing her tail. Even though her blue scales matched well with the color at the bottom of the pool, anyone could see her for what she was. To explain would be another conversation worth avoiding.

"It's simple," John said. "Martin, you call your uncle and say you're sleeping over at my place. I'll tell my folks I'm staying with you tonight." He then turned to Naomi and me. "You both do the same. We'll all stay here. It'll be like summer camp."

"Or like a campfire," Naomi said.

"Are we going to tell adventure stories?" Cheryn asked.

Little had I realized that we were about to host the first official meeting of the Red Shoe Adventure Club. But it wasn't going to be over a campfire. No marshmallows.

"No, this won't be an official meeting," I said. "All meetings have to have a campfire and marshmallows. But I think we should all stay."

"We'll need something for dinner," Martin said. "And stuff to sleep with."

"And some kind of pop or water," Naomi added. "Not to mention swimsuits."

"Yes," I said. "Swimsuits for all."

"Okay then." John headed for the exit. "We've got work to do."

~  ~

Naomi opted to stay with Cheryn while I made a trip through town. I first headed back to the house and left Dad a note about my plan to stay at Naomi's. Then I made sure Tim was set for the afternoon and apologized for pushing him around earlier. He took it as well as little brothers can. Tim's put up with so much since my folks had broken up, I hope he didn't get too caught up in those games of his. Distraction is good, but reality trumps video games every time.

Before I left the house, I collected a change of clothes, a pillow and a sleeping bag. Then it occurred to me. Where would Cheryn sleep? What kind of bedding would work underwater?

Since I wasn't sure what would work, I instead collected my own supplies and gave the problem my best guess. From my closet I selected a thick fleece blanket that I used in the winter months, hoping the heavy fabric could survive a night in the pool. Given the weight of the blanket, I was glad to have a rack on the back of my bike. With a second pillow ready to go, I strapped everything to the bike with a bungee cord and headed towards town.

There were a few stops I had to make. First, I had to get something else for Cheryn to wear. Naomi would want her grandmother's skirt back eventually. Since the school swimsuits would be impossible for Cheryn to wear, I stopped at Miss Hathaway's consignment store. Since I couldn't bring myself to buy only the top half of a swimsuit, I ended up buying both pieces, disregarding the size of the bottoms. Scanning the many options, I picked out a simple bikini top with a blue and yellow swirled pattern that looked to be about her size. Then it occurred to me. Her blouse was frilly, and I wasn't sure what size her chest was underneath. So I bought another top that was that was magenta and yellow and slightly larger just as a backup. Both suits, tops and bottoms combined, were priced under $20. Miss Hathaway offered great deals.

My second stop was the juice bar. John had suggested bringing a few sandwiches. Although the sandwiches there weren't anything special, they would work in a pinch. Plus, the shop was still open and we could split the sandwiches amongst the five of us without much difficulty. Thomas and Hannah were working. Apparently, it had been an ordinary shift. I opted for three sandwiches, one with ham, one with turkey, and one with roast beef, along with five bags of chips and some cookies. When they asked why I gotten such a big order, I said I was bringing the sandwiches home as a surprise for the family. It wasn't completely a lie. Although the order cost almost $30, the expense was worth it. As far as I was concerned, the cost was an acceptable sacrifice toward the mission to keep Cheryn safe. When I had gotten my credit card at the start of that summer, Dad had made me promise to use it only for emergencies. This was an emergency.

After leaving the juice bar, I swung by Naomi's house. Her mother was home, naturally, as Mrs. Rovan was a quilter and Mr. Rovan was still at work. She asked where Naomi was.

"She's at home watching Tim until Dad gets home," I said. "But I needed to come by and pick up a few things for her. We were talking about going swimming. Do you mind if she sleeps over tonight?"

"No, that's no problem, though she should plan ahead next time."

"Yeah, it's kinda a last-minute thing, I needed someone to watch Tim—" I began.

"Well, okay then," Mrs. Rovan replied. "Have her check in later, okay?"

"Will you kids be okay tonight? Everyone's worried about that missing girl. I'm sure your father knows—"

"He won't be working that late, the store closes at 8," I answered. "We're okay."

"All right," she said with a slow nod. "But be careful tonight."

"We will."

I wanted to tell Naomi's parents what I saw in the lab, but decided against it. They should know, but not until we had a better idea of what actually was being studied there. She was right to be worried for us. Rachel had been missing for several days now, and frankly, Dad should've kept closer tabs on me. But it'd be worse for Cheryn if we were caught.

At last, I returned to the school. I brought my bike inside, as Martin had made the suggestion before we split up. That way, none of us would have to worry about our bikes outside all night, though nobody on the island ever seemed to steal. More importantly, nobody needed to know we were harboring a mermaid.

I brought everything into the pool area, including the sandwiches. John and Martin had yet to return, so I gave Cheryn the swimsuits to see which was a better fit. She had no shame when it came to modesty. The skirt was off, the blouse was off, and both were soon folded nicely on the pool deck. Suddenly I realized the smaller suit wouldn't fit.

"Are all mermaids as much as an exhibitionist as you are?" Naomi asked.

"Geez Naomi," I muttered. "It's not like you haven't seen boobs before."

"We're not in the locker room either," Naomi replied.

It didn't long for Cheryn to figure out the mechanics of the bikini top. The magenta and yellow suit proved to be a perfect fit.

"How's this?" Cheryn asked. "Do you think it'll do for winter wear?"

"Perfect," Naomi said. "Maybe not for winter, though."

I was compelled to agree. She looked good in the magenta and yellow top. "It brings out the highlights in your hair."

"Are you both ready to come in with me?" Cheryn asked. "Or should we eat first?"

"We should wait until the boys get back," I said.

"I'm getting my suit on," Naomi said as she headed for the girl's locker room. "Not about to pass this up."

Actually, Naomi, I was referring to the sandwiches. Either way, point taken.

Before I knew it, Naomi was in the water with Cheryn and both were splashing about. Even though I had my swimsuit, I kept my street clothes on in case anyone unexpected arrived while Naomi and Cheryn began a race competition. By the time Martin and John returned, Naomi had already lost two legs of a 100m freestyle. Had I a brought a stopwatch, I might've determined that Cheryn had beaten the school record of 53.34 seconds, which was posted on the wall. Cheryn was right about being a pro. Even though I was ready for dinner, I soon had my suit on as well and tried my best to win. Though I'm hardly a competition swimmer, I at least beat Naomi.

Naomi had just lost another race when she proposed a new challenge for Cheryn.

"Okay," Naomi said as she caught her breath. "Last race before dinnertime. I'm going to do two laps and you're going to do four. First one to finish wins. Deal?"

Cheryn smiled. "You're doing great, Naomi. I've been in the water all my life."

"This time will be different," Naomi said as she climbed out and onto the starting podium. "Martin, count us out."

Cheryn moved low in the water so she could kick off the wall, and Naomi readied herself.

"Three. Two. One." Martin hesitated. "Go!"

John and I cheered on Team Landlubber as Team Aqua went into full gear. I hate to say there wasn't any competition between them, since in a normal race Cheryn won every time. But now, Naomi actually seemed to be gaining on Cheryn. Naomi used a smooth forward crawl, while Cheryn swam with a smooth undulation, keeping her arms tucked to her side and kicking with her fin. The only time I saw Cheryn falter is when she reached the end and had to use her arms to push against the wall before flipping head over fin for the return leg of the race.

John leaned over the edge as the two competitors neared the finish line, with Cheryn on her fourth lap and Naomi on her second. It was remarkably close. Both reached out for the wall...

"And it's Naomi by a nose!" John cried.

"What? Impossible!" Cheryn gasped after surfacing. "Really?" Her disappointment soon changed into a smile. "Congratulations!"

"I beat a mermaid in a swimming contest!" Naomi jumped and cheered before giving Cheryn a big hug. "Great race, Cheryn."

"Great race, Naomi."

Once Naomi and I had a chance to dry off, we tucked into the sandwiches, splitting them accordingly. Cheryn seemed to enjoy the roast beef. I opted for turkey. Everyone had their fill and there were few leftovers. She joined us on the pool deck while we ate. The whole meal was just like a picnic, if certainly one of the most unique places to have one. There were no views of the beach or the park, but I couldn't begin to wonder how I'd ever top the experience.

We let the meals digest and gathered in the spa. I could hear my mother over my shoulder, telling us to wait an hour before swimming, but then we weren't actually swimming. Martin lowered the lights in the room so that the only light came from the pools, making the atmosphere match a campfire.

"Here," John said as he took a lighter and lit the flint, holding the flame above the center of the spa. "Campfire."

"Cute," Naomi said before blowing out the small flame.

"Did you make a wish?" Cheryn asked.

Naomi shook her head. "It's not my birthday."

"I still think we need marshmallows," I said.

"What are marshmallows?" Cheryn asked.

"Small white balls of sugar and air," John said as he tossed the lighter onto the pool deck behind him. "You heat them so they melt, and then put them into a sandwich of chocolate and graham crackers."

"And, chocolate?" Cheryn asked. "That's the sweet brown stuff?"

"Chocolate is of the greatest discoveries ever," Naomi said. "Mmm."

"You're all making me want to go out and get marshmallows," Martin said.

I shook my head. "We be okay for tonight. Are we telling stories?"

"Can I go first?" Cheryn asked. "I loved the one with the water spirits the other day."

John laughed. "I knew it!"

Martin shook his head. "And I thought I knew all the local legends."

"Okay, Jessica," Cheryn said. "How does this go? What are the rules?"

"Welcome, all, to this unofficial meeting of the Red Shoe Adventure Club," I said. "All attendants must present a story, preceded by the phrase 'For Your Consideration'."

"Official meetings usually have a campfire, but the churning waters of the spa will do nicely," Martin said.

"Meetings must not last later than midnight," John said. "I remembered our charter. But tonight, since the meeting's unofficial, that rule might not be enforced."

"I'm not planning on staying up that late," Naomi said. "It's already been a long day."

"Hopefully that race didn't tire you out," I said. "You have the honor, Cheryn."

"Okay," she smiled. "For your consideration, I present the story of *The Three Mermaids.*"

There was a cavern in the subaquatic depths of the Bering Sea that few mers ever traveled to, for this cavern was enchanted. Legends had said for generations that the cavern could grant a visitor their deepest wish, but there was a catch. For while this cavern may grant a visitor their deepest dreams and desires, it would also grant their greatest fears.

One summer season, three mermaids from the southern Pacific headed north and came to this cavern in hopes of achieving their dreams. Each had hair, scales, and a personality that all matched in lovely harmony. All had vowed to enter this cave, no matter the cost, setting aside any thought of fear. Undaunted, they each took their turn.

The first mermaid, a bold mermaid with red hair and red scales, ventured forth first. "I'm not afraid of any cave, no matter what hides inside." With that, she swam inside.

When this red-headed mermaid entered the inner core of the cavern, she discovered a great current swirling inside. She heard a voice within her head.

"The greatest gifts come to those who must suffer their greatest fears. All that you dream may come true, but so may your nightmares. However you decide to choose, know that you do so at your own risk."

Bravely, the redhead swam forth and entered the torrent. She quickly succumbed to the currents, and gave into her senses as they ferried her deep into the cavern. When she opened her eyes again, she discovered there was no water around her, for she was floating within a cavity of air. Sun was filling the cavern from a vast unseen opening and creating an inviting warmth. Was she on the land? Was this the surface? The floor of the cavern was coated in a green, carpeted plant and there were palm trees with large coconuts.

She recognized the place immediately, as it was her favorite spot to tan near her home. Before she could swim over to the grass and relax, she discovered something odd.

Her tail was gone. Her beautiful fins were nowhere to be found. Two, subby, fleshy legs were in its place. She could not recognize her beautiful body, and she was stricken with fear.

"What has happened to my body?" she asked the empty room.

Suddenly the scene didn't look nearly as inviting as before.

She loved to tan, but as herself. Humans were such clumsy creatures, and to be human was her worst fear.

Abandoning her hopes of tanning and relaxing the day away, she found the exit to the cave and swam as fast as she could. The illusion was cast aside and she glanced behind her to see her fins restored, having never been altered. Somehow, the cavern had input the dream into her mind only as long as she had been inside its walls.

Outside the cavern, her two companions were ready with questions.

"What happened?" the mer with green hair asked. "Did your dreams come true?"

The red head refused to share her experience. "Go see for yourself."

Undaunted, this second mermaid brushed aside her long, luxurious green locks and swished her matching emerald tail. She entered without any reservation, believing herself courageous enough to conquer the fears that her companion shared.

When the green-haired maid entered the current, she found herself inside of a grand underwater palace of stone and coral. This mer adored sparkly treasures, and this palace was laden with all kinds of jewels, pearl necklaces, glittery coins and all manner of gemstones. She swam up to the nearest pile and ran her fingers through them, discovering the jewels heavy and smooth. A ransom of treasure was here, yes, but how could she show her friends?

Suddenly, she discovered herself to be far from alone. From a corner of the palace, two great white sharks entered the chamber. They sniffed out the green-haired mermaid and zeroed in her position.

"Sharks!" She hated sharks most of all. Especially ones as territorial as these.

They chased her out of the room and back to her worried friends. Had she ignored the sharks, she might have had a moment to enjoy her deepest desires. Instead, her hair was frizzled and her wits escaped her.

"Well?" The red-haired mermaid waited with baited breath.

The green-haired mermaid shook her head. "There was nothing in that cavern for me."

Their third companion, a shy mermaid with blue hair, swam towards the cavern. Perhaps if there had been nothing of interest for the others, maybe what lie inside was specially for her? There was only one way to find out.

She entered the cavern, located the torrent, and swam inside.

When the currents subsided, the blue-haired mermaid gazed around to find a colorful coral reef filled with all of her favorite flowers. Purple sea lilies, golden coralettes, rosary pink anemone flowers, and a rainbow of fish painted a scene filled with color and life. Many of her friends, including those who waited outside the cave, were here also. On a table of stone in the center of the coral garden was a setting for seaberry cake, served with sea sprout salad and cups of seaberry juice. The water was clear and the cavern was so large that she couldn't find an easy exit, not that she would want to leave so quickly.

It was then she remembered the cavern's warning. Before her was her greatest desire: a chance to enjoy a quiet setting with friends in a beautiful place, filled with no worries. But here too would be her worst fear. From a shadowy corner of the reef they entered. Four humans, two young men and two women, walked into the garden and sat down at the table. They appeared stern, and fierce, and seemed to have a frightening aura about them.

The mermaid with the blue hair was about to turn away. She didn't, however. She looked at the humans closely, and looked at herself. Was she so different from them? Perhaps not. Here, they were sitting down at her table with all of her friends. Her friends didn't seem to mind their company. How bad could they be?

Abandoning her fears, the blue-haired mermaid joined the party. And she had overcome her fear to enjoy the best party she had ever experienced.

"The end," Cheryn said. "How was that?"

"Wonderful," I said. The group gave their applause.

"Interesting how four humans fit in." Naomi said. "I wonder if that's a coincidence."

"Could've used a few more reef monsters," Martin said. "But I like it."

"That must've been a beautiful reef," John said. "Have you been around Hawaii? There are some great snorkelling spots."

"You'll have to show me some time," Cheryn said.

"It's a date," John replied. "Who's next?"

Martin adjusted himself in the spa. "I remembered what you folks said the other day, and I came up with a better story. This one is more of a thriller than yours, Cheryn."

She smiled. "I welcome it."

"Okay," Martin said. "For your consideration, I present *A Tale of Accidental Science.*"

~ ❀ ~

Dr. Bryant was working hard in his Seattle laboratory as part of a member of the University of Washington's chemistry microbiology division. For several weeks now, the determined doctor was working on the next great medical breakthrough toward the treatment of cancer. While in another part of town his fiancé was fighting through the treatment of an advanced stage of the disease, he devoted every waking moment of his time to his latest treatment. The use of a yet unknown strain of bacteria, derived from a cold-water sea sponge found only in the Straits of Georgia, had proven too great a discovery that would lead to a drug capable of combating the crippling disease.

His fellow researchers had recognized his obsession and felt for his situation. His fiancé was going through tough times, and a few members of the team suggested he instead spend his time at her side. The doctor had resorted to sleeping in his own office, taking his meals there, and abandoning his own hygiene in the quest toward discovering a cure.

For years, Dr. Bryant had observed several control specimens and tested a combination of serums in hopes of curing his beloved. At last, Dr. Bryant perfected his solution exceptionally early in the morning of the day he had picked to plan their wedding. They had delayed the ceremony as far back as they could, for she had lost her hair and had been taking steady treatments of chemotherapy, radiation and nearly any treatment her doctors attempted. Even with the success of this latest discovery, the odds of her becoming cancer free for the nuptials seemed unlikely, as did any hope for them to enjoy their lives together. Time was growing short.

The results of his ongoing studies convinced him that the serum would save his fiancé's life, but the serum was untested. Nobody would allow him to test the final serum, and there were many obstacles. Legal. Ethical. Emotional. No, he would never convince her doctors, her parents, or even his fiancé herself, that the drug could be used successfully.

Desperate and beyond comprehension, Dr. Bryant prepared the injection of a disabled strain of cancerous cells into his own bloodstream. Unable to find a willing assistant, he prepped his own tourniquet, injected the cancerous cells, and allowed them to mingle in his bloodstream for a period of one hour. He then injected the serum, hoping the two would be nullified and his serum would become a success.

Eight hours after the injection, after what was the first full night of rest in nearly three weeks, Dr. Bryant slipped into a coma. His assistants rushed him to the hospital and immediately began to notice interesting changes. They monitored his condition and sealed the door, keeping close tabs on any changes.

In the meantime, the doctor's fiancé began to recover. She had gone through the worst of it and was declared cancer free a month following Dr. Bryant's injection. Although she still needed to take treatments to prevent the disease from spreading as well as adjust her medication to help restore her system from the damage caused by all the treatments, she soon recovered and no longer needed the proposed serum to return to her normal life.

Dr. Bryant, however, had become a subject in his own laboratory. He finally regained consciousness nearly six weeks after taking the experimental injection. Yet, his motor functions and mental processes were severely impaired. They ran several tests to determine the extent of cancerous cells from the initial injection, but they could find no trace. Instead, they discovered that the cancerous cells and the serum had somehow bonded, creating a rare strain of super powerful leucocytes that attacked both diseased cells and, to a lesser extent, any cells within his own body that might be considered 'weaker' or 'inferior.' The medical technicians couldn't explain it, and some of the greatest medical minds, some from far away as the Mayo Clinic in Rochester, Minnesota, came to study the findings.

Meanwhile, Dr. Bryant was up, walking, studying his own test results, and consulting with these experts, through hermetically sealed glass chambers and electronic communication systems. He was barred contact from anyone, his fiancé included, and was unable to continue any assistance with the wedding planning.

Dr. Bryant had become the patient, not the researcher, and was examined closely. Blood tests, MRIs, cat scans and X-rays revealed few answers. Even though his body was attacking and healing itself at an alarming rate, physically he felt fine and was as healthy as a horse. Yet, he could not have any physical contact with anyone, and was essentially cast from any hope of having a normal life ever again. Sadly, that meant his wedding would likely be cancelled.

Ultimately, the doctor threatened to take his own life unless the researchers came up with a way to extract these new leucocytes and allow him to marry his beloved childhood crush. Finally, on a rainy day when the hospital experienced a brief power failure, Dr. Bryant found a way to escape from his confined laboratory and access the hospital's parking lot. He commandeered a Chevy Yukon and drove straight to his fiancé's apartment, discovering that she had abandoned her promise to *him and instead found another doctor for her affections. For there stood his rival, the former captain of the football team, home at last from serving abroad in a distant conflict.*

In a bout of rage, Dr. Bryant raged and tore a marble counter-top from the kitchen, smashing it across the face of her new beloved. Both were notably surprised. While Dr. Bryant had almost expected a more physical reaction, the new object of his former fiancé's affection slowly succumbed to his injuries and perished.

For his actions, Dr. Bryant was taken by the police. Any hopes for happiness with his former fiancé were gone forever. How he had removed the countertop was a mystery, for there had been no changes to his physicality or form, only an increase in aggressive tendencies and physical strength. As his fiancé lay before him, dying at his feet, he gave up without a fight. They locked him into a far corner of the Groom Lake facility, sometimes known as Area 51, and behind walls of titanium, electric conduits and compressed iron, he has since been sealed away from society and subjected to increased scrutiny and examination. His research became property of the government, and was sealed away. He became a relic of his own rage.

Dr. Bryant only wished to save a life. As a result of his actions, he instead robbed a person of their life and sacrificed his own future, now doomed to a loveless future.

"The end," Martin said. "That has to be better than my last one, yes?"

"Sounds awfully sad," Cheryn said. "Could he meet another researcher sometime?"

"Maybe," John said. "Why didn't you go all Hulk with him?"

"That's already been done," Martin said. "I'd never be able to sell a story like that without upsetting the people at Marvel."

"Like they'd ever ask you for story advice," Naomi said. "You sure stole a lot."

Cheryn shook her head. "That doesn't seem like a fair thing to do."

"Sure he did," I said.

"No," Cheryn said. "To just lock up the doctor. It's not fair to him."

"How would you have ended it?" Martin asked.

"The doctor repents his actions," Cheryn said. "He requests another laboratory to continue his research and find a cure for his own situation. Somehow, he finds a way to nullify his condition, using his own cells as both a test platform and as a control. Then, one day, he walks out of the lab, takes one of the researchers who showed sympathy towards him, and joins a travelling circus while displaying his incredible strength and knowledge of science and magistry."

"Have you taken science classes?" John asked. "You really know applied chemistry."

"Either that, or a lot of comic books end up at the bottom of the ocean," Naomi said.

"No, neither," Cheryn replied. "I'm just going with what I learned from Martin's account of the science. I wouldn't know the first thing about chemistry or medical studies."

"Okay, maybe I didn't get it all right," Martin confessed.

"Yeah, but Cheryn, you seem to know the terms," I said. "What else falls overboard from those cruise ships? Medical brochures?"

"Stuffed animals," Cheryn said. "And a lot of cigarettes."

"I don't like the sound of that," Martin said. "At least you all can agree that that story was better than my last one?"

"Yeah," I replied. "Works for me."

"Agreed," John said.

"There's room for improvement, but I'll give it a pass," Naomi said.

The four of us applauded. Martin had his moment.

"Who would like to go next?" I asked.

"I might have a story that is similar to the one you told, Cheryn," John said. "Hope you don't mind a little redundancy."

"I don't mind," she replied. "But first, does anyone else need a break?"

"Is something wrong?" Naomi asked.

"Well, I'm used to water much cooler than this. But," she whispered into my ear something rather personal.

"Maybe I should've brought that wheelchair."

"What's the matter?" John asked.

I leaned close to him and conveyed what she said to me.

"Do you ladies object if I go into the ladies locker room for a moment?" John asked.

Naomi and I shook our heads.

"Will you carry me, John?" Cheryn asked. "I'm sorry."

All she said was that she had to use the toilet. Maybe it shouldn't be embarrassing, but if you think about it—actually, no, I'd rather not think about it. There must be some way to avoid swimming in—no, I'm not going to try to think about it. Curiosity would probably get the better of me, but some mysteries are best unsolved.

~ ❀ ~

Before we agreed to call it a night, John told a story that was indeed similar to Cheryn's. Instead of three mermaids, however, the story told of three golfers who were in search of the perfect drive. All of them had to cross a bridge to complete the tournament, and along the way they had to outsmart a troll who had been living under that bridge and feeding golf balls to a nearby crocodile. It was a sillier story, and we all seemed to have a better mood afterwards.

Even if it seemed earlier in the evening than we might have normally gone to bed, the four of us who could walk headed into the locker rooms and washed the chlorine off of our bodies and prepared ourselves and our sleeping bags. I had brought along my night clothes and was back from the locker room first to find that Cheryn had set up her cot and blanket on the pool deck.

"Cheryn, won't you dry out if you sleep there?" I asked.

She adjusted the sleeping bag I had brought for her. "What would happen to these if I put them into the pool? Would the chlorine dissolve them?"

I smiled. "No, not by tomorrow morning. In fact, I don't think I've ever heard of chlorine eating away at anything larger than dirty bacteria."

"Okay, but I don't want them to be damaged," Cheryn said. "Everything you have is very nice, and well cared for."

"You're kind to say so," I replied. "But I brought them for you to use. I said I'd do what I could for you, and that means not letting you dry out. You may not have noticed, but there are dryers in the locker rooms."

"What's a dryer?"

"For clothes or fabrics, it's a machine that dries them," I said. "It's a real time saver."

"Oh." Cheryn smiled. "Humans get all the toys."

I smiled. "I'll see if I can dry the bedding out tomorrow before I go into work."

"Will that work?"

I nodded. "And if they smell like chlorine or anything, that's fine too."

"Okay then." She pulled the cot, the sleeping bag and the heavy pillow all into the pool. Each item floated briefly before they sank slowly towards the bottom. Cheryn then ducked below, unzipped the sleeping bag, and laid it out flat.

"Looks like that will work," I said, even knowing she was

underwater.

Cheryn moved her mouth and spoke, but I couldn't quite hear what she said.

"What?" I said. "You can talk underwater?"

She surfaced. "You can talk in the air," Cheryn said. "All I said was that this works."

"Yes, but," I hesitated. "You seemed to speak normally, yet it became muffled. Why?"

Cheryn shrugged. "Sound travels slower underwater. If I speak with another mer, we're used to it and our conversation moves at the same speed as it does in the air." She hesitated a moment. "I guess I've never noticed anything different until you pointed it out just now."

"Huh," I said. "I can imagine that the question wouldn't come up in any of my science classes." I had nearly forgotten about the sleeping bag. "Anyway, will you be warm enough for tonight? Is everything comfortable?"

"Oh yes," Cheryn said. "In fact, I'm probably warmer than I would be at home."

"Wonderful." I tended to my own sleeping bag, unzipping it similarly to the way Cheryn prepared hers so that I wouldn't feel too trapped.

"Jessica, I should thank you for arranging all this," Cheryn said. "It means a lot."

"John and Martin deserve the most credit," I said. "Thank them."

"You really are a nice person."

I smiled. Guess I have done a lot for her.

A moment or three later, John came back from the locker room. Cheryn climbed out of the pool and leaned onto the deck. "John?"

"Yes?" He came over. "What's up?"

"Come here."

"What?" He leaned closer. "Is everything okay?"

What was she up to?

Cheryn held onto his shoulders. "I want to, to, whoa!" She had pulled herself onto him and dragged him forward, causing him to lose his balance. In an instant, both of them fell backwards. John could not react before both of them pitched into the pool.

"Cheryn!" I gasped, getting up. "John!"

Both recovered a moment later. John was first to surface. "What was that all about?"

Cheryn surfaced, giggling like crazy. "Oh John, I'm so sorry!

I just wanted to give you a hug for suggesting all this tonight. Do you forgive me?"

His shock slowly melted and turned into a smile, even though he had been wearing lighter clothes for bed and was completely drenched. "You're such a nut."

"And Jess," Cheryn said. "Thank you for doing all this too."

I smiled. "You can hug me later."

The evening really had been like summer camp. John ended up wearing his other clothes to bed, and most of us were wired after all the excitement. Still, we knew there were things to do tomorrow, and somehow the five us drifted off to sleep. There was no reason for anyone to keep watch, as the school was locked and there were no surveillance cameras anywhere except the lobbies, the hallways and the main exits.

I'll admit I might not have slept as well as I would have at my bed at home, since the cot above the hard pool deck was hard and cold. Yet, that was probably one of the best nights of the summer. Confident that Cheryn would be safe, at least for tonight, I drifted asleep.

The Red Shoe Adventure Club

Friday July 10th, 2009
Friday Harbor Herald

Authorities from the University of Washington are offering their services and broadening the spread of their search for the missing teenager Rachel Arlen. Yesterday, a team of divers came to Friday Harbor and began searching for any sign of the teen as surface support teams continued the search along the coast. The United States Coast Guard service has been activated and is working with ground-based teams to conduct a search from the air as well. Residents are encouraged to assist with the search where they can. Contact the police department for details.

In the meantime, Friday Harbor Police continue to uncover the story behind the disappearance. An ongoing investigation has identified several subjects. Officer James Roberts respond-ed to our inquires, stating "Our investigation is moving forward with several persons of interest, but as of today we have yet to identify any suspects or motives that have led to either a conviction or evidence that will lead us to the missing teen. I have made a vow to the Arlen family that their daughter will be located safe and unharmed very soon."

In other news, Friday Harbor Hardware, located at 360 Spring St. was the target of a burglary last night. The owner, Dan Summers, reported a minimal loss of hand tools, water softening salt and aquarium supplies, as well as a broken security door. Surveillance cameras are being analysed toward identifying the responsible party. The total loss of inventory and damage to the business is estimated at nearly $1500. If you have any inform-ation concerning this incident, please contact Friday Harbor Police.

Readers of the Herald are also reminded to submit their writing contest entries by July 15th. There have been a limited number of entries and staff at the Herald would like to see many, many more.

When I first woke up in the morning, I expected the sun on my face. Somehow, I had forgotten where I was. Instead, there were few windows in the pool area and the only things making me wake up were the pressure in my bladder and a rumbling in my stomach. My phone had a message, but I ignored it to find the bathroom. I returned a moment later to take stock of the place. John's sleeping bag was gone. Martin had also left, but his bed things and backpack were still here. Naomi appeared to be sleeping lightly. I then checked the pool to see that Cheryn was laying at the bottom, still asleep underwater.

"Naomi?"

She stirred in her sleeping bag. "Oh, good, you're up."

"Where are the boys?"

"John had to go back to work for the day." Naomi stretched and sat up. "Martin said he'd be by after an hour."

"What time is it?"

"Quarter after nine," Naomi said. "They left pretty early, so I got some more sleep."

Oh no. It couldn't be a quarter after nine. "I work at ten."

"Huh?"

"I work at ten!" I jumped up, grabbed my clothes and ran for the locker room.

When I left the locker room, showered and dressed, I immediately went towards the exit to find that Martin had returned with a sack full of breakfast sandwiches he had picked up from the Shell gas station.

"Hey, you're up."

"Martin," I said. "I work at ten. Is someone going to stay and keep Cheryn company?"

He nodded. "Naomi and I are both staying, in fact. We agreed this morning. You and John both have jobs, after all." He handed me a sandwich. "Can you come by after you get off?"

"Sure," I said. "I have to go. If you come by, I'll take care of your lunch again."

"Don't worry about it now, go," he said. "You've got stuff to do."

"Thanks so much." I grabbed my bike and pushed it out the door. "Bye."

"Say, did Naomi tell you about—" His words were drowned out as the door closed.

Eating the egg and sausage sandwich along the way, I biked straight home to get my work clothes. There had been so much going on yesterday that, despite all intents and purposes, I might have thought I actually was at summer camp. Pity how the world continues on.

When I arrived at the house, it was unusually quiet. Dad was gone, but then he would have been gone anyway. Tim was also gone, and the TV was off. That was probably the most unusual side of the equation.

Unfortunately, there was no time to waste. I stuffed my blue vest and blue cap into my backpack and locked up the house.

My arrival at work couldn't have been any closer. No sooner had I locked my bike to the rack behind the shop did Melissa arrive on hers.

"Am I on time?"

I nodded. "Good morning."

"You're out of uniform, boss." Sure enough, Melissa was wearing her blue vest over her clothes and the blue visor. "Aren't you trying to set an example?"

I held up my bag. "It's all here. Can't wrinkle it."

"No, I suppose not."

~  ~

Of course, stuffing my uniform into my bag hadn't been the best idea, and I did have to smooth the fabric before opening the store. But, that aside, the juice bar was quickly up and running, as it usually is, and I was expecting a call from the delivery man when the phone rang. However, it was not the delivery man.

"Jess? Hey."

Dad? "Yeah, hi. Is someone watching Tim?"

"He's here, with me, at the store," he said. "Did you get my message?"

"No," I replied, having forgotten to check my phone. "What's up?"

"The store was broken into and robbed last night. I've been awake since about four when the alarm company called."

"What?" I couldn't believe it. "What did they take?"

"Not too much. According to the video tapes, two figures wearing dolphin masks broke into the back door and took a bunch of buckets, fastening tools, painting tarps, clear plastic hose, two large sacks of water softener salt, a 125-gallon fish tank and related accessories," he explained. "Oh, and a rubber ducky."

I smirked. "Cute."

"I suppose it could have been worse," Dad continued. "The safe was untouched, as were my records or anything in the office. The burglars were polite, according to the video footage."

"Still, nobody ever seems to steal on this island," I said. "I hope the police find them."

"The images from the video should help," he said with a sigh. "I've raised you with the mindset that if you needed something, you earned it. Apparently, someone else doesn't subscribe to that idea. How'd it go at Naomi's?"

"Good," I said. "We mostly watched movies." I brushed aside the hair from my face. "Dad, is there anything you need me to do? Anything at all?"

"No, sweetie, you've got your own job to worry about. I've been talking with Deputy Hammond and everything is under control here."

"How long will it take to repair the door?"

"It's already fixed," he said with a chuckle. "I had all the necessary equipment in stock."

"Okay, sure," I said. My dad knew tools, no doubt there. "But if it's fixed to the same way it was before, couldn't someone get in the same way again?"

"Don't worry about that, sweetie. I'll bring you lunch today, okay?"

"You don't have to do that."

"See you soon." Click.

Guess I didn't have a choice in the matter. At least there'd be free lunch involved. But why were these crimes occurring? First Rachel went missing. Then a plane crashed. Now there was a break-in at Dad's hardware store. Life on our little island was growing worse by the day.

About an hour later, the lunch rush picked up and I found myself making sandwiches. Thomas, my co-manager, had arrived in the nick of time to help with the extra orders. With Melissa working the blender, Miss Jackson and Thomas working the register, the line of customers cooled off quickly. Fridays in Friday Harbor always seem busy. Soon the line drew short and the shop emptied out, as most customers chose to take their orders outside. At the end of the lunch line, Officer Roberts came up to the counter.

"Hi! What can I get you?"

He glanced up at the menu board. "How about a cup of coffee and some information." He then looked me in the eye. "Unless you have any doughnuts?"

"Sorry," I said with a smile. "They go fast in the morning."

"Just the coffee, with cream. Where can we talk?"

"On the patio," I said. "What size?"

"Grande." He laid down a five-dollar bill. "Bring the change?"

Once the order was complete, Melissa took over and I brought it outside.

On Saturday Square, I brought the coffee and handed over the change once I found him at a patio table overlooking the harbor. "Nice day today, huh?"

I gave a nod. "Is there something else I can do for you, officer?"

"Heard about your dad's place." Officer Roberts had that way of talking that was a combination of straight-line winds and raw facts. Hence, he wasn't asking me a question.

"Yes," I said. "He's a little upset, but okay."

"Rest your feet a moment."

I had been on my feet for some time, and it felt good to sit.

"Yep, yep." He glanced out across the empty square. "Pity this place hasn't been cleaned up since the carnival left, isn't it? Every year, those tourists leave more trash across our fair city. Then, more clues are washed away, I suppose." After a sip from his coffee, he focused his attention back to me. "So has anything else happened since we last talked? Anything that might be useful toward that Arlen case?"

My mind avoided any thoughts about Cheryn. "I can't think of anything."

"You hear about that plane crash?"

I nodded. "I went by the site on my way home. Awful."

"Indeed." The policeman sipped from his coffee again. "Seems a lot of your friends are joining in on those search groups. Greg himself went down to Cattle Point today."

"They're still searching, then?" I asked. "With my recent promotion—"

"Did you get promoted?" he asked suddenly.

I nodded. "Assistant manager. Mr. Bridgewater thinks I can handle it, though I'm still waiting for the delivery guy today."

"Gotta have fresh fruit for fresh juice," he said. "Congratulations."

"Thank you." I adjusted my bangs as I adjusted my blue visor. "Some of the fruit is frozen, but we do get small shipments three days a week."

"I can't have fresh guava juice?"

"Sorry," I smiled. "Not unless it's in season."

"Can't put in the java anyway." Another sip of coffee. "Greg said something about a bogus tip-off at Camp Caution."

"That's awful," I replied, knowing full well that it was Martin who had been responsible. "At least some people are taking the search for Rachel seriously."

"Have you joined them?" the officer asked.

"I haven't had a chance to join any search groups with the extra work," I answered.

"Sure, you're a hard worker." He sipped from the coffee again and adjusted himself in the chair. "You know, since you're talking about things being in season, it brings up a similar point about investigation. In order to understand the criminal mind, you have to also understand everyday processes that happen, anywhere in the case. How things move in a given place, for example. Logistics, that sort of thing. If something is happening outside of the norm, the good detective takes note." He glanced toward the marina. "Does Gary ever come by the shop?"

I had to think a moment, as I always called my boss Mr. Bridgewater rather than by his first name. "Maybe a few times a week. Monday mornings he checks inventory and receipts, and occasionally if he needs a roll of paper for the registers, but beyond that, he spends most of his time at the marina. Leia takes care of everything else."

"Yes, Miss Jackson," the officer nodded. "Do you ever visit Gary at his house?"

I shook my head. "No. I call him on the phone once in a while, but that's all."

He sipped from the coffee again. "How's that Douglas Rovan? Any idea?"

"At work," I replied. "Is he being investigated too?"

"Oh no," Roberts said. "We used to golf back in the day."

I nodded. "John's the golf expert."

"And his old man," the officer replied. "You ever go by the research camp?"

Did he suspect something? I quickly shook my head.

"Young girls get curious, you know. You into science and biology?"

"I enjoy it, I guess."

"But you wouldn't go anywhere where you're not welcome, or anything?"

He did know. My eyes darted towards the water where a diver had just dove in. I hoped my distraction would somehow hide my worry.

"Good girls don't bypass security or anything," he chuckled. "Right?"

"I don't know what you mean, sir."

He smiled. "Nah, you wouldn't, you're an open book."

Had one of the security officers said something to the police? Other researchers came and left from the docks all the time. I hadn't done anything nobody else had, as far as I was concerned. I had too many other secrets to keep right then.

"One more thing," he said after another sip of coffee. "If your boss were to ask you to do something, anything, would you do it?"

"Depends," I said. "I mean, for the business, I'll do just about anything, within reason, I suppose. I wouldn't do anything illegal, sir. Do you think Mr. Bridgewater is hiding something?"

"Oh, I don't know," he said as he rose to his feet. "Probably not. Anyway, I should probably get back to the beat. You know, you can always call my cell if you see anything."

"Sir?" For some reason, I felt like I should say something. About Cheryn. If there was any connection with her and Rachel, now would be the time. But I couldn't.

"You know, anything that might help me find Rachel."

I nodded. "Of course, sir."

He glanced at the storefront for the juice bar. "No missing poster in the window."

"Oh, right," I said with a smile. With everything that had been happening, along with our group chasing Cheryn around town, the task had more than once slipped my mind. "I'll take care of that right away."

"Good." He gave the table a firm pat. "Right then. See you later."

As I watched him leave, I wondered if he had suspected myself, Naomi or Martin, for going ashore into the research camp yesterday. There were no signs banning anyone from going ashore there, as it wasn't exactly a secure facility. Unless you were coming to stay in one of the cabins and work on a specific project, you could go in and out just by showing an ID or signing a clipboard at the security station. It was true, we hadn't done that, but people have probably been doing it for years. People my age, especially, would often head up to Lookout Point on Friday nights to make out with each other. Surely teenagers had been going there as long as my parents had, those many years ago. No doubt the whole island knew, the police included. Why ask?

I could at least be certain of one thing. There wasn't any reason to fear for myself or the others, because if Officer Roberts wanted to arrest us for trespassing, he would have done so by now. But he had brought up a good argument about the square. Flyers from the carnival, along with tickets, cups and candy wrappers were all over the place. Rachel had been last seen by the Tilt-A-Whirl, which had been located between the juice bar and the marina's boat house, where Mr. Bridgewater had his apartment. Could my boss really be responsible?

At the same time, the delivery guy for today's shipment was late. The order was almost always in before eleven, after the ferry arrived from Anacortes.

I had an idea for a little investigation of my own. But first, I would have to finish my shift and figure out where the delivery guy was. But I couldn't start it until I got off work. And-

"Jess!" Dad had just arrived onto Saturday Square holding a pair of Styrofoam packages that gave off the scent of cilantro and cumin. "I brought burritos!"

Even though I'm sure he would've wanted to know, I avoided telling Dad about the conversation with Officer Roberts. He left before I could ask about the robbery or anything else, as he had to get a burrito to Tim. There was much that I wanted to tell him, but as with the officer, the timing was wrong. After all, what could I say? I saw them harboring a mermaid at Jaquim Labs, oh, and I'm hiding one at the school? Until I knew more, there was nothing I could say. Plus, I had obligations for work that came first.

"Hello, this is Gary Bridgewater."

"Mr. Bridgewater, it's Jessica at the juice bar." I was sitting in the office at the desk as I spoke on the phone. As we talked, I pulled up the Friday Harbor Police webpage and printed out the missing poster for Rachel Arlen.

"Yes, what's up?" Mr. Bridgewater asked.

"The delivery guy is running late today, and I was wondering if you had heard anything."

He hesitated a moment. "No, I haven't heard any news. Hasn't been by, eh? I'm sure I saw the *Seath* go by, oh, maybe half an hour ago."

"Then, is there any way I can call the company? See if the driver missed the ferry?"

"I have the number here," Mr. Bridgewater said. "Leave it to me. In the meantime, just do your best with the fresh fruits. If you run out, you run out."

"Okay, sir."

"Thanks for bringing this to my attention."

"You're welcome, sir."

I felt bad not telling him that the police were investigating him, but then, he might already know. Maybe it was best I didn't involve myself any deeper than I already had. But I needed answers, and I could only get them one way. By going deeper.

~ ✿ ~

Halfway through the afternoon we ran out of fresh strawberries. Anyone who wanted strawberry in their fresh juice order was out of luck. Because we used frozen strawberries for smoothies, however, customers could still be satisfied. Most were, considering they knew we were on an island and could only get what we could get. The delivery guy never came.

Since the shop closed at four on Fridays, I locked up and recorded the receipts before putting the day's deposit into the safe. By 4:30, I was done and able to begin my investigation.

First, I circled the square and tried to recreate where everything had been. Since the carnival had arrived on the island several days before the Fourth, I was able to recount their placement rather easily.

The Roller Coaster had been located on the south end of the square. Midway games and food trucks filled in the center area. The Ferris Wheel was located on the east end, angled so when you rode you were almost parallel to the harbor. Other game stands, including a ring toss game and a dunk tank, had been out in front of the juice bar on the northwest corner. That meant that the Tilt-A-Whirl would have to have been located in the northeast corner.

Surely the officer had interviewed the carnival company every way from sideways. Otherwise, somebody on the newspaper staff would have noticed it by now. But the location of the ride suggested Mr. Bridgewater could have been involved, as the only other nearest structure is the juice bar. But it's unlikely, for even our walk-in cooler was too small to hide anyone. If the police suspected anything, they would almost surely take him into custody.

Yes, there was some trash still strewn about. But I didn't see anything ground-breaking.

Realizing that no clues would be acquired here, I unshackled my bike and headed home to check in with Dad.

While I coasted down the driveway, I realized I would have to leave home again to keep an eye on Cheryn. Maybe we wouldn't all have to, but I had been the one to suggest it.

Dad was sitting on the deck and looking out toward the channel. There was no avoiding him before I could go inside.

"There you are," he said. "I've been waiting for you."

"Sorry," I said as I climbed up the steps. "What's up?"

He glommed onto me and hugged me tightly. "Just this."

I embraced him. "Sure, Dad. Have a rough day?"

He explained a series of phone calls with his insurance company, with the security company for the hardware store, and several phone calls with police. Sounded awful.

"At least you got through it," I said. "Nothing else was taken?"

"Nothing else was taken," he repeated. "Though I'm tempted to set up a cot overnight just in case anyone gets grabby."

"Oh Dad—" I trailed off. So dramatic.

"If it wasn't for your mother's sense of reason, knowing what was best for you kids, I wouldn't have either of you," he said with a sigh.

Uh oh. This sounded like one of those epic conversations. "Has something else happened between this afternoon and now?"

He shook his head. "You and Tim are all I've got. I still don't know how it happened."

I leaned back into the nearest chair. There was no getting out of this.

"Christmas came and New Year's went, Jess, and then your mother went to Seattle for the weekend. Business trip, she said, just a business trip. She'd taken trips like it many times."

I nodded. Mom had made many of these trips, as she worked as an internet controller for a major aerospace company in Seattle. Basically, she managed online systems that managed equipment transfers between divisions and customers. The job could be performed remotely from here, which meant we were set up with a T3 internet connection that I don't use much, as I only seem to use the internet to reserve books at the library. I never quite understood Mom's job, but it meant she had to make trips to Seattle fairly often, usually once or twice a month.

"January came, and she moved out," Dad said. "Just like that. Three years later and I still don't know how it happened, Jess."

I knew how it happened, and so did Dad. She had moved out on him, I knew that. Saying so wouldn't change anything now. That was that, and Mom made her choice. Was it worth discussing? Maybe not. Nothing could change what had happened, as far as I was concerned. Not having Mom around was strange, more than odd, but a lot has happened in those years since. Guess I've had plenty to focus on in the meantime.

"Dad, she made her choice," I said. "She told me herself, she doesn't think any of us did anything wrong. Especially you."

"That doesn't stop it from hurting," he said.

I couldn't argue with that. Maybe it was time to break that news, but there were other things to be said first. But even so, I couldn't say anything that would compromise my investigation. I still had work to do, and Cheryn's safety depended on it.

"Dad, I might be heading back to Naomi's tonight. We're working on something."

"Oh?"

"A 3000-piece jigsaw puzzle," I said. No, it wasn't time to break *that* news. But a puzzle? Where did that come from? Suddenly I was lying to my father, much like my mother had lied to him. "It's a large picture of fireworks."

Dad hesitated a moment before nodding slowly. "Wow, that must be a tough puzzle."

I shrugged. "The box art's pretty epic."

"At least you're using your summer vacation to the full."

"I hope you're okay with this."

He nodded, much more confidently this time. "You're on your way to becoming a successful adult, Jess. Don't let anyone tell you otherwise." He gave a wave to the kitchen. "I brought a pizza from Van Go's if you're hungry. It's in the fridge."

"Okay," I said. "Thanks, Dad."

"You're a growing girl, Jess. Make sure you pay attention to the world around you. Okay? Don't let people who are close to you stray too far away."

"Should I stay here tonight?" I asked. "Home?"

"Go have fun. That's more important."

Somehow, I felt it was a loaded suggestion. "Are you sure?" He nodded. "Go on. Get out of here."

I had been given marching orders, so I had to go back to the school. Before I left, though, I called Naomi to see if I needed to bring anything for her or Cheryn. Along with something for dinner, Naomi suggested I borrow Dad's portable DVD player and a film. Guess which one.

On my way outside, however, Dad handed me something. A letter, with an oddly stamped rendering of my name, though it was misspelled.

"Say, I almost forgot. This came for you in the mail today," he said. "Doesn't seem to be any return address. Any idea who sent it?"

"No," I replied. "Thanks."

"Have a good night," he said before adding, "But I'd like to see you tomorrow night."

"Oh?"

"For a family campfire," he said.

I nodded. "Okay. See you tomorrow."

"You're such an independent young woman."

If only I had realized how much Dad needed me that night. He had become very accustomed to having Tim and me in the house, especially when he himself slept alone. Getting robbed at the store had taken that sense of security from him. It must be an awful feeling.

Before riding away, I tore open the letter. Inside was a cryptic scrawl on a single sheet of paper. It was a message stamped in large letters, much like those ransom letters you see in movies.

WE KNOW YOU HIDE RACHEL. YOU BETTER HIDE TOO.

The quality of the threat was somewhat questionable, and looked like it was made in Photoshop. However, to say I wasn't startled by the message would've been an understatement. In lieu of utter panic, I folded it up, stuffed into my backpack, and waited to show it to Naomi. To be honest, while I imagined they had intended the message for me, I wondered if they had indirectly directed the threat towards Cheryn. After all, she had been the person anybody would have seen. Clearly, this was more than a simple case of mistaken identification.

Since Naomi knew I was coming, she opened the school door and allowed me to bring my bike inside. For the moment, only she and Martin were here, but Martin would not be staying the

115

night. John had family obligations, while Martin hadn't been able to come up with an alibi to remain on school property overnight without telling his folks where he would be.

Though I was relying on my credit card a lot lately, I was able to pick up a few pita sandwiches from the Greek deli on Market Street. I decided that they might be something Cheryn had never tried before.

"Good, pita bread sandwiches," Naomi said. "These will be great."

"There's something else." I presented the letter.

Naomi looked it over. "Uh oh."

We walked into the pool area to find Martin and Cheryn sitting along the edge of the pool.

Cheryn gave a wave. "Hi Jessica. How was work?"

"We have a problem."

Once each of us had a sandwich and some chips, the issue of the letter became the primary focus. Certainly, this was a problem that needed immediate attention.

"This Rachel girl," Cheryn said. "What's she like?"

"Shy," I said. "Spends a lot of time in the library, like I do, but we don't talk."

"Who could have sent this?" Martin asked. "That Kelsey girl?"

"Only if they still think Rachel became a mermaid," I said. "Or the reverse, I suppose."

Cheryn giggled.

"What?"

"I always giggle when I hear how humans think we can grow legs."

"Then, you can't?" Martin asked.

She shook her head. "We're happy enough being who we are. It's naïve to think that every non-human creature aspires to be human."

"Then, all those stories?" Naomi asked.

"Nope," Cheryn replied as she patted her lap. "This is me. No hiding who I am."

"And all those little girls who want to be mermaids?"

"Probably not," Cheryn said. "Though many have tried, I suspect."

"Those stories you talk about are written by humans," Martin said.

Naomi nodded. "Maybe I grew up wanting to believe them."

"This is still a threat though," I said as I held up the letter.

116

"We stood outside the school for twenty minutes yesterday. In all that time, anyone who drove by would be able to connect the dots and confuse Rachel for you."

"I still think we look nothing alike," Cheryn said.

"At any rate, if they think you're Rachel, this may not be a safe haven any longer," Martin said, turning to me. "Did you see any evidence of divers in the harbor?"

"I was at work all day," I replied. "But yes, a diver came in and ordered a smoothie."

Cheryn sighed. "Darn."

"When I left to head home for lunch, I looked toward the harbor but didn't see any more boats than usual," Naomi said. "It's not likely they'd keep looking after two days."

"Actually, they may keep looking," I disagreed. "Until they find her, they'll keep looking."

Martin climbed to his feet. "As long as there's still sunlight, I should look around. While it's not likely they'd keep searching into the evening, I might be able to find a few clues."

"You'll let us know on your shell phone if we need to leave, right?" Cheryn asked.

Naomi giggled. She hesitated a moment. "I always giggle when mermaids call things the wrong names."

"What?"

"It's a cell phone, not a shell phone," Naomi replied.

"Like dinglehoppers," Martin said.

"What's a dinglehopper?" Cheryn asked.

We had our giggle, though it felt wrong not to let Cheryn in on the joke.

"Anyway, I should go," Martin said. "You remember the code for the security system?"

Naomi nodded. "Can I set a level for the doors but not the interior?"

"Probably, but don't mess with it," he said. "Just remember that the cleaning guy is coming to clean the place in the morning. You'll want to set your alarm."

"What time?" I asked.

"He usually comes after eight. Make sure you clear out by seven."

"We'll do that," Naomi said.

"Will John come by with his golf cart?" Cheryn asked.

"I'll remind him," Martin said. "What's the plan for tomorrow?"

"Tomorrow," Naomi said hesitantly, "Tomorrow we all start looking for Rachel."

"Agreed," Martin said. "You work tomorrow, Jess?"

I shook my head. "Only four days a week."

"Great," he replied. "Good night."

"Good night," we repeated.

For the next hour we swam together, though Naomi and Cheryn had exhausted their competitive spirit. Afterwards, Naomi and I took turns in the shower before hooking up the portable DVD player. It was a small screen, but the three of us were able to watch *Aquamarine*. I hadn't been worried about the wish idea, but the wish promise inevitably came up.

"Is that where that wish idea came from?" Cheryn asked. "I feel like humans have entertained an idea like that for years, but longer than—" She held up the DVD case. "Longer ago than the year 2003."

"This movie just plays into popular legends," I said. "It's a good chance that the writers of this film didn't have a mermaid as a creative consultant."

"Jess, did Cheryn promise you a wish or something?" Naomi asked.

Cheryn giggled. "I might have."

"And?"

Cheryn shrugged and put the case down before sliding into the pool.

"Well?" Naomi stood up. "You're not going to get out of my question that easily."

Cheryn swam to the far side of the diving well and sat in the corner, giggling to herself.

"Come on!"

"I think we're going to have to give up on it for now," I said.

"I'm going in after her." Naomi threw off her shirt, dropping to her swimsuit. "Back me up on this, Jess."

"How?" I asked.

Naomi dove in before she could answer. Soon, the two were chasing one another, swimming in circles around the bottom. Naomi surfaced a moment later, and I could hear Cheryn giggling the entire time. It was a little comical, but I also worried that Naomi might forget to breathe. She could be pretty determined when she made up her mind.

"Come on!" Naomi cried before diving under again.

After a few more laps, Cheryn began to build up speed and emerged from the pool, jumping twenty feet into the air and towards the lap pool, landing and swimming into a circle before circling around and surfacing. "Are you finished?"

I had instinctively ducked when Cheryn made her leap, even though she wouldn't have been close enough to hit me. She was completely in control.

Naomi, however, surfaced and pounded the water with her hands. "Not fair! Foul!"

"I'm enjoying this game," Cheryn said. "Unless you'd rather go another round?"

"Stupid mermaid," Naomi said.

"Clumsy human," Cheryn giggled.

"I think it's time I gave you both a time out," I muttered. "Gosh I sound like my Mom."

Cheryn swam up to the edge and pulled herself up. "Did you bring any other movies?"

"No more movies until you fess up!" Naomi cried.

"I might have one other," I said.

Dad had left a copy of *Miracle* in the player, so that was the film we watched. I had to bring Cheryn up to date about the game of hockey, not to mention the concept of frozen water, since the straits don't freeze over in the winter. Overall, I think Cheryn enjoyed the film.

"Has the United States hockey team won gold medals since this film?" she asked.

"Don't think so," I said. "I don't really follow hockey all that much."

"I'll tell you more about them if you tell us how we get a wish," Naomi said.

I sighed with a yawn. "Try not to chase each other again."

Cheryn didn't give into Naomi, and was rather mum for the rest of the evening. I wondered if she had intended only to grant a wish for me, though it felt awfully selfish of me to think that way. Then again, the other possibility was that Cheryn never possessed any magic of the sort, and that she was, as she had said, herself and nothing more. It seemed less likely that she would have some magical seashell that granted wishes.

For the next half hour or so, I brought out my book light and read while Cheryn and Naomi went to sleep. I knew that the small police squad on San Juan Island wouldn't investigate any tip-offs in the middle of the night, and as soon as I was confident that nobody would try to get inside, I turned off my light and succumbed to the darkness.

The Red Shoe Adventure Club

Saturday July 11th, 2009
Friday Harbor Herald

In the ongoing search for Rachel Arlen, the family has announced a stipend of $1000 for any information that leads to the discovery and homecoming of the teenager. Accordingly, the Herald staff would like to remind people that Rachel Arlen is described as sixteen years of age with dark blonde hair and blue eyes. She was last seen wearing a Friday Harbor High School letter jacket and blue jeans with grey and blue tennis shoes.

Search teams have expanded their search to western portions of San Juan Island as well as in the waters of the harbor and surrounding channels. Any with information are encouraged to contact Friday Harbor Police. Searchers are welcome to contact Roche Harbor Police, who have joined in the search.

As a result of increased search efforts, today's annual Paddlethon Regatta has been postponed. The canoe race that circumnavigates San Juan Island will be postponed until further notice. Participants are encouraged to check with race management, as well as enlist with active search teams.

In other news, Dr. Gregory Pruitt has announced that his seven iron was successfully returned. Staff of the Herald were unable to determine how, according to unconfirmed sources, the shaft of the club bent. The doctor has vowed to uncover this mystery, and has launched an investigation.

While I was deeply immersed in slumber, the piercing bells of my cell phone began to ring, causing Naomi and I to stir. The time was six thirty, and both of us were groggy.

"It's too early," she said.

"Remember what Martin said?" I asked. "The pool cleaner will be here soon."

"Okay," Naomi said. "Time to wake up. Her too."

I stood up and walked to the edge of the lap pool. "Cheryn?"

As I looked toward the bottom, Cheryn was comfortably sleeping, leaning slightly to the side. She seemed incredibly content. I hated to do it, but I pulled a golf ball from my backpack that was a leftover from a tournament two weeks ago, and dropped it onto Cheryn.

The ball landed on her stomach. Hole in one. She moved around and picked up the ball.

"They say you're supposed to play it where it lies," I said. "But it's time to get up."

With a swish of her tail she moved to the surface. "Already?"

"Afraid so. You don't want to be here when the pool guy arrives."

"Okay." She tossed me the golf ball. "I can get up. Are there any blueberry muffins?"

"Nope."

"Darn."

"Agreed," Naomi said, turning to me. "Why didn't we bring muffins?"

With Cheryn's help, I pulled her bedding from the pool and put everything into dryer in the girl's locker room. Naomi and I then packed up everything else, such as the portable DVD player, and waited for the sleeping bag to cycle through the dryer. As for the camp pad Cheryn had been sleeping on, it would've fallen apart in the dryer, so we propped it up against the wall to dry.

As we waited for the dryer to finish, I sent John a text. He called a moment later.

"Good morning," I said.

"And to you," John replied. "Everyone awake and chipper?"

"Only if you are. We could use some transport."

"I'm on my way. See you in fifteen minutes."

When I removed the bedding from the dryer, it occurred to me that it'd be best to leave it for another cycle. There was no time for that, so out it came and I wrapped it as tightly as I could, as the scent of chlorine permeated from the fabric. Everything else had to be wrapped up as quickly as possible, because John was here. Naomi let him inside, and I brought everything into the main area. Cheryn was sitting up on the pool deck, patting herself dry above the waist. Her blouse, skirt, and sun hat were nearby.

"Good morning," John said. "How was your stay? Comfortable?"

"I finally got used to the chlorine," Cheryn said. "But I'm ready to go home."

"We didn't have a chance to hear from Martin," Naomi said. "Are they still searching the harbor? Are there still divers?"

John shrugged. "Maybe they're starting the search after breakfast."

Cheryn began to button up the blouse, having left the bikini top on as a brazier. "If there are still divers in the bay, won't I have to come back here?"

"Martin said the swimming class only goes until two," John said. "You said something about searching for Rachel?"

"Yes," I said. "If we can find Rachel, they won't look for her anymore." I removed the letter I received yesterday. "Plus, we'll get someone else off our back."

John looked at the letter. "Is this for real?"

"As real as Cheryn is," I said.

"Can you help me, Naomi?" Cheryn had the blue skirt in her lap.

Naomi kneeled and assisted her with clasping and securing the skirt. "I'm convinced it was Kelsey who sent that letter."

John shook his head, a sceptical look on his face. "Anyone could have driven by and mistaken Cheryn for Rachel. They do look alike."

"Still not convinced," Cheryn said. "Different hair, different legs—"

"At any rate, it's time we cleared out," John said. "Can I carry you?"

Cheryn smiled. "Please."

As John took her into his arms, the telephone in the pool office began to ring.

"Should we answer that?" Naomi asked. "It might be Martin."

"I'll get it," I said. "Start packing everything, Naomi."

"I can't wait to go home again," Cheryn said. "I can taste the water already."

I answered the phone. "Hello?" There was nobody on the line. My eyes drifted toward the window overlooking the school parking lot. A patrol car had just pulled up with its lights blazing. Had the phone call been a warning? The police were here!

"We have to leave! Now!"

"What?"

"Come on, let's go!"

The three of us who could run did, and Cheryn held onto John tightly as we headed outside. I jumped into the driver seat of the golf cart, and John loaded Cheryn into the passenger side. There was no time to set up the wet towel.

"Take my bike, John, once you deal with the police." I hit the gas pedal and propelled the cart forward. "See you soon."

"Go!"

I didn't stop to look behind me as Officer Roberts and Deputy Hammond came up behind us. While I'm sure John loved riding a girl's bike, there really was no time to lose.

"Freeze! Stop right there!"

Were they aiming their guns? Maybe it was just their go-to threat? I didn't stop to find out. Instead, I pushed the golf cart as fast as it could go and pulled onto the road. At least there wouldn't be heavy traffic on the island until the first ferry arrived. Behind us, I could hear yelling, but it was muffled out by the hum of the cart's tiny motor. I assumed they would chase.

Cheryn held onto her hat with one hand and the bar along the outside of the seat with her other. "We forgot the towel."

"Yeah." I spotted her tailfin emerging from beneath her skirt. "You said it yourself, Cheryn, you are yourself and there's no disputing that. We'll just have to take our chances."

"Can we outrun them in this?"

I glanced behind me to see that the police cruiser was pulling out of the school lot.

"Jess?" Cheryn asked. "I've never been in a high-speed chase before."

"This is a low speed chase," I replied. "Hang on!"

Making it to my house seemed both impossible and a mistake. I also didn't want to take the golf cart down Spring Street, just in case anyone was awake and might see I had a mermaid with me. As I came down Second Street, instead of turning onto Spring Street I went straight towards an alley between the real estate office and the cafe.

"Are we heading for your house?" Cheryn asked. "Would the police know where to go?"

I didn't answer, instead turning towards the waterfront and following the alleyway toward the ferry station. The morning ferry had already left, and there were no vehicles in the queue. I steered us toward Saturday Square. In the distance I could hear the sirens approaching.

"Head toward the water, Jess," Cheryn said. "How long can you hold your breath?"

"Not very long," I said. "You're the expert swimmer."

"Leave it to me, okay? You'll be safe with me."

"Okay," I said, even knowing I couldn't hold my breath forever. "I trust you."

I drove onto the empty Saturday Square and navigated the picnic tables toward the dock that lead to Mr. Bridgewater's boat house, where his second-story apartment was located above the harbor. Trash leftover from the Fourth of July scattered as our speed disturbed the area, and did little to aid the cleaning effort.

"They're coming!" Cheryn said as she looked behind. "Take that dock!"

The police cruiser drove onto the square and closed quickly. One of the officers got onto the loudspeaker. "Pull over!"

"Where?" The suggestion seemed silly, as there were no curbs. Driving onto the narrow dock, there was no escape now. We were about to run out of dock, for there was nothing ahead of us but harbor. John wouldn't be happy with me.

Cheryn gave a nod. "Take a big breath, Jessica, and take us in."

"What about the golf cart—"

"There's no time!"

She was right. I sped up. The next thing I knew, we were driving head first into the harbor. I gasped for air, and held my breath as I was overcome by water. A moment later, I felt a sudden yank as Cheryn grabbed me by the collar, pulling me away from the golf cart and into the open harbor as the cart sank into the bay.

"Hold on, Jess! Hold on!" It was Cheryn's voice, and I heard her clearly. Perhaps I was crazy, or dreaming, or dying. She was right, I could hear her just fine. "Stay with me!"

Cheryn swam fast and frantically, and I pursed my lips as the oxygen slowly released through my nose. Everything I saw was moving away, swiftly fading into green bubbles. The movement was smooth, yet obviously hurried. As my view was facing backwards, I could only see an occasional view of Cheryn's fin as the sunlight reflected off of her shimmering scales. Were we going deeper? Did the light seem dimmer? Or was the air escaping me?

"Just a little longer, Jess. Stay with me a little longer."

My lungs craved air. A tunnel formed in my field of view as oxygen escaped my senses. This adventure would be ending soon, and I wouldn't be able to tell anyone what it was like. Everything began to blur.

"Jess! Wake up!"

Had I blacked out? I couldn't remember the last several moments. Air filled my lungs and I rested on the beach. As I slowly sat up, Cheryn was supporting me. I recognized the view of Brown Island and the channel towards Vancouver. Mt. Baker was shining beyond the horizon above the distant islands.

"I'm home," I said. "Aren't I?"

"Yes," Cheryn said. "You did great. Really great."

"Really?" I blinked several times, and felt like I might have water in my ears. "How long was I underwater?"

"Maybe two minutes," she replied. "But you made it."

"Good," I said. "Where are the police?"

"I don't know," she replied. "But we might not have much time. Can you launch your canoe again?"

"The canoe?" I asked. Maybe I was still hazy from blacking out. "You want to go for a ride in the canoe again?"

"Yes," Cheryn said. "Right away. If we head across the channel right away, we can check to see if there are any divers near my grotto."

"Are you sure?"

She smiled, boosting my confidence. "You said you trust me. I've trusted you this far."

"I trust you," I said again. "Okay, the canoe."

Inside of five minutes I launched the canoe and collected an oar and a life jacket for each of us. I also grabbed a package of cold cuts from the house and some bread before tossing them into the cooler, having skipped breakfast. This time I remembered to grab a beach towel, the nearest of which had been left hanging in the garage. The orange and white towel gave off a pungent musk, but it would hold water.

Cheryn pulled herself into the front seat and dunked the towel before wrapping it loosely around her fin. "Are we ready?"

"Ready." I pushed the canoe into the water and jumped in as it left the beach. Cheryn used the oar to propel us past the tidal basin and into the open water, and soon we were both taking turns with the oars. "Where'd you learn to paddle?"

"I'm a quick study, plus Naomi's a great teacher," Cheryn said. "I think she has Lummi ancestry. They used to traverse these waters by canoe all the time."

"You're familiar with the Lummi tribes?" I asked.

Cheryn turned and gave me a smile. "Naomi told me all about them last night. Were you asleep or something?"

"Guess so," I said. "How long were you both talking?"

"Quite a while," she said as she eased up on her paddle work. "We got to talking about acrobatics. I haven't lost that dream, you know."

"Why should you?" The idea didn't seem all that silly. "I'm sure lots of people would pay good money to see a mermaid acrobat performer."

"That's the only part of my dream that wouldn't have to come true," Cheryn said.

I found that surprising. "You want to be an acrobat, but not to perform for people?"

"Nah," she said casually. "I wouldn't need to have an audience."

At this point, I realized that we were heading straight into the open channel toward Shaw Island. "Say, are we going the right way?"

"Yes, keep us straight of your dock toward that next island," she said. "I can usually make this swim in ten minutes."

"Even with the currents?"

"The trick is following the ones that move you along faster and skipping past the ones that send you into a different stream," she said. "It's much easier than it sounds."

I shook my head, exasperated. "Ever the professional."

Crossing the channel by canoe took much longer than ten minutes. Even following her advice and bucking the current took nearly an hour. No wonder Dad said not to go this way. But now that we had, we were committed. As the current subsided and I felt we could relax a little, my stomach began to rumble. Breakfast had yet to be discussed.

"Gosh, are we there yet?" I smirked at myself. "Glad I grabbed that lunch meat."

"Are we stopping?" Cheryn rested her oar and dunked the towel in the water before replacing it around her fin. "We need to go a bit further, just to the far side of the point."

"I'll make you a sandwich if you want to keep rowing." I opened the cooler.

She picked up the oar again. "Are these sandwiches like from the other day?"

"Not nearly," I said as I slapped deli ham between two slices of bread. "No toppings, no lettuce, no cheese. Here."

"Thank you."

Once we both had a sandwich, we found it easier to traverse the channel.

"Remind me, what do humans eat?" Cheryn asked. "Was that ham?"

"Right. Comes from a pig," I replied. "Beef is from a cow, and chicken is chicken."

"I've seen all these meats in the menus, but you must go to a lot of trouble to get them pressed flat like that."

"They're sliced." Apparently, it was time for the food discussion. "Do you eat fish?"

"I go hunting twice a week with a coral spear my father gave me," she replied. "Mostly I'll snare shellfish and the occasional trout."

"Do you eat them—" I hesitated. "Raw?"

"Not exactly," Cheryn replied. "There's a spot in my grotto where the water is warmer than everywhere else, and when I put the meat onto a rock it cooks the meat a little. Enough so I can use my knife to add the meat to a sea kelp salad."

"You have a knife?"

"I can show you when we get there. I only use it around my grotto, and it's very old. My father found it in a shipwreck a long time ago. Has a sheath and everything."

"Sure," I said. "I guess I imagined all mermaids are vegetarians or something."

"Because we're all friends with fish and crabs?"

It was hard to hide my smirk. "It's easy to make up stories."

"There are lots of things about us that humans don't understand," she replied. "We make tools with what we've got. After all, a girl's gotta eat." She used the oar to direct us east. "At the

127

point we should start to turn right."

"I guess it seems silly to bring it up."

"In the few days I've met you, I've learned as much about you as you have about me," Cheryn said. "That's the other thing Father told me. Never stop being curious, and it's never silly to ask a question you don't know the answer to."

"Good advice," I said. "My mother tells me that too."

After a few more moments, I turned the canoe into Parks Bay, a picturesque little nook along Shaw Island that was made up of little nooks and lagoons. The water was calm, and all of the nearby shoreline was comprised of trees and rock. Other than a few houses on the north end which were blocked by a row of trees, there was no evidence of human habitation.

I found myself rather awestruck, having been so close to this area and yet never visited.

"Beautiful, isn't it?" Cheryn said as she put her oar in the bottom of the boat. "You should see it from below."

"Yeah, I don't think I've got my diving certification just yet."

"At least we're free from the divers here." She sighed and looked over the edge of the canoe as we drifted further into the bay. "You're going to wait in the canoe, then?"

"Are you leaving?"

"Just to check on things. Unless you're worried?"

"No," I said. "Though I know from experience it's tough to climb into a canoe."

"There's a shallow beach in the furthest inlet," Cheryn pointed towards the southeast. "Years ago, there was a house, but nobody lives there now."

"Should I wait for you there?"

"That would be good." She removed the life jacket and dropped it into the canoe. "I won't keep you for too long."

"Okay," I said. "Can I have the hat?"

She smiled and handed it to me. "Of course."

I put it on. The hat fit okay, even though it didn't match my blue flannel and jean shorts.

"Okay then." She used her arms to move herself in the seat before pushing off and jumping into the bay. I had to steady the boat with the oars, and managed to avoid tipping.

She surfaced a moment later. "That was exciting!"

"Maybe for you," I said.

"Sorry, I didn't know it would tip that much." She put the soaking wet beach towel into the bottom of the boat. "Give me about ten minutes, okay?"

"Sure," I smiled. "I'll be at that inlet."

"Don't worry, I'll find you." She ducked under and was gone.

Now I found myself alone. I gazed toward the north end of the bay and saw a pair of orcas slowly cruising by. A moment later, they too were gone. If there was one thing this bay offered, it was wildlife.

I pulled out my cell phone. One bar, but that would do. The screen had cracked slightly, but despite having gone under-water, the thing worked. It was time I checked on John and Naomi. I dreading telling John about the golf cart, and decided to call his phone first.

The phone rang twice before a baritone voice answered. "Jessica Summers."

I couldn't contain my sigh. Guess who had answered it. "Officer Roberts."

"Nice to know you survived your little swim."

"Thank you. May I speak to John please?"

"I'm afraid that won't be possible."

"Then I don't know if there's much we can talk about," I said.

"Can I speak with Rachel?"

So, they did think Cheryn-

"I know you had a passenger, Miss Summers. Put her on the phone."

"She's not here," I said. "My passenger is checking things at her home."

"Are you aware that Miss Arlen is a missing individual? Continuing to harbor a victim like that constitutes holding a prisoner against their will."

This was getting ridiculous. Everyone thought Cheryn was Rachel. It was time I said something and stopped dancing around the issue. Mermaid or not, she was her own person.

"Her name is Cheryn," I said. "My passenger's name is Cheryn, okay? She has reddish brown hair and blue eyes. She looks nothing like Rachel, and I can prove it."

"Cheryn," Officer Roberts replied. "Does this Cheryn have a last name?"

I hesitated. Do mermaids have last names?

"Miss Summers?"

"She hasn't told me what it is yet."

"How inconvenient." He spoke away from the phone a mom-ent. "Run a search on the name Cheryn." He drew the phone closer again. "How do you spell that?"

I spelled it out for him.

"Interesting." A moment later, Officer Roberts spoke again. "Your friends are all here at the station. Bring Rachel here and we'll drop any charges against you."

"That won't be possible," I said. "I don't know where Rachel is."

"There's no record of anybody named Cheryn in our files."

"No," I said. "There wouldn't be any records of her."

An obvious huff of frustration sounded across the surface of the phone. "You're leaving me few options, Miss Summers. My choices are to either put out a warrant for your arrest, which includes requesting a search warrant for your home, or you come in to the station, with this Cheryn of yours, and we figure this out."

I hesitated. My friends had been open to meeting Cheryn. To introduce her to a public official, especially in an open legal case—

"Miss Summers, I've got the police radio in my hand. All I do is send out an all-points bulletin, and if you set foot on any public road on this island or otherwise, my staff bring you in with steel bracelets."

Behind me, I heard a soft pop. Cheryn had surfaced. She was holding an impressive hunting knife in a leather sheath, as well as a sleek metal spear with a sharp coral tip.

"You have thirty seconds, Miss Summers."

"Cheryn, would you like to speak with Officer Roberts?"

She looked back with a nervous expression. "What happened, Jess?"

"Put her on, Miss Summers."

I offered Cheryn the phone. She wrapped the weapons around her left wrist before holding herself higher above the water by hanging onto the canoe. With her free hand, she took the phone and held it up to her ear.

"Hello?"

For a moment, Cheryn stared blankly into the bay, turning away from me. I couldn't hear anything the officer was saying. Eventually, she spoke.

"I understand, officer. Please don't arrest Jessica. I was never in any danger with her, and she's not responsible for the other girl's disappearance." Cheryn nodded. "Certainly, sir. I don't want any of my friends to be in trouble over this."

I couldn't believe my ears. Did Cheryn just agree to meet the police?

"Officer, I'm happy to meet with you, but only at Jessica's house. Okay?" She turned back to face me, giving me a smile and a nod. "Certainly. We'll be there soon. I'm looking forward to our meeting." She listened another moment. Finally, she handed me the phone back. "He wants to talk to you."

"Officer?" I asked.

"I won't release your friends until I get to the bottom of this. Understand?"

"Yes," I said. "See you soon. We're not actually at my house yet, but we're on our way."

"You have a half hour." Click.

I put away the phone and released a deep breath. "Oh man."

"Did anything happen above shore here?" Cheryn asked.

"No." I glanced around the empty bay. "Let's bring the canoe to the shore first so you can get back into the canoe."

"Should I put these away?" She held up the knife and spear.

"I think that would be best," I said. "As a habit, it's not a good idea to bring weapons to a meeting with police."

"Just a moment," she said. She dove under.

In the meantime, I picked up the oar and rowed backwards so the canoe would have a stable foundation to climb into. No sooner had I hit the sandy shore at the inlet did Cheryn re-appear. She used her momentum to flip over the bow, using her hands and twisting her body to land with a thump in the chair.

"That's incredible!" I gasped. "How?"

"I told you, I want to be an acrobat someday," she said with a wink. "May I have the hat again, please?"

"Of course." I took it off and put it on her head. She was already putting on the life jacket.

"This seems silly," she said as she snapped the latch on the jacket, "but I guess we have to keep up appearances until we get back."

"I guess so." I used the oar to push off from the bottom and directed us back into the bay. "Cheryn, do you have a last name?"

"Harvin," Cheryn replied. "It used to be Hardfin, but we changed it many years ago."

"Why change it?" I asked.

Cheryn picked up the towel and dunked it in the water before replacing it around her fin. "I don't know, it was my father's idea. Sounds more streamlined, I guess." She patted her scales. "Not only that, I'm very flexible, as you may have noticed. It's more floppy than rigid."

"Fair enough," I said. Harvin. Sounded very close to Arvin, which felt too convenient to be a coincidence. I kept telling myself that there was no way their two families could ever be related as we rowed back into the channel.

Forty minutes later, we approached the dock at my house. I could see a pair of police cruisers in the driveway. Dad was sitting on the bench at the end, and both Officer Roberts and Deputy Hammond were leaning against the railing of the deck near the house. John, Martin and Naomi were nowhere to be seen. I hoped they were inside either patrol car.

"Ten minutes late," Dad said. "Where were you?"

"Parks Bay," I replied. "Dad, meet Cheryn Harvin. Cheryn, Dan Summers."

She reached up a handshake, and Dad returned it. "Hello."

Cheryn removed the life jacket. "It's nice to finally meet you, sir."

"The feeling's mutual, though I haven't heard anything about you," he replied as he kneeled and held tightly onto the side of the canoe. "Climb on out, both of you."

"She can't," I said. "Cheryn can't walk, Dad."

Cheryn unwrapped the towel from around her fin, revealing herself.

"Dear me," he replied quietly. He kneeled to the dock, shock-ed.

At that moment, Officer Roberts walked onto the dock. "You're late."

"We had some distance to cover," I said. "Cheryn, Officer Roberts."

"This case just became interesting," Officer Roberts replied as he looked over Cheryn. "How about that."

Cheryn sat on the edge of the dock, facing the house with her tail in the water while Officer Roberts stood nearby. Dad had pulled the canoe onto the shore and collected a pair of chairs to bring out to the end of the dock, while I chose to sit cross-legged next to Cheryn. I had yet to see my friends. Tim was sitting on the deck watching us. And now the world knew that mermaids were real. There were only so many mysteries left, one of them being Rachel's location and how she continued to factor into everything. What had been a secret between friends would surely leave this yard now that the police knew.

"I think we've established you're not Rachel Arlen," Officer Roberts said.

"Thank you," Cheryn said.

I put my arm around her. "We met on the Fourth, a few

hours after the fireworks."

"Before we get ahead of ourselves, officer, please tell me you're not going to arrest Jessica," Cheryn said. "She has been nothing but a friend to me, and I'd hate to see her in jail."

"Assuming you could visit," Roberts replied. "Nobody needs to go to jail here."

"This isn't over, though, is it?" Dad asked. "How can we even report this? We'd be a laughing stock and plastered across the news channels."

"I'm not ashamed of who I am," Cheryn said. "I made a choice to introduce myself to Jessica, and I stand by that."

"You can't stand by anything," Officer Roberts replied. "Well, not physically—"

"Come on already," Dad muttered. "This is ridiculous."

"This isn't a costume, Dad!" I was so upset with my father and the officer. "Why can't you people accept the impossible?"

"Enough," Officer Roberts waved his arms and shook his head. "You're right, Jess. We're not here to discuss the legitimacy of mermaids, not while one's sitting in front of us. Tell me about the past few days and why you were keeping Miss Harvin in the school pool."

"There were divers in the bay," I said. "Looking for Rachel. If she stayed, they'd find her. And then they'd add her to the tank with the other mermaid." I gasped at myself. "Oops."

"What did you say?" Officer Roberts pulled up the second patio chair. "What's this about a second mermaid?"

"We think there's another mermaid being held at that laboratory complex," Cheryn said. "I myself did not know she had been taken. Perhaps I suspected something was going on at the lab, but I did not suspect one of my kind would be there. In fact, I'm not even sure who she is."

"They never covered this in training," Officer Roberts said as he picked up his radio. "Hammond, I need you out here." He clipped the radio back to his uniform. "It'll be hard to define human rights when two of the suspects aren't human."

"Cheryn has the same rights as anyone else," I said as I sat upright. "She has thoughts she has dreams; she is as much a person as anyone else is."

"Do we have to debate human and mermaid rights right away?" Dad asked. "We still don't know what the press will say about this."

"The press doesn't have to know," Officer Roberts said. "They only want a name."

"I wouldn't mind having my name in the paper," Cheryn

said. "But maybe my fins can stay out of the limelight for now. I've worked very hard to remain hidden."

"Hell, the tourist industry would love to know there are mermaids living offshore," Dad said. "Not that there aren't enough tourists here already."

"Enough about her being a mermaid," I pleaded. "Where are John and the others?"

Deputy Hammond walked onto the dock. "Huh, look what the catfish dragged in." Much like Officer Roberts, Hammond always had a flatbush way of speaking out the side of his mouth. Although he seemed to grunt a lot more than Officer Roberts did and never seemed to fully open his eyes, I always had thought that he was a true detective.

"Sir, I'm beginning to think we have a more complicated situation than a simple matter of a missing persons report," Officer Roberts said. "Should we release our suspect?"

"Which suspect?" I asked.

"Huh, she doesn't know," Hammond replied. "We arrested Gary Bridgewater shortly after your dive into the bay."

"You brought in Mr. Bridgewater?" I asked. "He had nothing to do with Cheryn. He's never even met her."

"Is this for real?" Officer Roberts asked.

"Of course," I said. Did I have any other reason to lie? They already knew Cheryn's secrets. They were standing across from a real live mermaid. We had nothing else to hide.

Hammond picked up the radio. "Officer Jepson, do you copy?"

I had heard the name a few times, mostly in the newspaper. Jepson was the desk officer who often processed forms at the police office and also answered dispatch during the day.

"Jepson here, go ahead Hammond," the officer's voice came over the radio.

"Have you questioned Gary Bridgewater?"

"Yes sir, according to your instructions."

"Huh, good," Hammond said. "As soon as I wrap up things here, I've got a few questions for him, but I have it on good authority that he is not involved in the Arlen case."

"Do I copy you right, Deputy?"

"Affirmative. I'll be at CO in ten minutes. Hammond out."

"Yes sir."

Hammond clipped the radio back to his uniform. "What else ya got, Roberts?"

"They think there's another mermaid being studied at Jaquim Labs." Officer Roberts looked at me for confirmation.

"Right?"

I nodded.

"Yes, we're sure of it," Cheryn said.

"Huh," Hammond replied. "How does this relate to the Arlen case?"

"We're not sure yet," I said. "For all we know, none of them may even be involved. The only reason why Cheryn was at the school was because there were divers in the bay."

"Huh," Hammond said. I didn't realize that was his catchphrase. "I thought mermaids were better at hiding than that."

"There's nothing magical about us," Cheryn said. "If there was, I wouldn't be here."

"Right then," Hammond said with a nod. "Regardless, we can't move on the labs without more proof or cause. Judge Keilor will never grant a search warrant over a suspected mermaid."

"No?" Cheryn looked upset. "Officer, she's likely being held against her will, much in the way Rachel is being held wherever she is."

"Police can't just barge in and take stuff," Hammond said. "The fourth amendment bans unlawful search and seizure without due cause. Even if there was suspicion of a human being held there, the law says we can't go in without any evidence to back it up."

"All we can do for now is release your friends and keep any existence of what Cheryn is to ourselves," Officer Roberts said. "Ordinarily, I'd bring you to the station to file a few reports, but I guess if we've got no case, we've got nothing to sign."

"Lieutenant," I said. "Who tipped you off to the school?"

"Anonymous caller," he replied. "Someone slipped a letter through the door when we came into the office this morning. Jepson should be completing the trace soon."

"Can we at least see our friends?" Cheryn asked.

Hammond gave a nod and started for the shoreline. "Roberts, bring Summers down to the station and let's get on with this. Let her ride in front."

"I'll drive her." Dad rose to his feet. "Cheryn, you can come too if you want."

"Who would watch Tim?" Cheryn asked.

We had almost forgot about him. He was still watching us from the deck, and almost never broke eye contact with Cheryn.

"Your friends are all at the station, and they're pretty much free to go," Officer Roberts said. "We'll meet you there."

Dad gave a nod. "I suspect there's more to this case yet. Who knows, maybe the robbery at the store is part of this too."

"This will be one of the biggest cases in Friday Harbor history, the way things are shaping up," Roberts said. "Come by anytime." He then gave Cheryn a nod. "Nice meeting you, miss."

Cheryn smiled.

The officers took their leave. Once they were out of earshot, Dad turned to me.

"How long were you going to wait to tell me you met a mermaid?"

"I'm sorry, Dad." I couldn't talk my way out of this one.

"If anything, Dan, it's my fault for asking her not to," Cheryn said.

I owe you one, Cheryn. Actually, I probably owe you two.

"I guess going to the police station is more public than staying here, huh?" he asked.

"Seems like Tim can't keep his eyes off of me," Cheryn said. "I can keep an eye on him."

"A mermaid babysitter," Dad shook his head. "Wonder what your mother would think."

"I think she'd be thrilled," I said. "Can I tell her about you, Cheryn?"

"At this point, it's hard not to," Cheryn said. "I trust you'll know what to say."

Although Dad was sceptical about leaving Cheryn out of the water, she assured him that she'd be okay. She put the wheelchair into use once more, keeping the spray bottle handy. Tim would probably be asking her questions all the time, but I had confidence she could handle him. With things well in hand, Dad and I went down to the station. As far as I was concerned, riding in Dad's truck always made a rough day better.

Inside the station, there was no paperwork to file and no forms to sign. Once we were able to talk outside, John held back what he had been waiting for.

"I can't believe you drove the golf cart into the harbor," he said. "My dad's going to flip when he sees the news."

"Sorry," I said. "Will it be okay?"

John shrugged. "Probably, once we change out the batteries. If nothing else, I've got a good story for next week's campfire now."

"Did Cheryn make it back to the harbor okay?" Martin asked.

"Yeah?" Naomi asked. "Is she safe?"

"Fine," I replied. "She's keeping an eye on Tim."

"The police must've been taken for a loop," Martin said. "They know about her?"

"As soon as they saw her, they dropped any kidnapping charges," I replied. "Did you leave everything at the school?"

"There wasn't any time to pack anything," Naomi said. "What about the lab?"

I leaned closer, checking over my shoulder to see that Dad was on his phone in the truck. "It's up to us. The police can't perform a search without a warrant."

"Then I guess we know what our afternoon entails," Martin said.

John shook his head. "Not me. I've got to go fishing."

"For what?" Naomi asked.

"The big one," John replied. "I wonder what kind of bait you use for a golf cart?"

"A really big hook," I replied with a giggle. "And maybe gummi worms."

~ 🌸 ~

Naomi and Martin rode in the back of Dad's crew cab as we rode over to the school. Swimming lessons were taking place, but our stuff had been moved into the lobby and was otherwise undisturbed. Once everything was loaded, Martin stayed behind to explain to the coach why there was bedding in the pool area. He said he'd fess up after assisting with the lessons.

Since it was coming close to lunchtime, Naomi opted to check in with her parents and said she'd call me later. Hopefully she didn't have a lot to explain.

Lunch involved mac and cheese, Tim's favorite. He insisted on adding a can of tuna to the mix, thinking the girl on the can was a friend of Cheryn's. It was a thoughtless gesture, but the combination worked well enough and we had a good lunch.

Cheryn and I sat together on the deck after everything had been cleaned up. The gathering clouds suggested rain in the future.

"What did you two talk about?" I asked after a sip of ice tea.

She sprayed herself with a cascade of water. "He's a curious boy, and asked about my grotto, what kind of foods I like, how I cook food, all sorts of things."

Dad came out and interrupted our conversation. "I feel like I should give you $20 for watching Tim, but I don't know if you'd be able to do anything with it, Cheryn."

"I'm sure I could," Cheryn smiled. "But that's okay, Dan."

"Are you two plotting anything? Going to the lab, maybe?"

"Why would you think that?" I asked.

"Because when I was your age, I'd probably be planning it." He folded his arms. "The kid in me says do what you have to do, but the adult in me says don't."

"Have you been keeping up with the case in the news, Dad?"

"The *Herald* and Channel 7 news ran a story on the progress of the investigation." He leaned against the side of the house. "Washington State Police located the owner of the carnival that came here. After questioning the staff, they determined that the operator of the Tilt-A-Whirl was not responsible for Rachel's disappearance. Accordingly, the carnival owner had no knowledge of the missing girl, and was sorry to hear of it."

"And the carnival was here until Monday?" I asked.

He nodded. "Doesn't mean much to the investigation how long they were here, though. As far as the police are concerned, their only suspect has been Bridgewater."

"What about the searchers?" Cheryn asked. "Didn't you say groups of people have been searching the entire island, from tip to tail?"

I nodded. "They must've found something."

"Only two things," he said. "A green pearl earring and an eight-pronged comb."

"A comb?" Cheryn asked. "I lost a comb a while back."

"Really?" Dad chuckled to himself. "They posted a picture on the newspaper website."

"It could be one of mine, I tend to lose them everywhere," Cheryn said. "Occasionally I find one again, only to lose it later. My favorite ones have eight prongs and a scallop handle."

I pulled out my phone and pulled up the webpage, showing a picture of a worn brass comb just like the one she described. "Is this it?"

"Yes!" Cheryn said before pursing her lip. "I'm never getting that one back, am I?"

"Probably not," Dad said. "At any rate, I don't want either of you doing anything illegal."

He had a good point.

"I don't think Jessica would ever do anything illegal," Cheryn said.

"She's surprised me before," he said warningly.

"At Christmas," I said. "Birthdays, Father's Day, but come on, never—"

"Just don't let me find out about anything from the papers," he said as he shook his head and walked away. "At least give me a heads up or something. I still want to see you at the family campfire tonight."

"I'll be there," I said. "Are you going back to the store?"

"Anders is going to hold the fort for the rest of the day," he replied. "But I can tell nothing I say will stop you from going to the lab."

It felt terrible to lie to my father. So, I didn't say anything.

"Should I give you a ride?"

"No," I replied. "We won't be able to get in past the guard gate anyway."

"Just don't get arrested."

"Thanks for lunch," Cheryn said. "Tell Tim it was a good idea adding the tuna."

He gave a worried nod and headed inside. I couldn't imagine how disappointed he was.

"Well?" Cheryn asked. "What are your plans?"

"I'm not sure yet." It was an honest confession. "But I know we can't get in while the sun is up. We'll have to go tonight."

"You can't go while the researchers are there?" Cheryn asked.

I nodded. "Maybe I should get some rest."

She agreed, rolling her wheelchair towards the steps. "Maybe I should too. When will your deck be handicap accessible?"

"Soon," I said. "I'll talk about it with Dad."

"Keep me from falling out."

I stood up and tipped the chair back, gently helping Cheryn down the steps. She then rolled herself along the walk toward the dock.

"I'd like to be a part of this adventure tonight," Cheryn said. "But I hope I won't just slow you all down."

I made my way out onto the dock and all the way toward the end. "I don't know how I'll even be able to get inside. Maybe Naomi has an idea."

"I've never been to a laboratory. Are there guards?"

"Probably."

"And alarms? Cameras?"

I hesitated. "What do you know about cameras?"

"I told you," she smirked. "If it goes overboard, it's ours."

We reached the end of the dock. "Is there something you want to tell me?"

"Not yet," Cheryn said. "I'll be back around sunset."

I shook my head. "Dad wants to have a campfire, remember?"

"Later, then." She moved the wheelchair up to the edge and

applied the brakes. "When is Tim's bedtime?"

"Eight," I replied.

Cheryn nodded. "I'll be around after sunset." She leaned forward in the chair. "I didn't thank you for helping me get away from the divers."

"Don't worry about it," I said.

"Same for you," she said, turning toward me. "Don't worry about tonight. If you're able to get into that lab, you'll be doing me and my kind a real favor. We've gone to great lengths to keep ourselves hidden, and while friends are hard to find underwater, we still have to be careful."

"Guess that makes us friends, then," I said with a smile.

She nodded with a smile. "Guess so." With a firm push, she jumped out of the chair and made a heavy splash into the bay.

Maybe she wasn't always that graceful. Or maybe she wanted to be noticed.

The rest of the afternoon was fairly quiet. While I wanted to get a nap and be alert for tonight, I couldn't seem to relax. I had to know who had called the school and warned me about the policemen. There were three possibilities. After letting Dad know I'd be out for a while, I rode my bike to the least likely source first. He didn't ask me where I was going.

I crossed Saturday Square and locked my bike at the rack that I always used when working. There was a salvage arm crew cruising away from the end of the dock that lead up to Mr. Bridgewater's boat house, and the golf cart appeared to be on board. The crew may have just recently finished the recovery operation. Aside from a few loose strands of kelp, the cart appeared to be fairly intact. Hopefully it would still run and John wouldn't hate me. Luckily, John and his father weren't around for me to explain myself.

A bell rang above the door as I entered the juice bar. The store had a few customers, but the crowd was nothing the crew couldn't handle.

"Hello!" Melissa gave a wave. "Oh, hey Jess. Need a smoothie?"

I shook my head and called to Thomas. "Hey, Tom? I need Melissa a moment."

Outside, I picked a table on the edge of the square. Melissa came out and stood.

"Take a seat, you've been standing all day," I said.

"Is this about work?" She continued to stand across from me with a worried expression. "You didn't report me for skipping the other day, did you?"

"No," I said with a smile. "I wanted to discuss how the search went Wednesday."

"I think they discovered something out there in the harbor," she replied. "Must've watched them working all morning—"

"They recovered a golf cart, but it has nothing to do with Rachel. Where did you say you searched for her? Down near Mulno Cove?"

She nodded and sat across from me. "There must have been twenty of us, all fanning out from the shoreline. Julianna had us all stand in a line facing away from the bay and start walking, reporting anything we found with a shout and a yell."

"Julianna-?"

"She's a grade above us, in Mr. Barron's class. I think her last name is Gregorson."

I nodded. "Were you able to find anything?"

"We picked up a lot of garbage," she said with a shrug. "Plastic bottles, used condoms—"

"Okay, don't need to know about that," I cut her off. "I heard from the police that they found an earring?"

"Not our group," Melissa said. "Might've been the group from Point Caution that found it Tuesday, but that's all I know."

I had forgotten that it was mentioned in the Wednesday paper, and couldn't have been reported in the paper until the story broke. "Oh, right." I refocused my questions. "Did you discover anything yourself?"

She shook her head. "Nothing that seemed to indicate Rachel had been there. I picked up a large fish scale, but I can't identify what kind of fish it came from."

"A scale?" I asked. "Are you sure?"

"Julianna and a few other nearby searchers looked it over with me. They couldn't identify it either. Someone thought it might have been a discarded guitar pick, since there are always groups hanging out at the beach there. So, I put it into my pocket and brought it home."

"You're sure it's a fish scale, though?"

She nodded. "Don't know what else it could be. It had a dark green hue to it and sparkled in the sunlight. Have you seen anything like that before?"

Maybe it was a fish scale. But for Cheryn's sake-

"Can't really say if I have, without having it here in front of me."

Melissa nodded. "Of all the things we found that day, it was the most unusual. It had been on the beach, and was partially buried in the sand."

"Could have been there a day or a week, then."

"Why the sudden interest?" Melissa asked. "Are you planning on joining the search?"

The thought didn't seem like a bad prospect. "No, but I've got my own search going on." Maybe she had something useful after all. "Any chance I can get a look at that?"

"Sure," Melissa reached into her pant pocket. She then showed the fish scale to me, inside of a small plastic baggie that you might keep a spare button from your new pair of shorts in.

"May I?"

She allowed me to pick it up. Maybe she had oversold its girth, as it was closer to a quarter in size but not perfectly round. Rather, one end was rounded and iridescent, while the other was rougher in appearance, square cornered and jagged in the middle. Sure enough, its overall color was a deep emerald or forest green that faded in color from the rounded edge down. Maybe the scale wasn't Cheryn's, but there was a familiar resemblance to its pattern.

"Quite a find," I said.

Melissa gave a nod and put it back into her pocket. "I'm hoping to bring it to the lab after my shift and then pick it up on Monday."

"Are you giving it to someone you trust?" I asked. "After all, you may never find another one exactly like it."

"Don't worry," she said. "I'm hoping it belongs to a green sturgeon. They're pretty rare."

I nodded. She rarely seemed unsure of herself. "I'll have to contact Julianna and find out what she knows about the case."

"Anything else you need from me?"

"No," I said. "Thanks, Melissa. See you Monday?"

She nodded. "Enjoy your Sunday."

"You too."

Next, I tracked down Kelsey. I started at her mother's store, hoping I might figure out where her group usually hung out. Just like at the juice bar, the door to the Karma Korner opened with a bell. Inside, the space was thick with incense and sun-catchers. This was Friday Harbor's only source for Tarot, occult jewels, and wheatgrass tea.

"Namaste," a tall, thin, healthy woman who just happened

to be Kelsey's mother greeted me as I browsed a rack of necklaces that ranged from steampunk to skulls.

"Hello," I said. "Is it Melinda?"

She nodded with a bow. "You're one of Kelsey's friends. How might I be of service?"

"Sure," I said. "She's been busy lately."

"Oh yes," Melinda said as she arranged the necklaces on the display. "Forgive me, but I cannot recall your name."

"Jess."

"Of course. You came in looking for a seeker stone once."

I came into the store last summer on a scavenger hunt that Naomi came up with. At the time, I needed to find a seeker stone, which really can be any kind of stone that supposedly helps you find lost things. Never did find one, except in her shop. The one I picked out was a translucent glass paper weight that wasn't quite red and not quite purple. Cost me six bucks.

"Did you lose it?" Melinda asked. "They have a way of escaping us."

"No," I lied. Funnily enough, I misplaced mine about a month after I bought it, and I quickly decided that I didn't need another one. "I just need to talk to Kelsey about something."

"Of course. She is planning an event for her friends tonight. You may find her in her fortress of solitude."

Fortress of solitude? Give me a break. "And where might that be?"

"Our backyard, on B street." She smiled nervously. "She says it sounds much less magical when I call it our tool shed."

"If I visit, will I be disturbing her?" The last thing I wanted was to walk in and find myself hexed, or worse, laughed at.

"No," Melinda said as she held up a pendulum stone, a pointed purple stone with black flecks on a black rope, in the air above me. "I sense you are on a divine quest." She closed her eyes and let the stone settle. "A quest involving water and—" she hesitated as the stone came to rest. She smirked, apparently in response to some arbitrary chart that existed only in her mind. "Pearl? How interesting! You must be very blessed."

"Sure," I replied, moving out from underneath the jewel. "I have to go now."

"Be faithful on your adventure," Melinda said, opening her eyes. "And keep your friends close, for they will surely be your salvation."

"Thanks." I couldn't get out of the store fast enough. She sure took her job ominously.

I found Kelsey's house, a purple Victorian manor with a wrap-around porch, only two blocks away. The house was easy to recognize, because there were missing posters for Rachel plastered across the front porch accompanied by posters announcing Rachel's ascension from the SIREN group. I followed a trail of mossy stones into the backyard, where a smaller version of their house had a large banner of SIREN's logo on the front. Perhaps the building had been originally built as a custom tool shed, but Kelsey had turned it into her club headquarters.

From the inside of the building, I could hear a soft chanting. The scene of incense was just as thick here as the store, and wafted out of the open window.

"Kelsey?" I asked. "Can I have a word?"

The chanting suddenly stopped. "An unbeliever approaches," Kelsey said.

"Oh give me a break."

She pushed open the door from the inside, revealing herself and three of her friends, who I knew were named Lewis, Cecelia, and Drake. They were an eclectic bunch.

"Have you decided to join our ranks?" Kelsey asked with a bright welcoming smile. "We're planning a ceremony tonight."

"Another ceremony?" I asked. "Oh yes, I read about that in the *Herald*. Sounded like your meeting didn't go well on Wednesday."

"Our celebration was met with considerable resistance," Kelsey said with a sigh. "We will not be deterred, however."

"Sure," I said. "I was wondering if you had any luck finding Rachel."

"There is no such thing as luck," Lewis spoke from the shed. "Those who try fail. Only those who welcome success earn what they seek."

"Sure." And everyone knows that Jedi don't bleed. "Did you join the search for her?"

"Our efforts have been unwelcomed by those who wander the isle," Kelsey said, continuing to speak officially. "But do not worry, for we believe that there needs to be no proof to know that Rachel has succeeded. Not just anyone can complete a quest like that."

"Sure." They still believed the impossible. In all fairness, I hadn't expected to find anything useful clues here. "Thanks."

"Will you be joining our ceremony tonight? Since our last attempt was spurned, we're going to try again tonight, but in the middle of the harbor."

"No." It may have been an afterthought, but I said it anyway before leaving. "Good luck with your ceremony." I didn't stay around to hear their response.

Finally, I headed back to Saturday Square and biked out to Mr. Bridgewater's boat house. I had only been up to his apartment a few times, and while it wasn't exactly off-limits, he didn't seem to enjoy company, especially from employees. Swallowing my apprehension, I climbed the steps up the side of the boat house and crossed the balcony to the front door.

Two knocks later, a determined grumbling emerged. "No rentals today!"

"Mr. Bridgewater? It's Jessica."

Two moments later, he answered. He hadn't bathed, and appeared quite unlike his usual pressed and clean-shaven self. To my chagrin, he had been drinking, as I could smell what was surely whiskey on his breath.

"Haven't you already clocked in twenty hours this week?"

"I have, sir. Can I come in a moment? I'd like to talk to you about this morning."

"Sure," he said with a nod. "You know you're always welcome here."

Inside the apartment, Mr. Bridgewater had several specimens of seashells on display, ranging from a large pink conch to one of the largest blue scallops I had ever seen, though when I first interviewed for the juice bar job last summer, he informed me it was a fake. The rest of the open-concept apartment's walls were covered with photos he had taken on his many vacations.

"Take a seat anywhere. Want some Coke?"

"I hope you mean pop," I replied.

He chuckled. "The only Coke dealer I know stocks the soda fountain, of course." He procured a glass and filled it from a 2-liter bottle from the fridge. "What's on your mind?"

I sat on a chair near the door. "Were you arrested this morning?"

"Yes," he replied. "No doubt you spoke to the police sometime after they chased you into the harbor. Sounded like they fished out a golf cart." He motioned toward the window that overlooked Saturday Square. "Saw me the whole thing. You okay?"

I nodded. "I'm a good swimmer."

He poured another glass of Coke, making no effort to hide

from me as he added a shot of Jack Daniels before capping both bottles. "They came in here after your little swim, saying I was hiding someone at the school. They cited all kinds of vocal accounts and hearsay, but couldn't produce any solid evidence. I got back by ten." He sipped from the draught. "Don't tell me they didn't talk to you?"

"Officer Roberts was waiting for me, and I answered his questions as honestly as I could."

"And?" Mr. Bridgewater asked. "Surely they didn't chase you for exceeding the speed limit on a golf cart?"

"No," I replied with a smile. "My friends and I were at the school, but we weren't hiding Rachel there. None of us know where she is, but hopefully she'll turn up soon."

"Is that right?"

"Yes sir." Had I just confessed to something? I had tried to pick my words carefully. Yet, I had to backpedal, and immediately. Telling Bridgewater about Cheryn was the last thing I wanted to do. "I wish for Rachel to be found soon, as does everyone else."

"Of course," he said. "But you say you were at the school this morning? Early?"

"Briefly," I said with a nod. "Met a classmate there."

"Would this classmate be that young lady I saw you with last Thursday?" He sipped from the cup. "The one with the long red hair?"

"That's Cheryn," I said, before catching myself and coming up with a quick alibi. "She's my cousin, who is just visiting. Came to stay for about a week."

"Yes, indeed," Mr. Bridgewater nodded. "There are too many tourists on this island, but you gotta make room for family where you can." He sipped again. "She live on the mainland?"

"Yeah, Vancouver," I replied, knowing it was adding to the lie.

He gave another nod. "Interesting taste in late 18th century dress."

"She's a traditionalist," I smirked. "Did you have to get a lawyer or anything?"

"No." He shook his head. "Honestly, there's not much else to tell. But I'll say you can't do much of anything with handcuffs on your hands, unless you're into the kinky stuff."

"I'm not, sir," I said quickly.

"That's right, you're a good girl," he replied quickly. "Good girls don't own leather."

"Is there anything else about Rachel you might know, sir?

Did you ever go to the carnival or even the juice bar last Sunday?"

"You're starting to sound like a cop," he chuckled. "That's good. Ambitious. You're going to be a detective someday, Jessica." He then sipped from his drink.

Since he dodged the question, I assumed he wouldn't be very reliable for any more questions. But I had one last one that needed to be addressed.

"Did you use your phone call, sir?"

"Phone call?" He shook his head. "Didn't get no phone call."

"Before the police arrived at the school, the telephone rang."

"Nope," he gave me a clear expression. "Can't use the phone when you're in handcuffs, either. That's just something that happens in the movies, unless you're incarcerated."

I nodded in response. Whomever called me had been brief, but they would've at least used their hands. Mr. Bridgewater could not had tipped us off. "Thanks for the drink."

"Anytime, sweetie," he said with a chuckle. "Anytime."

As I made my way up the dock toward Saturday Square, my cell phone began to ring. I felt like I had more questions than answers, but maybe Naomi had some answers.

"Hey, you around?" Naomi asked on the phone.

"Heading home. How are your folks?"

"Oh, fine, they were just happy to see me," she replied. "Cheryn with you?"

"She went home for the afternoon. I've been scouting around town for some information." I told her what I had discovered.

"I don't see how your boss could've tipped us off," Naomi said. "But I'm not surprised that Kelsey would try their stupid ceremony thing again."

"I'd like to check one more lead. Do you know where Julianna Gregorson lives?"

"Sure, she's my neighbor," Naomi replied. "About three houses down from me. Shall I meet you there?"

Ten minutes later, Naomi and I knocked on the house at the end of her block, a ranch style house with a large front porch. As I waited, I noticed a canoe in the front yard that had been converted into a planter. After another moment, a tall grizzly fellow answered the door with a modest grunt. As evidenced by his thick beard, red flannel and bushy black leg hair, I could tell he shared my taste in flannels but had little interest in shaving.

"Mr. Gregorson? Hi, I'm Jessica Summers, and this is Naomi Rovan."

He gave a nod. "Are you selling something?"

"No sir, we're wondering if Julianna is around," Naomi said.

He shook his head. "She's in Roche Harbor today. You know, continuing the search." He hesitated a moment. "Are either of you on the cheerleader squad?"

"No sir," Naomi replied. "But we're also looking for Rachel."

"Julianna's taking the search very seriously, since—" He trailed off, abandoned his original statement, and started again. "Those two seem to do everything together, after all. Yearbook, cheerleading, photography club, you name it."

"I didn't know Rachel was a cheerleader," I confessed. "We're in different classes."

"Nah, she's just the equipment manager," Mr. Gregorson said. "Julie's the captain, of course, but Rachel's always been too shy to actually perform on the squad, though she could probably do it if she chose." He hesitated again. "Did you want to get in on the search? I'd be there myself too, you know, if not for my gout."

"Sure," Naomi began. "We're searching on our own too."

"We'd like to check with Julianna to see if she found any clues toward finding Rachel," I said. "Pool our resources and discuss our findings."

"Sure, sure," Mr. Gregorson said with a nod. "It'd sure be something of a tragic day if anything were to happen to Rachel. Give Julie a call on her cell if you have any questions." He gave me her number. "She's determined to find her friend."

"Hopefully Rachel will turn up soon," Naomi said.

The bear of a man gave a curt nod.

"Thanks very much, sir."

He closed the door without fanfare. Guy liked his privacy, I guess.

We walked along Turn Point Road together as I called Julianna. She didn't have a lot of time to talk, but when I asked about the search for Rachel, she reported very little evidence. Aside from strengthening her enthusiasm that Rachel would be found, Julianna didn't have much else to say. If she knew anything about the seashell comb that Cheryn lost, she didn't say. I didn't prod.

Martin called us just before we arrived home. Twenty

minutes later, the three of us began to plan our raid at Jaquim Labs. Naomi hadn't been proud of her actions, but she had already gotten a hold of her father's ID card for the lab. With luck, it would get us where we needed to go. Martin brought along his camera, since my phone's camera had yet to be fixed. We would arrive by canoe and search for a way inside, hopefully undetected. Our plans were decidedly vague, but then, going to the lab at all was a gamble. We had to prove that our sighting was genuine.

While there was a good chance we were about to something highly illegal, not to mention dangerous, Cheryn's future was at stake. Tourism on the island was already out of control, and more tourists would come hunting mermaids if word of their existence was released to the world. Plus, the longer Rachel went missing, our own freedoms would also be in jeopardy if our parents decided to crack down on curfew.

That evening, just before sunset, the Summers family had a campfire. There were no adventure stories, though Dad tried to get us to sing together. I resisted, but gave in once s'mores became involved. At least he sang on pitch for once.

Tim went to bed around nine, and I brought a book out onto the deck while I waited for Dad to go to sleep. Finally, around a quarter after ten, I was alone. I sent Naomi and Martin a text each, and both were soon on their way. Cheryn showed up shortly thereafter, as she had been watching me from a safe distance.

By eleven o'clock, the four of us had assembled and were ready to leave for Point Caution. Each of us had a flashlight, and wore our best burglar black. Mine was a plain black sweatshirt that my father owned. Cheryn, of course, wore her usual blouse and skirt. If she had a full wardrobe of discarded clothes from shipwrecks, I decided it wasn't the time to ask.

"Can the four of us ride in this canoe?" Martin asked.

"It's got a capacity of 800 pounds," I said. "But it'll be tight."

"I can swim beside the three of you," Cheryn said. "In fact, that might be best. Did you leave the sun hat behind?"

I nodded. "No sun at midnight."

"Are we really going forward with this?" Naomi asked. "I don't want to have a criminal record. It might affect future college applications."

"This is for Cheryn," Martin said. "And her friend."

"You're all wonderful for doing this," Cheryn said. "It means a lot to me."

"If I'm going to commit a felony," Naomi said, "I'm glad I'm doing it for you."

Cheryn smiled. "John should be here too. He's part of our adventure."

"I put him in enough trouble already," I said. "Hopefully he won't be mad at me for the rest of the summer."

"Depending on what you find," Martin said, "we may all become a part of the local folklore. People will talk about us for centuries."

Naomi pulled the canoe along the dock. "Well? It's now or never. All aboard."

Martin sat in the back of the canoe, while I sat in front. Naomi rode in the middle, while Cheryn swam beside us on the starboard side. We were on our way, with only the waning moon to guide us. I was glad to be scared, otherwise I'd have been fast asleep.

~ ✿ ~

As we approached the university research camp, I was pleased to see the place was quiet. There were a few cabins with lights on, but most were dark. Nobody was walking about.

During our cruise, we had been talking quietly. Closer to our goal, our desire for conversation dragged. By now it had to have been almost midnight.

"Should we go to the dock or the shore?" Naomi asked.

"The shoreline, definitely," Martin said, steering right. "Just like last time."

"Can I climb in?" Cheryn asked.

I shook my head. "Not yet. Let's get to shore first."

We coasted to a quiet corner of the camp, past a grove of trees. I had expected a fence or No Trespassing sign, but neither were to be found.

The canoe hit bottom and we were jostled. "Land ho." I then climbed out, digging my oar into the ocean bottom to keep myself steady.

Naomi followed behind me and left her lifejacket in the boat.

"I could use a first mate," Martin said. "You're sure that it's better to have fewer people? I mean, we could even carry the captive girl home if all three of us came."

"No, I'm sure," I said as I turned to Naomi. "The police said we need evidence. What's the stronger form of evidence? A fish scale, or a live mermaid?"

"Fair enough," Martin replied.

"Got that ID card?" I asked. I knew she did, since we wouldn't get far without it. Still, it settled my nerves to be sure.

"Of course," Naomi said. "But it may not get us into the lab if they've changed all the access information. Also, there may be regular doors or padlocks inside."

Cheryn gently kicked her fin and climbed into the front of the canoe, plopping on the seat as quietly as she could. No acrobatics this time. She then reached for the life jacket, fumbling in the dark. "Where—"

"Here," Martin said. "Seems silly, doesn't it?"

"Shh," I shushed them. "We should probably be quiet."

Cheryn leaned forward in the chair and kept her voice low. "The trick to stealth is slow movements. If you move with a gentle, smooth pace, you might do better at avoiding attention."

"Right," I said. "Good advice from an expert."

Cheryn latched the life jacket on. "At least now I won't drown."

"Okay, that does seem silly," Naomi said.

"Shush!" I said again. "Not so loud!"

"My phone is on vibrate. Yours?" Martin asked quietly.

"Yes," Naomi replied under her breath. "And I have a flashlight."

"And I have the camera," I replied with a whisper. "We're committed. Let's go."

Naomi pushed the canoe into the bay.

"Jess," Cheryn said softly. "Mariana has dark green scales, if that helps."

"Mariana?" So that was her name. Had Cheryn known this all along? "Hang on, she has dark green scales? Why—" Suddenly it all made sense. It was never a guitar pick that Melissa found, it was a fish scale. It had to be.

"What is it?" Naomi asked.

"Nothing, later." We had other things to worry about.

"Do either of you have gloves?" Martin asked.

We nodded.

"Why?" Naomi asked.

"To keep your fingerprints off of anything, in case you both are implicated," Martin said.

"You're saying this now?" Naomi gasped. "I thought we planned this?"

"Forget it," Martin said. "Just be careful. You hear an alarm, you run. Got it?"

"We will."

"Right," Martin said. "Good luck."

We stayed along the tree line, avoiding any lit pathways or hardscapes. We made sure to be careful for any twigs, leaves, or anything that might draw attention to us. Any sound could turn even the most distracted ear. Naomi and I were too afraid to even speak. I remembered Cheryn's advice, and it seemed like I made less noise with every step. I was so nervous, I swore that even the simple movement of my legs brushing together would give us away.

Near the north end of the camp we approached the back side of the lab building, the same place I had scouted several days earlier. There was minimal lighting coming from the windows on the upper levels of the four-story structure, but all the windows I had looked through were blocked with thick tarps. Could these be the tarps that were stolen from the hardware store?

"Well? There's only one way we're going to see inside," Naomi said. "Do we proceed?"

"Yeah," I said. "We may not get another chance."

Naomi nodded. "Okay then, follow me."

I followed behind Naomi as she had me stay low behind a hedge, following the side of the outdoor patio on the east end of the building. The square wasn't impressively lit, but to enter there would cost us the cover of darkness.

"The entrance is on the southwest corner," she said quietly. "If we stay between the hedge and the building, I think we'll be better off."

Not one to argue, I continued following her lead. Our progress was slow going, but as we made our way around the building it became clear the windows on this side of the building weren't as obviously blocked. Standard vertical business blinds were used instead, although not all of them were drawn. Perhaps only the windows to the Ichthyology Lab and the scuba area were blocked.

At the entrance, there were two sconce lights on either side, as well as a light on an awning above the door. Beyond that, there were no floodlights. It was as good as we could hope.

"I should've worn a mask," I said.

"Hush," Naomi said. "If the card doesn't work, we run. Understand?"

I nodded.

Naomi then entered the light and emerged from the thicket to approach a panel on the side of the entrance. She pulled the

ID card from her pocket and looked for a slot.

"There's no slot? How did Dad even use this thing?"

"Touch it," I said. "Try touching the back of the card to the pad."

She did so, and a small green LED light illuminated on the left side. The lock on the door clicked. All those droll nights of watching CSI had finally become useful after all. Naomi waved for me to approach as she pulled the glass door open.

"Hurry!"

We both rushed inside, and heard the door lock again when it closed behind. Now, we were inside the lobby, the same lobby we had shared conversation with Dr. Gardiola. Here, too, the lighting was minimal, but we were no longer so innocent. A camera was facing the door.

"Quick!" Naomi pulled me out of its line of sight. "Don't look directly at the cameras."

"Have you done this before?" I asked.

"Just come on. The scuba area is this way." She brought me past the security desk, which was unmanned, and used the ID card again to enter the hallway. This was the central hallway in the building. On our left were a pair of elevators before an open staircase in the northwest corner. Naomi went straight to the right, however, ignoring both.

"Keep your head down," she said. "Don't look up."

I did so. This hallway was too public, but there was no other way. The space was lit minimally with recessed lighting along the edges of the ceilings, but I still felt exposed.

"I'm surprised they don't have a stronger security system," I said as we passed several rooms. They ranged from public restrooms to the Hydrogeology Lab and the Hydroponics area. "Motion sensors, that sort of thing. All that CSI stuff."

"They must not think they need that," Naomi replied. "They have cameras and ID cards, sure, but they also have a team of guards. Plus, everyone who enters the gate signs in."

About halfway down the hallway was the security door for the lab's Scuba Training Area. Another card pad was along the wall on the left side of the jamb.

"This is it," I said. "Let's get out of the hallway."

Naomi held up the ID card. "Just like outside." She touched the card to the pad. From a tiny speaker, the pad buzzed and displayed a red light across the face.

"No good?"

Naomi tried a second time with the same result. "Hmm... hey! There's a door that connects to the Scuba area through the

Ichthyology Lab. It leads to an upper level observation area. Do you remember? We were there for a tour during school once."

"Are you sure?" If we had ever taken a tour here, it was years ago. But the longer we stood there, the idea of standing here in the hallway on camera seemed a worse idea. "Let's try it before they spot us on the cameras."

"I'm positive. Sometimes they bring larger fish into the scuba area—" She trailed off and grabbed my hand. "Oh just come on!" Naomi quickly took us to the last door on the north side of the hallway, the Ichthyology Lab. She touched her father's ID to the pad and it blinked with a green light before the lock clicked open.

"After you, Miss Rovan."

Naomi gave a nod and pushed the door open.

Inside the space was lit with minimal lights, though none of them appeared to be for safety lighting or even basic security. Instead, the only lights came from scone lights surrounding the entrance while others were above specimen tanks. As soon as I entered, I felt like a rat in a cage as the light coming from the walls was a dark amber that illuminated only the doorway and cast hash marked shadow on the walls and the floor from the grated fixture. Fortunately, the specimen lights in the large lab space came from several aquariums in an area beyond an iron rack and glass partition that resembled a waterfall. The partition had thick, wavy, blue glass that cut down the amount of light that could come through, though in this light, it had no other use than to appear decorative. As far as I decided, the design of the wall made the space feel more inviting.

Directly in front of us was a tall cylinder of a specimen tank that was obscured by large canvas tarps that had been tied together with rope. A thin amount of dim light escaped the edges of the tarp, displaying the silhouette of a large creature with fins.

"Is that her?" I asked. "Mariana?"

"That's the sablefish," Naomi said as she took out her flashlight and checked a large trash can located behind the partition wall.

Since Naomi had probably spent more time here than I have, I didn't question her.

"Look at this!" Naomi pulled out a package for a paint tarp that had a price tag on it. "Friday Harbor Hardware. Didn't the police say they were broken into the other day?"

"Yeah, they stole an aquarium and all kinds of supplies."

Confirming my suspicions, there were more packages in the trash. These contained most of the packaging for the aquarium accessories. "This links the laboratory complex to the robbery, but not the guilty party."

"I wonder why someone from my father's division would steal?" Naomi reached into the canister to remove the packageing.

"No," I said. "Leave it. Don't touch anything, remember? Fingerprints."

"But this is evidence that implicates someone!" She hesitated. "I hope my father's not involved in this."

"The evidence stays," I said. "We can't make it look like we've been here or else they've got us for more than breaking and entering. The picture will be enough. Okay?"

She nodded. "Okay."

I reached into the pouch of my sweatshirt and removed Martin's camera. Lining up the shot, I then snapped a picture. The flash was blinding. I blinked a few moments before my eyes recovered. By then, Naomi had used a stairway constructed of open iron grating to access a catwalk surrounding the top of the cylindrical tank.

"You coming, Jess?" Naomi said quietly.

"Coming."

I quickly followed her around the top to a more secure platform on the north end that traversed the area above the research stations and cubicles below. At the end of this ran the exterior windows on one side and a drywalled room on the other. On the left was a single controlled door that had a pad and a sign that read BREAK AREA. I continued past that to join Naomi at the end of the passage where a set of double doors had its own control pad. The sign here said OBSERVATION AREA. Inside, I thought I heard voices. They echoed in the room, but had been much quieter at the other door.

"Naomi?" I whispered. "Do you hear that?"

"Yeah. We'll be quiet. Here we go." Naomi pulled the ID card from her pocket and touched it to the pad. It beeped with a green light. She then slowly opened the door.

"—week's worth of chlorine will affect anyone negatively, she can't stay in there any longer," a man's voice spoke, having a heated argument with another person. "No, Brooks, there's nothing to be gained by leaving her in there any longer than we need." He hesitated. "Why didn't we change the tank water with bay water? Or even aquarium salt water?"

We quietly closed the door and stayed low. This was indeed

the observation area, and the safety rails were drywalled, though there were benches to either sit or stand on. Naomi and I stayed low as the conversation unfolded.

"There was no time," a woman's voice said. I thought for sure it was Dr. Gardiola. "Gentlemen, we're in the process of freeing up a tank in the Ichthyology lab next door."

"And tomorrow is Sunday, yeah?" A man with a Boston accent was now speaking. Presumably this was Brooks, unless there were more men in the room. "So what happens when the workers come in Monday morning and see her?"

"Leave that to me," Dr. Gardiola replied. "We will have this tank drained and prepped with an environment replicating bay water in less than twenty hours."

"What will happen to my subject in that time?" the first man's voice spoke. "My associates have spent a lot of money toward this project to fund your research, doctor."

"And they will be fairly compensated, Dr. Wilson, should the subject expire under my care," Dr. Gardiola answered. "We are not prepared to pursue a vivisection, but we will proceed with a complete autopsy only if nature lets us. Though I assure you, we have done everything we can to keep the subject comfortable and healthy. We have no interest in killing her."

"Yes," Dr. Wilson replied bluntly. "Which is why she is dying."

I covered my mouth and hid my gasp as best as I could. Presumably, there was a lapse in their conversation as well. While I did not approve of Dr. Gardiola's words just now, if I were her it is likely I'd have glared at him too.

"Sir, we signed a contract," Gardiola said firmly. "We are all patrons of science, and what we have here is the greatest maritime discovery of all time. As I stated to you the other day, and I shall remind you again, that I share your admiration of the world's oceans and its creatures. Our first task is to appreciate and respect our subjects, regardless of truth or fantasy."

"Of course, if you hadn't convinced me as such when your discovery was verified, we would not be here," Dr. Wilson said. "A pity we could not find a more reliable pilot."

"Indeed, and when our work is finished, I shall be glad to provide airfare," Gardiola said.

"We'll all need airfare," Brooks said with a chuckle. "To Stockholm to accept our Nobel Prize in biology."

"Perhaps she'll ride in the cargo hold, though," Dr. Wilson muttered.

The three doctors quietly laughed. I couldn't believe my ears.

"Speaking of which, how soon can we move the subject?" Dr. Wilson asked.

"I say we move the subject as soon as she is stable," Brooks said. "Tomorrow morning."

"Agreed," Gardiola said. "Mr. Trom and I both will assist. Won't you, Jason?"

Naomi's eyes widened. Mr. Trom was in on this as well?

"Absolutely, ma'am. The subject's worth a lot to me."

"Good," Gardiola clapped her hands once. "Gentlemen, it's very late and we all have our own tasks to do tomorrow. Shall we retire for the evening?"

"Yes," Dr. Wilson said with a yawn. "Time to get back to my hotel."

"Of course, forgive me for asking you to continuing to meet with us so late. This way."

"After you," Mr. Trom said.

We continued to lay low as someone shut off the lights in the room, leaving only a few sparse lights on in the pool, casting a hypnotic reflection of moving water onto the ceiling. Finally, several uncomfortable moments passed before Naomi and I were convinced the room was clear. Only then did we move to our feet and find the stairway leading to the main level. Although there was a rope gate in place that was designed to curtail tour groups from accessing private areas, we passed under it and made our way down.

"Can you believe those people?" I asked quietly.

Naomi nodded. "They have no regard for life. If they really meant what they said, they would have let her go at once."

"Is someone there?"

Naomi and I both jumped. Could that be Mariana? Where had the voice came from?

"Who said that?" Naomi asked. We both looked toward the tank, which had a thick layer of kelp and seaweed across the surface. In addition, it had been covered with several large sheets of acrylic so that nothing inside the tank could surface. There was an access gate, but it had several padlocks with brass and iron bars. An open grating allowed things to be dropped inside, but getting anything larger than a minnow through the narrow slits would be impossible.

"The audio system must be off." Her voice was soft and ethereal, much like Cheryn's. "If you can hear me, use the switch on the wall."

"Naomi, use your flashlight," I said. "Look for a switch."

We both scanned the walls, making our way around the

room to a control area on the far side of the tank. Unable to find anything other than water controls, I descended a few steps where I was able to see inside the tank. That's when I saw her. She was floating upright in the water, staring at me from behind a thick wrap of kelp. Mariana's long brown hair was so silky that it seemed to tangle within the weeds. Her scales were emerald, but several had almost been peeling off in several places while others were completely gone, leaving a rough bare patch. In addition, her skin had several blemishes that were a sickly grey. If that evidence wasn't enough, her expression and deep blue eyes told a story of deep suffering.

Mariana seemed to be pointing to a computer panel. I sat down and looked over the panel, finding a toggle switch that controlled the sound system, MIC. I flicked to toggle switch to the on position, expecting an alarm. There was none.

"Good, that's a relief," I said.

"I can hear you now," Mariana said. She moved aside the kelp to get a better look at us. "You're not part of her team?"

"No," I said as I turned to look at her, now realizing that she had no clothing except for a matte black bikini top that must've been given to her by the researchers. "Are you Mariana?"

She narrowed her eyes and looked me over through the acrylic wall that was several inches thick. "How do you know my name? Even the woman doesn't know, but then, she's never been courteous enough to ask."

"Cheryn told me about you," I said.

Mariana opened her mouth, awestruck. "Cheryn? Do you know Cheryn?"

"Yes," I said. "She's with a friend of mine, and she's safe."

"How can she be safe?" Mariana looked away. "You must have captured her as well."

"No," I approached the tank to look at her. "In fact, she approached me first. Cheryn's my friend. I'm not like the doctor."

"She's right," Naomi said. "Neither of us are."

"There are two of you?" Mariana turned to look around. "They obscured the surface of this tank once the woman thought people could see in from outside, but it only made it harder for me to see them. But I know what they're up to."

"Jess," Naomi said as she came down to join me. "There's no way for her to leave the pool. We're not getting through these locks."

"That's not surprising," I said with a nod. "It's a shame they didn't use every piece of iron they could find."

"You said Cheryn approached you? The lady said they

searched the bay."

"There were divers," Naomi said. "She had to come ashore."

"Cheryn came ashore?" Mariana asked. "She always was reckless."

"Even mermaids can survive out of the water for a little while, Cheryn has proven that to me," I said. "She's proven a lot of things to me, I suppose."

"She's only the craziest mermaid I've ever met," Naomi added.

"What else did she ask you to do? Ask you to help me escape?" Mariana asked. "Because unless you brought her here, I'm not sure if I trust either of you. I don't trust anyone who won't tell me who they are."

"Jessica," I said. "My name is Jessica and her name is Naomi."

"We're both friends with Cheryn, and have known her for over a week."

Mariana nodded. "We mermaids identify each other by the sheen of our scales. If you tell me what color her scales are, then I will believe you."

"Blue," I replied without hesitation. "A bright sapphire blue that matches her eyes."

"Correct," Mariana said with a smile. "Very well, I trust you have met her. How do you propose to release me?"

"I don't think we can," I replied. "Not without the right tools."

Naomi groaned. "Or without setting off about a dozen alarms."

"Oh, well, that's okay," Mariana sighed, crossing her arms. "You came all this way just to say hello. How worthless. You're as worthless as the lady and her team."

"Now hold on a moment," I protested, before realizing she was right. How far was I willing to go? Cheryn went on land and revealed herself, and her entire race, when her natural instinct might have been to remain hidden. "There has to be a way—"

"Cheryn put her trust in you," Mariana said quietly. "I question her judgement. I'd sure like to talk to her, if nothing else."

"That's possible," Naomi said as she walked back around to the access panel. "I can slip you my phone through the bars."

"Yeah," I hesitated. "But Naomi, you'll never get it back, and you'll ruin your phone."

"What's a phone?" Mariana asked. "You humans have such weird technology. I mean, I can scarcely understand how we're talking as we are. They called this an audio system?"

"It's complicated," Naomi said. "And it would be too, for you to talk to Cheryn." She came back over to me. "Jess, this isn't going to work. We're not going to be able to get her out tonight, nor is there any way she can talk with Cheryn."

As the plan thus far had been an improv session, I didn't have any better ideas. "You're right. And we certainly can't bring Cheryn here."

"Is there no way I can speak with Cheryn?" Mariana asked. "No way at all?"

It was time to prove how far I was willing to go. I took my phone from my pocket and climbed onto the top of the tank.

"Jess? What are you doing?"

"My phone's camera may not work, but it still makes phone calls." I slid my finger along the screen and dialled Martin's number. "We didn't come all this way just to give up."

Martin answered a moment later. "What's wrong?"

"Nothing. Put Cheryn on."

A moment later, Cheryn answered. "Hello? Jess?"

"Cheryn," I said. "Someone wants to speak with you." I slid the phone in between the narrow slits and let go as Mariana took it.

"What do I do?" she asked as she floated along the surface as best she could, even though she was pushing up against the panels which were locked in place and would not budge.

"Hold it to your ear," I said. "And then say something. She'll hear you."

Mariana had to put the phone slightly under the surface to do so.

"Cheryn?" Mariana said. "I'm sorry."

There was a moment where I wasn't sure if the line was still open, or if Mariana might have cancelled the call. I was lucky that she wasn't holding the phone correctly, allowing me to hear their conversation, brief as it was.

"Okay," Cheryn replied. "Don't worry, you won't be there much longer."

"Thank you." Mariana handed the phone back up through the bars. "Will it be okay? I hope that it's not damaged."

"I need to replace it anyway." I took the phone back and patted it against my shirt before returning the phone to my ear. "Cheryn? Where are you and Martin?"

"Cruising the bay. It is very quiet, but Martin thinks he heard a motor start earlier."

"Okay," I said. "We'll head outside soon. Talk to you later."

"Be careful."

I cancelled the call and replaced the phone in my pocket before climbing back down from the top of the acrylic cage.

"Hey, Jess?" Naomi whispered to me. "You heard what the researchers said, right? About her dying?" She turned to Mariana. "How do you feel? Have you eaten anything over the past few days?"

"No," she replied. "They started leaving smelt. I ate one, but—" She gagged.

Naomi and I both wretched with equal contempt. "Ugh," Naomi said.

I regretted not bringing a granola bar or something more substantial. "Do these pool chemicals bother you?"

Mariana nodded. "The water tastes awful. And several of my scales have fallen out."

"Okay, Naomi," I said, turning away. "Let's look around for anything that might be useful. Look for a sling, or a candy bar, or anything."

"Right. I'll look topside," Naomi replied. While there were life-saving rings and a Shepard's Hook for pulling swimmers out of the water, there was little else that could cut the padlocks or penetrate the acrylic shell. "Jess, how does a sling help us when we can't access the pool anyway?"

"Stupid me," I grumbled. I must not have been thinking clearly. "Let's at least try to find her something to eat. What's next door? Was there a break room back there?"

"Yes," Naomi said. "Mariana, we'll be right back."

"Okay," Mariana replied. "I'm obviously not going anywhere."

"Wait!" Naomi stopped me before climbing the stairs. "The camera!"

"Right." I went up to the window looking into the tank, where Mariana was looking at me with mixed confidence. She might've backed away from the sight of the camera, but I took the photo and rushed up the stairs.

The mermaid blinked from the flash. "What did you do? Steal my soul?"

"I took your photograph," I said. "I'll explain later. We'll be right back!"

"What's a photograph?" she asked. "Did I have a photograph?"

After returning to the Ichthyology Lab, I walked past the entrance to the break room to search the offices of the researchers below the grated catwalk. Around the outside wall of the lab space below were a row of cubicles, each one containing the work of an individual employee that had been left as is since the previous work day. Nobody had food sitting out, however.

"Naomi, I think it's clear that the staff was sent home on Monday because of Mariana," I said as I descended the stairs to the main level. "I mean, I don't know when they found her, but surely they would've wanted to hide her as much as possible while bringing her inside."

"Seems likely," Naomi replied as she leaned over the rail above. "We'll have to ask how long she's been here. As for food, check my Dad's office, he usually has a jar of little candy bars. He won't mind if you take a few."

When I came to Mr. Rovan's cubicle, I saw a jar of Hershey's Miniatures with a tight lid. Removing the lid was easy enough, so I took five or six pieces before replacing it.

Naomi had since headed back upstairs next to the break area. "Maybe someone left something more substantial in the break room."

With several candies in hand, I went back up to the catwalk. Naomi had just tugged on the door to the break room, finding it was locked tight.

"Last time I was here, the lock was open," she said. "There was a refrigerator and everything, and even a television and an apartment in case researchers stayed late."

"Why would they lock the break room?" It didn't seem remarkable to me. There was a reinforced security door, complete with a pad for the ID card. "I mean, Mariana's next door. Maybe they wanted to protect the food from the guards?"

"Sure," Naomi smirked. "Guess we'll try the card."

Red light. It buzzed with a cold reception.

"That's not good," I said.

"Did I do it wrong?" she asked.

I shook my head. "Your father must not have clearance."

"Let me try it again." She touched it a second time, same response.

Messing with this door seemed like a bad idea from the start, especially since the scuba area was the only place large enough to hide Mariana from the public.

"It's not working."

Naomi touched the pad a third time. Three was the magic number. Not only did the pad buzz, but a siren began to sound in the room as a red caution light activated near the celling. We had just worn out our welcome.

"What did you do?" It was time to go. "Come on." I pulled her and began to sprint down the catwalk. "This way!"

"I didn't know the system would trigger a general alarm!" Naomi cried. "Who does that?"

We reached the exit to the hallway, finding the door had somehow sealed itself. Naomi touched the card to the pad, but it didn't respond. Maybe security had locked it out so that any intruder wouldn't be able to leave.

"What do we do?" Naomi pounded on it. "The door won't open!"

"Calm down," I said. "There must be another way out. Fire exit, or something."

Both of us scanned the lab space, and indeed there was another way out. There was a fire exit on the western wall behind the partition wall, along with an impressive array of aquariums. There were at least fifty. One stood out from the crowd and was placed on a wooden palette, away from the others which were all mounted on solid steel stands. A 125-gallon tank that still had product stickers on the side, along with a heater and a light. Three large fish were inside, including a striped shark, a massive steelhead, and a white sturgeon.

"Jess! Do you think this is the stolen fish tank?"

"Probably. We have to go!"

"Use the camera!"

I paused to take another photo. I don't know if the image would show anything incriminating, but took one more, using the camera's flash. Suddenly I couldn't see.

"Jess, what about Mariana?" Naomi asked.

"There's nothing we can do for her now," I said as I pushed the door open. Beyond was a short dark hallway that turned to the right before a door leading outside. Now back into the night air, we ran straight into the woods. Security lights flooded the area, and we didn't stop to see if anyone was coming. After all, we didn't want to be found.

"This way," Naomi said. She led me through the thicket and toward the east. "Can you call Martin?"

"Yeah." I pulled my phone out and dialled. He answered quickly. "Martin? Yeah, you can probably hear the alarm, huh? Look for us on the east end of the point."

"This way," Naomi said. "Keep moving. Don't look back."

"Head toward the point. You'll be there? Good." I hung up. "He's almost there."

"Good. Keep moving!"

People were waking in the camp. In the distance, I heard voices and more sirens. Of course, they were intended for us, but we had done worse than incriminate ourselves. Naomi's dad was now involved, as we had used his identification card. He had been completely innocent, and would likely get a phone call. Worse, we had been on camera. Then again, Dr. Gardiola and the men were on camera as well. Certainly, they weren't innocent.

"Wait," Naomi said. "We're making too much noise."

"How can we not?" I asked. "Keep going."

We proceeded as quickly and quietly as we could. I heard dogs barking behind us. We had to leave the area, and now. Finally, we emerged from the woods and found the point. Cheryn and Martin were there in the canoe, a few yards off-shore.

"Hey," I said in a hushed voice. "Good."

They rowed in closer, and I grabbed the bow along the rocky shoreline.

"Climb in," Martin said. "Let's get out of here."

"Agreed," Naomi said. She climbed in first, sitting in the bottom behind the middle seat.

I climbed in behind Cheryn, who was using the towel.

"Let's head toward the house," I said.

"No," Cheryn said. "Let's head toward my grotto. Across the harbor they'll see us."

"They'll see us anyway!" Naomi cried.

"Not in the main channel," Cheryn said. "Head towards Parks Bay."

"Agreed," Martin said. "Tell me where to turn."

"How did she look?" Cheryn asked. "Was there any chance of helping her?"

"She's starving," I said. "I wish we could've done more for her."

Cheryn nodded quietly. "You will, but that's not the wish I plan to grant. Thank you for giving me the chance to talk with her."

"Yeah." Once again, we were talking about wishes. Personally, I was beginning to care more about their relationship than any wish I might want. What mattered was that the two mers had been given a chance to reconnect with one another.

The canoe sat low in the water, but Cheryn and Martin kept their rowing even and soon we were crossing the channel toward Shaw Island.

Sunday July 12th, 2009
Friday Harbor Herald

On the morning of July 11th, the Clambert Salvage Company recovered a stolen golf cart from the Friday Harbor Country Club, believed to have been involved in a low-speed chase that began somewhere along Roche Harbor Road. The owner of the club, Mitchell Donaldson, reported that the golf course had no knowledge that the golf cart was missing. At press time, Herald staff were unable to determine the cause of the chase. Our re-quests for information from Friday Harbor Police were returned without comment, citing privacy concerns over an open investigation.

In a related story, Friday Harbor Police did release a statement to the press that Gary Bridgewater, owner and supervisor of the Friday Harbor Marina and the Saturday Square Juice Bar, was arrested on suspicion of kidnapping charges. Although police did not specify a specific case, witnesses to the arrest believe that the charges are related to the disappearance of Rachel Arlen, who has yet to be located. However, Bridgewater was released later that morning due to unreported circumstances. The search for the missing teen is ongoing. Friends of Arlen are confident that she will be found soon, safe and sound. Herald staff would like to inform our readers and all active search teams that the $1000 reward has been increased to $1500 for information leading to Rachel Arlen's safe return.

Paddlethon Regatta officials report that the race will recommence Monday, July 13th at 1 p.m. as was previously scheduled this past Saturday. Racers are asked to arrive by 11 a.m. for registration. Regatta staff are confident that the race will convene as planned, provided weather does not become an issue.

We reached Parks Bay quickly, having to simply cross the channel between San Juan and Shaw Islands rather than cruise north from the dock at my house. Twenty minutes later, the four of us finally had a chance to relax, despite a feeling of dread. All the same, we weren't in the clear yet. It was one in the morning, we were tired and hungry, and we couldn't sleep knowing the police might come at any moment to arrest us all.

"You're home, Cheryn." I gave her a pat on the shoulder. "You should probably go hide in your grotto before the police arrive."

"I'm not leaving you now," she said. "We're all in this together."

"They wouldn't arrest her," Naomi said. "Or even Martin. Right?"

"Actually," Martin said, "We might be liable as accomplices."

"Did you say Mariana is starving?" Cheryn asked. "I should have sent something with you. You have the camera, yes? Can I see her?"

"Sure." I pulled out the camera and showed it to her.

Cheryn smiled with a giggle before handing it back. "She looks so surprised!"

Naomi smiled, but the smile quickly faded. "She also looks very ill."

"You both did your best to find her," Cheryn said. "I cannot thank you both enough."

"I'm sorry to say it, but the police will still come for us," Martin said. "If you ask me, we're worse off than before."

"You still owe us a wish, right?" Naomi asked. "Can't you get us out of this?"

"Wishes?" Martin asked. "Genies grant wishes, not mermaids."

"Exactly what I've been saying," Cheryn said. "Sorry, Naomi, but it's like I told you. I'm just me. Forgive me, but I do not have the power to grant wishes."

"I knew it," I said. Movies didn't always get their facts right.

"At any rate, what are we supposed to do, stay here for the

rest of our lives?" Naomi asked. "Stay until dawn? I'm missing my bed right about now."

"Perhaps I should go check the harbor for police boats," Cheryn said. "Is that okay with all of you?"

"Yeah," Martin said. "On the surface, there's no cover."

"Can you, please?" Naomi asked.

Cheryn undid the skirt and lifted herself up from the seat before letting the garment slide into the canoe with a flick of her tail. She was getting pretty good at that. Then, she leaned toward the edge of the canoe and, shifting her weight in the seat, flipped into the water. "See you soon." She ducked below the surface and was gone.

Naomi shook her head. "That's getting annoying, how she does that without even taking a breath before diving away?"

"She's a pro," Martin said. "Tell me what happened in the lab. What did you find? Any opportunity for award winning pictures?"

As we waited, Naomi and I summarized our conversation with Mariana. He also saw the photographs of the items that were stolen from the hardware store. A moment later, he turned off the camera and gave it back to me.

"Cheryn is right, there is nothing remarkable about them," Martin said. "We use these photos to convince the police, but the photos cannot leave our circle. Agreed?"

"Agreed," Naomi said. "It wouldn't be fair to treat Mariana any more like a specimen than she might have been already."

"True," Martin said. "If I've learned anything from talking to Cheryn, I've never felt the need to send off photos of her to the National Enquirer."

"And you'd better not," I said. "Photos of her are private property. No posting them on Facebook either."

"Also agreed," Naomi said. "I only want one photo of us from the waist up that I can put on my nightstand. She's our friend, but it should be her decision if the world knows mermaids are real. Hers and Mariana's."

There was little else to talk about in the meantime. Although we were glad to be away from the guards, I began to wonder what might happen to Naomi's dad. By using his identification card, it was clear he was now implicated in our adventure. It was an uncomfortable feeling that served to keep me awake.

Cheryn finally returned a few moments later, just as Martin and Naomi were starting to nod off.

"Sorry I took so long," she said after surfacing. "You're not going to believe this."

"Actually, I might," Naomi said. "After all, I believe certain other things."

She smiled, realizing what Naomi had meant. "There aren't any police patrolling the harbor, but there is something else going on. There are four small canoes in the center of the bay, with two boys and two girls, all facing each other and chanting in some silly language."

I knew it was Kelsey and her crew right away, especially since she had hinted toward a ceremony over the water earlier in the day. "It's the SIREN group."

"Some sort of mermaid ritual?" Martin asked. "Or another attempt to denounce what we've been doing this whole time?"

"I think it's time we introduced them to the water spirits," I said as I carefully climbed into the front of the canoe. "Cheryn, can I count on you?"

Cheryn grinned enthusiastically. "I'm in."

"Wait, wait," Naomi said. "You're not going to introduce them, are you?"

"Of course not." I put on the life jacket. "We're going to have a little fun with them."

"This should be interesting," Martin said.

Following my instructions, Martin, Naomi and I stayed a short distance away from Kelsey and her group, who were chanting just like Cheryn had said. All four of them were kneeling in their kayaks, which were tied together along the west edge of the channel east of Brown Island. At the moment, Kelsey faced south, Lewis west, Cecelia faced north, and Drake faced east. Each wore a black robe with a hood of a different color. Kelsey wore purple, Lewis wore red, Cecelia wore green and Drake wore blue. All four had their eyes closed. No doubt all four took their séance seriously, but from my perspective the scene appeared rather silly.

"Mermana aquata trebara," they spoke in a single voice. "Acendia astral sucessana."

Suddenly, Kelsey's kayak began to shake violently. All four of them opened their eyes.

"What was that?" Kelsey asked. "Was that a tremor?"

Drake's kayak began to shake in the same manner. "We've awakened the spirit!"

It was time to move in. All four were shaking in turn now, though only one of them ever seemed to shake at any given time. Of course, Cheryn was rocking them from underneath.

"What kind of party is this?" Martin asked as he slowed his

rowing. "Playing with spirits again? Or calling to the divine powers so you can all get a real hobby?"

"As a matter of fact," Kelsey spoke up loudly. "This is our ascension—" she held onto the boat suddenly as it shook violently. "Ahem! Our ascension ceremony."

"Celebrating Rachel, right?" I asked. "Thought someone didn't appreciate that."

Drake's boat shook next, so much so that the bow dipped into the water slightly.

"We have a presence in our midst!" he said.

"Indeed," Kelsey said as she looked to the moon. "Focus! We must all focus."

Cheryn must have held up for a moment, because Kelsey was expecting a sign.

"It's official," Naomi said. "The four of you need to discover Facebook."

"The aquatic spirit is here," Kelsey said, raising her voice again. "You three are making her uncomfortable!"

"Oh really?" I watched Cecelia hold on as her boat shook violently. "Doesn't seem like your spirit is scared at all."

"I'd say it has nothing to fear," Naomi said.

"Perhaps you should all fear the spectre hovering over your heads," Lewis said.

"What are you talking about?" Martin asked.

"The spectre of justice," Lewis said bluntly. "Can't you see it?"

Cheryn must've been listening too, because she stopped shaking the boats.

"Justice? Against whom?" I asked.

"You," Kelsey said as she reached into her robe and pulled out a familiar object. "All of you. Perhaps you recognize this, Miss Summers?"

In the thin light, I recognized the green scale that Melissa had shown me earlier.

"How'd you get that?"

"Our organization has a budget for necessary artifacts related to our activities," Kelsey said. "Your fellow co-worker needed the money."

"Aren't you an assistant manager now?" Cecelia raised her hood slightly. "You should give her a raise."

"Okay, you bought a giant fish scale," I said. "So?"

"This is no ordinary fish scale!" Kelsey cried, holding it up to the light of the moon. "Our sister has found her true calling, and this is the proof."

"Proof," Naomi muttered. "Proof that you're delusional."

"Not true, Miss Rovan," Kelsey said. "Proof that you, Jessica Summers, have harbored the spirit of a liberated individual who craves the power of the sea."

"The power of the sea," Naomi repeated. "Power of the stupid."

"Disbelievers," Cecelia said under her breath. "You are all disbelievers!"

"Agreed, my proverbial sister of the cloth," Kelsey said. "This magical fish scale holds the truth. Rachel Arlen is here, beneath us. She shakes our foundation, calling forth the grim spectre of justice!"

"I'm going to be sick, and nobody's shaking my boat," Naomi said.

"This will never hold up in court," Martin said. "You can't prove anything with a fish scale that might've came off a green sturgeon."

I began to notice more of a commotion in the water. Did I see a snorkel in the water behind Drake's boat?

"What comes here?" Drake asked, turning.

Behind him was an orange kayak, without a pilot, slowly drifting toward the group. Inside the craft upon the seat beneath a folded purple shirt was a small chime, mounted on a wooden handle with three tubes and a hovering ball between them. The ball was safely secured, as it was mounted on a wire. The handle was ornately decorated, and had a red rabbit's tail on the end. Though the item looked ordinary, the SIREN group began to recoil from its approach.

Kelsey gasped and instinctively retreated into the stern of her boat. "It can't be!"

"Your accent's slipping," Martin said.

"What spooked you?" I asked Kelsey.

"Can it be the Chime of Catastrophe?" Kelsey asked.

Now the other SIREN members were recoiling in their boats.

"Yes!" Cecelia gasped. "It must be!"

"You said it didn't exist anymore," Lewis said to Kelsey. "You said Rasputin took it with him to the after world!"

"That can't be real," Drake said. "Can it?"

"Its very presence has disrupted our ceremony!" Kelsey dove for the front of her boat and scrambled to untie herself from the others. "We must flee before the world ends!"

Suddenly all four of the SIREN members were scrambling, and Kelsey was the first to flee, using her oars like a woman possessed. The other three followed behind, not even bothering to loosen their leads. They struggled, but were soon away. Meanwhile, the orange kayak slowly followed them in a zig-zagged heading.

"It has come to claim us! Hurry!" Kelsey gasped as she continued to row into the distance. "Get away!"

Suddenly, our canoe began to shake. "Cheryn?" I asked.

John surfaced, much to our surprise. He was wearing a snorkel and his swimsuit. "Well? I'll bet you didn't expect that, huh?"

"John?" I couldn't hide my smile. "Did you know we'd be out here?"

"Nope, but I knew they would. I had planned on breaking them up anyway, but then Cheryn came by. She didn't tell you anything about me, did she?"

"Not a word."

A moment later, Cheryn arrived. She was swimming along the surface and pulling the kayak behind her. "Well? What do you think of my performance?"

"Fooled them," Martin said.

Naomi smirked. "Fooled us!"

"Anyone can be a water spirit," John said. "All it takes is a snorkel and the cover of darkness."

"And you have to be a little creative," Cheryn said as she gave John a pat on the back. "Well done. You'd fit in fine down here."

John grinned. Apparently, he enjoyed his little swim with a mermaid.

We headed toward Brown Island first so John could get back into his kayak before heading back to my dock. Turns out the chime was just an ordinary chime that he had at his house. Adding the rabbit's foot was strictly ornamental, but apparently it looked enough like something Kelsey had in one of her books of magical artifacts. Perhaps it was a gamble on John's part, but the deception worked. He later explained that he had overheard them talking in one of his classes. Since the Chime of Catastrophe was real enough to the SIRENS members, the ruse worked.

On the way back, we got John caught up with our visit to the lab. He was disappointed about not being a part of the operation, but he was at least able to forgive me about the golf cart.

Once we reached home, Cheryn climbed onto the dock and helped Naomi exit the canoe. "I'm beginning to think I'm encouraging everyone to stay up late."

"It's my fault," I said. There I go again, pretending to be my mother.

"What time is it?" Naomi checked her cell phone. "Three AM."

"Guess you can all crash here," I said. "Though we may still hear from the police."

"Jess, I'll be nearby," Cheryn said. "This is as much my fault as yours."

"Cheryn," I began. "By helping us, you'll give yourself away to the world."

She shrugged. "I already have. I'm committed too."

"Maybe the thing to do is head to the station tomorrow," John said as he looked toward Naomi and me. "You'll both have to fess up about trespassing."

"If it helps Mariana return to the bay, it'll be worth it," Naomi said. "I just hope there won't be any jail time involved."

"Yeah," I said. "There must be more to this than a matter of breaking and entering."

"Mariana will at least appreciate it," Cheryn said. "I will too."

Inside of ten minutes, all the boats were pulled clear of the water and our band called it a night. Although I knew everything we had done was done in defense of Cheryn and Mariana, all I could keep thinking about was those steel bracelets Deputy Hammond had mentioned.

While the others got comfortable in the living room wherever they could, I turned off the light above the sink in the kitchen. That's when I noticed the answering machine on the house land line had a message. Adjusting the volume, I played the message. The call came from Mom, who had left a very sombre message.

"Dan, I hesitate to tell you this, but I've decided it's time I was honest with you. I've been seeing Harry Wellerson on my many visits to Seattle, since last April. It became physical, and everything that has happened since, well, it's been my fault. I can't begin to apologize for the way I've treated you, and if it's unfair to Jess and Tim, it's most unfair to you. Perhaps I should be saying this in person, but I'm ready to own up to my mistakes. You are a fantastic father to each of our children, and you did nothing to deserve this. Of course, it goes without saying that neither Jess nor Tim is responsible either. I should have said this years ago. I won't ask for your forgiveness, as I don't deserve it. I'll contact you soon and we'll sort this all out. You are still my first love and greatest adventure." Beep.

Maybe I was very tired, or maybe I had enough to lay on Dad

right then. Martin was right. It was time I stood up for myself, much like Mom had done. I sincerely hoped that Dad hadn't heard the message, because with everything I had done tonight, it would break him.

I found myself doing something I might regret. I deleted the message. Dad had enough to deal with at the moment, and knowing the truth about him and Mom was something he didn't need to hear. I would tell him myself. Yes, I had known since Mom told me last spring, on a trip to Seattle over spring break. It had been tough to hear, and I grew up that day. But after everything that had happened since, especially tonight, there would be a better time.

With everything on my mind, it was a miracle that I fell asleep.

~  ~

There was a bit of explaining to do when morning arrived. Dad was rather surprised to see the four of us, but even more surprised to realize how late it had been when we had come home. Guess there were some things that couldn't be hidden.

"Jess?" His voice brought me to consciousness, as none of us were in beds. I had slept on the couch, after all. "Why are all your friends here?"

"Listen, Dad." It was time to come clean.

"You did go to the lab last night?" He shook his head sadly. "Jessica, that's illegal. You know that's illegal! And I'm really disappointed you brought Naomi with you."

"They're holding a mermaid named Mariana," I said. "They're starving her."

"Starving her?" he asked. "Another mermaid. That's no way to legitimize—"

"It's true, Dan," John said. "I've seen her myself."

"Be that as it may—" Dad began.

"They stole from your store," Naomi said quietly. "We have photographs."

He stopped his tirade, but continued anyway. "You're not the police. None of you are adults yet, you don't realize—"

"We're going to the police station to turn ourselves in," I said firmly. "I'm prepared to stand for what I've done."

"Me too," Naomi said. "It was my idea."

Dad crossed his arms and huffed through his nose. I knew that look. "Very well. I'll drive you to the station." He looked toward Naomi, Martin and John. "The rest of you should go tell your parents."

"We're all in this together," Martin said.

John nodded. "Even me."

"You'll call your parents on the way?" Dad asked.

The three of them gave a nod.

"At least you're being responsible for yourselves," Dad said as he shook his head sadly. "What about Cheryn? Did you involve her in this too?"

Naomi nodded. "She agreed to join us—"

"No," I said. "I brought you all into this, Cheryn too. I asked you all to do this, all of our actions, and it's my decision. That's how we're going to tell the police."

"She said she'd be nearby," John said. "Do we bring her to the station?"

"I think we may have to," Dad said. "How do we bring a mermaid—"

"Mom's wheelchair is still in the garage," I said. "Cheryn's used it before."

"Fine," Dad said. "None of us deserve breakfast. Let's get this over with."

Although I had not planned on her coming, Cheryn was ready to go the police station with us. We retrieved the wheelchair, two towels, and her skirt from the bottom of the canoe. Within ten minutes, we all piled into the truck. The wheelchair rode in back, but Cheryn rode in front. The rest of us crammed ourselves into the truck's back seat. Seatbelts weren't optional in Washington State, but hopefully the police wouldn't add that to our list of growing infractions.

Dad and I went into the police station first as John and Martin helped Cheryn. Once she was wrapped up in the wheelchair, the rest of the group joined us. Deputy Hammond was reluctant to accept our confession at first.

"Officer Hammond, my daughter and her friend are here to admit to trespassing," Dad said. "She believes that the staff at Joaquim Labs are holding a mermaid against her will."

"Huh," Hammod muttered. "I thought we agreed to keep that fishy business private."

"I have a photo," I said as I showed the officer my camera. "We found evidence from the hardware store at the lab also."

"How about that." Hammond stared blankly at me while the others came inside. "Did you just admit to trespassing?"

"Yes sir—" I hesitated as the phone at the desk rang. Hammond answered it. I glanced down at the police office's phone, which listed the information for the call. It was Jason Thom calling from Jaquim Labs.

Hammond continued to stare at me as he listened to Trom, responding minimally with an occasional 'huh' or grunt. Finally, he said he'd investigate the alarm. "Huh," Hammond said after he hung up. "Sounds like you kids are making quite a mess of things. The security guard said that an alarm was triggered at 1:36 AM. That your work?"

I nodded. "Yes sir."

"Miss Rovan?"

Naomi nodded. "I triggered the alarm using my father's ID card."

"Guess we need to get Douglas Rovan out here too." He turned to the desk officer, Officer Jepson, a tall thin man with a narrow moustache. "Paul, get Doug Rovan on the horn. Have him meet us out at the lab gate."

Jepson gave a nod and picked up the phone. Naomi sighed, but held her composure.

"You came too, miss?" Roberts asked.

Cheryn nodded. "Are you going to arrest them?"

Hammond gave Dad a glance before looking over Naomi and I. Then, much to our relief, he shook his head. "If what you told me yesterday was true, there's more to this case. However, it's very likely that the laboratory will press charges."

"There's more," I said before telling them about Mariana. "They want to move her into the Ichthyology lab tomorrow."

"We've all seen her," Martin said. "You've seen Cheryn, too."

"If Mariana stays there, she may not survive," Cheryn said.

"She's really sick," John said as he showed the officers the photo on the back of the camera. "You have to believe us."

Officer Hammond and Roberts exchanged glances. "Huh."

"Okay," Roberts said. "Maybe it's time we procured a search warrant."

Hammond picked up the phone and called the courthouse.

A moment later, Hammond and Roberts were ready to go. They had their search warrant in hand, and we were all going to be a part of it.

"Shall we continue this at the lab?" Cheryn asked. "I know Mariana is waiting for us."

Hammond nodded. "But for official appearances, you two ride with me." He pointed at Naomi and me. They didn't put us into handcuffs, thankfully.

We agreed.

As it turns out, riding in the back of a police car was punishment enough. There are no cushions in the back of police cruisers, as well as no air vents, handles for the window or doors, or seatbelts. Take it from me, riding in the back isn't as fun as the movies claim.

Hammond exited the patrol cruiser and informed Mr. Trom that he had two confessed trespassers inside. He did not, however, mention the search warrant. A moment later, Mr. Trom opened the gate and drove his own golf cart as we followed him to the lab entrance. Dad followed in his truck behind us, along with Mr. Rovan who had drove his own car.

"Mermaids," Douglas Rovan said as he glared at his daughter as we assembled outside the lab complex. A larger man, Douglas was among the most level headed individuals I had ever met, and smart too. "To think, they're living here, off of Friday Harbor. Really."

"It's true, sir," Cheryn said. She hiked up her skirt to reveal the lowest part of her tailfin, just above her fin which was wrapped in the wet towel. "Naomi wouldn't have gotten involved in this if not for me."

Naomi smiled at Cheryn. "Thank you."

"Okay, okay," he said, shaking his head. "Can't dispute my eyes."

Mr. Trom looked at Cheryn with a sullen expression. "Somehow I feel like this isn't just a matter of trespassing."

"It's not." Officer Roberts held up the search warrant. "We're going inside, Trom. Either you let us in, or you get to join them in the back seat."

"They're not waiting in the car," Dad said. "Doug and I will see that to that."

Trom nodded quietly. "Fine. Let's get this circus over with."

A moment later, our group proceeded through the lobby and beyond the security desk. Aside from the light of the sun entering the atrium, the space had changed little since nightfall. From the other end of the hallway, Dr. Louise Gardiola headed our way. Beside her were two men wearing suits. One was wearing a neck brace and was older. The other was the man I had seen Wednesday, and still had a cast on his left arm.

"I hope you brought a search warrant, Deputy," Louise said. "Our time is limited."

"We're not leaving until we have what we need," Hammond said. "Who are they supposed to be?"

"Dr. Julian Wilton and his assistant Dr. Brooks Bagley," Louise said as she noticed Cheryn for the first time. "And who is this?"

"Cheryn Harvin," she said. "And you are Dr. Louise Gardiola."

Louise didn't respond. I wondered if there was something she wanted to say but couldn't.

"Mr. Trom, open this door," Hammond approached the door at the end of the hall.

"No search warrant, no entry!" Louise exclaimed.

Hammond unfurled the warrant. "As a policeman of Friday Harbor and an upholder of the laws of San Juan county, I order you to open this door."

Mr. Trom gave a nod and did so, using a special key that fit into a receptacle on the card pad. The panel lit with a green light and unlocked the door, and was disabled. Our large group filed inside, and as soon as we entered, we discovered the status tank was obscured by the tarp.

"Pull aside the tarp," Hammond ordered.

I could tell Dad had seen the tarp before. He didn't point fingers yet, though.

Mr. Trom went up the catwalk in the now fully lit laboratory, and allowed it to drop to the floor. Piles of green kelp littered the tank's bottom, but otherwise there was nothing inside. Not even a drop of water. Completely empty.

"There, Deputy Hammond, you see?" Louise asked as she gestured to the tank.

I didn't buy it for a moment, and neither did anyone else. "They must not yet have moved her. The only other tank large enough to hide a mermaid is next door."

"Yeah!" Naomi said. "She's in the Scuba area, and we can prove it."

"I saw her there also," Martin said.

"Same here," John added. "There was no mistaking her for a mermaid."

"Oh? And how can that be?" Dr. Wilton asked, speaking with a wrinkle in his voice. "Young women are gallivanting on that Internet all the time, flaunting fake tails. How can you be so certain of your young, foolish eyes?"

"Because," Cheryn said, "I'm the genuine article." She pulled the towel away with a flourish, revealing her sapphire blue fin from beneath her skirt.

"Impossible," Dr. Wilton stuttered. "A costume!"

"You knew this, didn't you?" Dr. Bagley asked. "We flew here expecting the truth!"

"You flew here because you captured a mermaid, stole from my store, and then studied her and starved her to death," Dad said.

"A lie," Louise said. "We know the laws regarding animal specimens."

"What about shoplifting?" I asked. "I have photos of a stolen fish tank, packages of aquarium supplies, as well as the stolen paint tarps."

Martin and John went behind the partition wall for a moment.

"And the rubber ducky," Naomi said.

"Lies, lies, lies," Louise continued.

Hammond spoke into his radio. "Roberts, Emmerton? You fellows here? Come in and bring a few handcuffs with you."

"You have no proof!" Louise said.

"Right here!" Martin said as he came back. "You didn't hide this."

Our group came around the corner where the 125-gallon fish tank had not been moved. The pump was still churning, and the three fish were still alive inside.

"Of course, it wasn't moved," Louise said. "There's nowhere to put them either."

"What about that room upstairs?" Naomi asked.

"What room?"

"The room upstairs," John said.

"That was the door that was alarmed," Naomi continued.

Suddenly Louise became very reserved. "That's just a break room."

"Then you won't mind if we search it," Hammond said.

Mr. Trom also became very quiet.

"Open the door," Mr. Rovan said. "It's been locked all week, and the staff were told to stay out. I want to know what's going on in there."

"I refuse to cooperate," Louise said. "You cannot enter that room."

"This search warrant says I can," Hammond said as Officer Roberts and Officer Emmerton arrived. Emmerton was a stout officer with sideburns and greying ginger hair.

"You called, boss?"

"Place Dr. Gardiola in handcuffs, along with Dr. Wilton and Dr. Bagley."

"What?" Gardiola gasped. "Why?"

"Because I recognize the men from my surveillance video,"

Dad said. "The neck brace is a convenient excuse, though."

"I nearly broke my neck in that plane crash!" Dr. Wilton exclaimed. "You think this is nothing but a stupid prop?"

"Then remove it!" John cried.

"Yeah!" Martin added. "Tell us why'd you remove it to rob a hardware store?"

Wilton hesitated, but did not continue to press the issue.

Officer Emmerton began to apply handcuffs to Dr. Wilton.

"That idiot of a pilot is to blame for this," Dr. Bagley said. "We might've even landed the plane if we hadn't smashed the pilot's head against the yoke," Dr. Bagley said before gasping audibly. "Maybe he didn't have to die."

"It was either that or pay him a million dollars," Wilton muttered quietly.

"Funny, we were expecting the results of that plane crash back from the FAA soon," Officer Roberts said as he cuffed the assistant. "I'm really looking forward to it now."

"Open that door," Hammond said.

"My boss ordered me not to," Mr. Trom said. "I refuse."

"Jason Trom," Deputy Hammond said, "I order you to open that door. Refusal to do so will result in your failing to comply with police and result in your arrest."

"Very well." He climbed the stairs as Hammond, Dad, John and Mr. Rovan followed him upstairs. I had to know what was in there too. Naomi and Martin stayed with Cheryn.

"You're not going to find anything!" Louise cried.

"Can it," Emmerton ordered as he restrained her. "We have more handcuffs."

At the end of the catwalk, Mr. Trom used his key to deactivate the security pad. He then pushed the door open and stood along the wall. Dad stayed outside to keep an eye on Mr. Trom.

Hammond, John and I went inside. This was indeed a break area, but to our surprise there was also an acrylic partition with a locked door separating the rest of the room from the main space. Several wooden posts had been used to support the wall, and had been erected in a hurry. But inside the wall was someone nobody had expected. A bed, a refrigerator, and Rachel Arlen.

Yeah, Rachel Arlen. Didn't see that one coming.

She was sitting on the bed, wearing a red tee shirt, blue jeans, sandals, and had her long dark blonde hair hanging loose below her shoulders. She was not hurt, bruised, or malnourished in any way. It looked like she was more bored than scared, and could not have been expecting any rescue party.

There was also another room behind her that had an open door.

"Rachel Arlen?" Hammond asked.

"What's going on here?" she asked calmly. "Jessica? John?"

Hammond quickly went into the hall and dragged Mr. Trom into the room. "Unlock this door, immediately."

Mr. Trom shook his head. "I don't have the key. Dr. Gardiola does."

"Why are the police here?" Rachel asked. "John? What's going on?"

"Don't you know?" he asked. "Everyone's been looking for you."

"I'm here," Rachel replied. "I'm not a missing person, am I? Dr. Gardiola said she'd contact my parents that I had volunteered for a study." She hesitated. "Though I don't know where they found the other girl."

"Who?" Hammond asked. "What other girl?"

"She must mean Mariana," I said. "See? We know what we saw."

Mr. Trom slowly started to scoot along the wall towards the exit and dropped his keys.

"You're not going anywhere," Mr. Rovan said as he blocked the opening.

Hammond gave a yell. "Emmerton! Get Gardiola in here!"

Officer Roberts brought Dr. Gardiola into the room after Mr. Trom was escorted from the room. Gardiola began to play the same song and dance.

"She is part of a control experiment. If I open that door, the results will be worthless."

"If you don't open the door, we will force it open and you'll be charged with felony obstruction of justice," Hammond said. "Don't make this worse for yourself."

With a long sigh, Louise reached into her blouse and removed a key from within. She then unlocked the plastic partition. John pushed her aside and went in first, though Rachel soon rushed up to him and hugged him tightly.

"I haven't been able to touch anyone in a week," she said quietly.

"I'm sorry that it has to be me," he said with a smile.

Hammond motioned to me. "Summers, you're with me." He then headed into the hallway and toward the observation deck next door, which he unlocked using Mr. Trom's key. We both walked out onto the observation platform. Perhaps it had taken her all night to clear the kelp, but we could see Mariana sitting inside of the scuba tank in plain sight. Her emerald green tail sparkled in the sunlight that streamed into the room between the loose edges of the painter's tarps.

Mariana smiled brightly at me. She didn't say anything, and didn't have to.

The next few moments were a blur. Dr. Wilton and Dr. Bagley were arrested for their involvement in the burglary at the hardware store, as positively identified by Dad. When they escorted Dr. Wilton outside, his neck brace snapped and fell off. Apparently, he hadn't broken his neck after all. Seemed strange that he'd hide it.

Deputy Hammond and Mr. Rovan helped Mariana out of the tank. Dr. Gardiola provided all the necessary keys. Martin found a second wheelchair in the laboratory lobby, allowing us to move her throughout the complex. Since Mariana was shivering and unaccustomed to the air temperature, I lent her my flannel. She put it on immediately and held it closed tightly.

In the flourish of activity, I hesitated as Officers Emmerton and Roberton escorted Dr. Gardiola outside to the waiting police cruisers. John waited with Rachel, while Mariana and Cheryn waited beside Naomi. Dad and Mr. Rovan stood by the policemen. I began to wonder if someone was missing.

As we all gathered in the main lab space near the empty status tank, Officer Emmerton came in from the hallway. "Sir, the security guard's gone."

Hammond grumbled. "Huh."

For the next few moments, our crew assembled in the laboratory lobby. John and I were directed to assist Mariana and Cheryn, making sure both were cared for and got something to eat. That meant basically waiting while Dad made a run for a sack of breakfast sandwiches from the gas station, which were still better than nothing. In the meantime, Deputy Hammond had already secured Dr. Wilton, Dr. Bagley and Dr. Gardiola outside in the two police squads. Officer Roberts stayed in the vicinity and contacted Mr. Arlen while making sure nobody else left in the meantime. Rachel sat quietly next to Cheryn and Mariana, while Mr. Rovan, Naomi, and Martin went to work ensuring that the specimens within the lab were well cared for. Apparently, they left Cheryn and Mariana to John and me, thinking we might have more experience with, what had been said in their words, *that* kind of wildlife. I'm sure they hadn't intended to be so literal.

"I'm glad you were able to receive my message," Mariana said to Cheryn as the two were sitting with their two wheelchairs close to each other.

Cheryn nodded quietly. "Yes, though you shouldn't have said so. There's no need for you to be sorry when none of this was your fault."

Mariana smiled, but it was a strained one.

"Did something happen between you both?" I asked. "A few months ago?"

"There was an argument," Cheryn said. "Everything was my fault."

"Yes, but that didn't stop you from going through with it," Mariana said. "For now, we are stuck with the results."

"Mermaids in the strait," Rachel chuckled to herself. "Imagine that."

"Rachel," I asked. "What was your role in all this? I mean, don't take this the wrong way, but if I expected to find anything in the room upstairs, it wasn't you."

"Saturday night, the Fourth of July, I was at the carnival going from ride to ride and having a funnel cake. When I got off the Tilt-A-Whirl, Dr. Gardiola came up to me and asked me if I wanted to volunteer for a science project, and that they'd pay me for my time. It seemed innocent enough."

"Then, could you leave whenever you wanted?" I asked.

She shook her head. "They said I needed to be observed, as a control for some kind of experiment. I didn't know anything else beyond that, only that I couldn't leave, couldn't see outside, and couldn't do anything other than crossword puzzles." She paused to brush her bangs from her face. "They took my phone and everything. I mean, there was plenty of food in the fridge, and every new day, I'd wake up to find three meals already prepared that I could heat up in the microwave. Aside from a big pitcher of water, there wasn't anything else to drink, but I had no idea they were studying a mermaid."

"Did you know there was another subject in the lab?" I asked.

Rachel nodded. "Dr. Gardiola did not say directly, but alluded to another test subject. Sounded like it was a girl, but why would I ever assume she meant a mermaid?"

"Because you're a realist," Cheryn said with a chuckle.

"I didn't know anyone else was in the lab, either," Mariana said. "I only ever saw the lady and the men. They never even told me their names. I watched them take samples of the water, of my hair, of my scales, but they never fed me anything."

"The whole time, you had no privacy?" Rachel asked. "Did they take a blood sample?"

Mariana nodded. "I remember one day they pulled me to the top of the tank and poked me with something pointy, along with a tube."

"That's a violation of basic human rights!" Rachel stood up suddenly. "They had no right to do anything like that."

Mariana shrugged. "We're not human."

"Officer!" Rachel ran up to him. "Officer Roberts, I have something to report."

Cheryn looked at me for encouragement. "Jess, this doesn't seem right. Does it?"

"No," I said without hesitation. "There must be some way to convince the police that they had no legal grounds to take blood samples without permission."

"I hope there's something that can be done," Cheryn said. "Ever since I met you, you've done everything to make me a part of your group. And I appreciate that."

I smiled. "Friends do what they can for each other, I guess."

"Jess! Come here!" Rachel asked. "Please?"

Cheryn rolled her wheelchair behind me as I joined her and Officer Roberts.

"Jess, he said there's a problem with pressing charges against the lab staff."

"What do you mean?" I asked.

Officer Roberts spoke with a sigh. "Officially, if I am to press charges against the staff, I will have to first establish in my report who and what Mariana is. Thus, in doing so, I will be announcing to the world that mermaids are real and live in the Strait of Juan de Fuca."

"Ugh," I said. "Cheryn? Are you okay with that?"

She looked down toward her chest. "We've worked very hard to stay hidden."

"But this is awful!" Rachel protested. "They violated you!"

Just then, Dad came into the room carrying two sacks of hot breakfast sandwiches. "Did anyone want something to eat?"

"Hey?" Mariana asked. "Do you have food? I'm open to human food. Please?"

Once everyone had a warm sausage or bacon and egg sandwich in their belly, I began to wonder about what Cheryn had said. Rachel was correct, too. In the eyes of the law, Cheryn and Mariana didn't have basic human rights. Did that mean they were legally treated like animals? That didn't seem fair. Below the waist they were fish, sure, but that didn't mean they were animals. Above the waist, they were human. They didn't breathe air exactly like us, but the flesh contained blood, organs and emotions that matched human ones. They spoke like humans. We were genetically distant, to be sure, but Cheryn and Mariana had a pulse just like mine. They deserved to be treated by humans far better than they had.

As I was going to ask Officer Roberts what my options were, he paused as Deputy Hammond contacted him on the radio. I missed most of the conversation, but Roberts explained to me what had been said.

"Miss Summers," he said. "Dr. Gardiola has agreed to resign her post as director of operations at Jaquim Labs, but she refused to admit to capturing Mariana. She has accused Jason Trom of bringing her into the laboratory."

"That's it?" I asked. "And then for imprisoning Rachel?"

"She claimed to have intended to contacted the Arlen family, but claimed that the conditions of the experiment —"

He stopped suddenly as another officer arrived with two people. I didn't quite remember their names at first, but they were Mr. and Mrs. Arlen.

"Rachel?" Mr. Arlen asked. "Rachel?"

"Daddy!"

"Rachel, my sweet child," Mrs. Arlen, a shorter but beautiful woman rushed over to her daughter. Soon all three were hugging each other tightly. It was a heart-warming scene, and I might've teared up a little.

"So yeah," Officer Roberts said as he turned back to me. "Dr. Gardiola also admitted to the robbery of the hardware store, since she claimed Dr. Wilton and Dr. Bagley had decided that Mariana couldn't share a tank with the three larger fish." He didn't finish his previous thought.

"Okay," I said. "So, can she be charged with imprisoning Mariana?"

He shook his head. "Only Rachel Arlen. Because Dr. Gardiola failed to contact the teenager's family and have them sign an agreement for voluntary scientific surveying, Mr. Arlen filed the missing person report. During that time, Dr. Gardiola had the opportunity to call off her experimental testing, whatever it was, but if she did, she would inadvertently risk revealing Mariana to the greater scientific community also."

"Officer," Cheryn said. "You've seen who I am, and you've seen who Mariana is. We know who we are, but we're not ready to let the public know. Close friends, perhaps, but not everyone in the world has to know about us."

"Yes, and you are entitled to that," Roberts replied. "But as the law is written, it doesn't include mermaids in its circle of protection. Thus, unless Mariana is stating her identity, providing a basis for her unique needs and situation, she cannot be included in the case. I'm sorry."

"Then," I began, "Then it seems this is all the further the law can help Mariana today."

He nodded, though I could see on his face it was a reluctant one. "I wish there was more I could do for you, I truly do."

"Thank you," Mariana said.

I turned around to see Mr. Arlen looking at me. "Hello."

"Jessica," he began. "I owe you an apology."

"What for?" I asked.

"For suspecting you were hiding Rachel," he replied before looking at Cheryn. "You both do look a little alike, but as beautiful as you are, Miss Cheryn, you're not my daughter."

Cheryn smiled.

"That phone call you received Saturday morning? It came from me."

I narrowed my eyes. The phone call could have come from anyone, but I wouldn't have suspected Michael Arlen for anything other than working to find his daughter.

"Yeah," he continued. "I wanted to tell the person who had my daughter what I thought of them. What kind of jury might convict them? The very flavor of gruel they'd be fed in prison."

"That's very perceptive, Mr. Arlen," I said. "Why didn't you say anything?"

"Because I was overcome by emotion. Because I wasn't sure. Because I was going on an anonymous tip, that I was too afraid to ignore. Because I was blinded by my love for my daughter, and blinded by my rage against any who would bring harm to her."

I nodded. "Luckily, no harm came to her. She was just kept away for a while."

"Yeah," he said. "That doesn't stop a few people from thinking otherwise."

"Who do you mean, sir?" I asked.

"That little red-haired girl with the SIREN group."

I nodded. Like everyone else who read the *Herald*, I had read about Mr. Arlen's involvement with SIREN on Wednesday, though he probably didn't know about last night's séance. Maybe it was better he stayed in the dark.

"I'm not defending Kelsey," I said, "But somehow I don't think she's worth your time."

Mr. Arlen nodded. "Let's hope your right. At any rate, I owe you some money."

"Money?"

"If you read the paper, you know there's a reward leading to Rachel's location. You did more than that."

"I'm sorry to interrupt sir." Officer Roberts asked. "Miss Summers, there was one thing we neglected to discuss. If I'm to file a proper police report, both you and Miss Rovan are going to be charged with trespassing. There's a sizable fine."

"Officer Roberts, consider their fines paid in full," Mr. Arlen said. "On our way home, I'll file with the courthouse."

"What?" I couldn't believe my ears. "That's awfully generous of you."

"I'll talk to your father about setting up a college fund. You both deserve it."

College fund? Wow. "Sir, I'm not sure that's necessary."

"Or maybe just a party for you and your friends. We'll talk." He turned to Cheryn and Mariana again. "In the meantime, you both probably have to return home? It was a pleasure meeting you, and I'm sorry you were both involved in this."

"Thank you, sir," Cheryn said.

Mariana held his hand a moment, and then he left. Rachel gave me a pat on the shoulder as she and her mother passed by. I was impressed that neither one of them seemed to realize that Cheryn and Mariana were mermaids, even though Mariana didn't have any clothes aside from the bikini top. Guess they thought they were costumes? Either that, or they were too happy to see their daughter again and were too overcome to care.

Rachel turned to me a moment before leaving with her parents.

"Call me about that party, huh?"

I nodded. "Sure thing. See you around."

Cheryn looked at me. "Are we done here?"

"I'm not sure. Officer Roberts?"

He nodded. "Make sure they get home safely. I'll clean up."

Dad later drove Cheryn, Mariana and myself home. We had all agreed that it was the best place to help both mermaids return to the bay in a place away from the press or the public eye. We picked the cove north of False Bay, which was perfect as the tide was in and the waters were receding. We took care bringing them to the water, but were glad to see Mariana home.

As for the rest of the crowd who had been at the police station, everyone headed home to explain everything to their parents. John had assured me that anything associated with the golf cart was in the past. Naomi rode home with her father, and later told me she'd probably be grounded after taking her father's ID card. Since she had acted with Cheryn and Mariana's best interests, there was a good chance she could still make an appearance at any proposed party with good behavior. Martin was already working on his story for our next campfire meeting, and promised to keep any talk about our local water spirits to himself.

And Cheryn? She said she'd bring the marshmallows. I told her not to go to any trouble. After all, I'd hate for her to spend her lifetime savings, probably comprised of loose change found in the bay, on a bag of air and sugar. That's before considering how she'd get to the store. I couldn't see her ever riding a bike, though after this past week, her ambition to be an acrobat seemed possible, if not guaranteed. Maybe she would ride side saddle.

When I asked Mariana about coming to our party, she politely declined. I respected her decision. She thanked me for everything, gave me a hug, and disappeared into the bay.

~  ~

Around nine that evening, I started a fire like always. It had been a long day and I was tired, but I had promised myself that I'd have a campfire every Sunday, with exceptions only for weather. Tonight's campfire would be performed for only one participant, however. Myself. John said to expect him next week, while Naomi was grounded, but just for the evening. Martin said he'd come when John did. Cheryn was safely home in her grotto beneath the bay. That left me sitting outside, in my red chair, alone.

Two logs later, Dad came outside and sat in the chair next to mine. Naomi's chair.

"Thought your friends would be coming over."

I tossed my bottle of water back and forth. "Guess it's been a long day."

"Tim was talking about you when I put him to bed. I think he's proud of his big sister."

There was no hiding my smile, even if it didn't last long.

"So what's bothering you?"

"Does it show?" I asked.

"You're not fooling anybody," he chuckled.

There never had been any hiding from my Dad. He may not have always got the story right, but he could read just about anyone, except my mother.

"I've known Cheryn for just over a week," I began, "And even though I can tell my friends, I can't tell anyone else."

"You could always tell me," he said. "Jessica, you can always tell me anything."

I nodded. "Mermaids can come on shore, but they can't have justice."

He nodded. "It doesn't seem fair, does it?"

"She's done so much to remain true to herself, and only wanted a few friends."

"Maybe I'm not the one to talk to about that."

"What do you mean?" I asked.

"I can't seem to understand why things work out the way they do sometimes. Like your mother and me."

"You didn't do anything wrong, Dad. Don't blame yourself."

"Joan and I were friends in high school. I started working at the hardware store, the store your grandfather owned and operated, and began taking classes in business. We loved each other. We got married on a sunny April day. You came along, and later, Tim, and things were okay. One day, things became too ordinary. Maybe we were trying to find that spark we had when we were first dating—" He trailed off.

"But you said it yourself, Dad, things were okay," I said. "And they are."

"Are they?" He patted my knee. "I guess as long as you and Tim are home safe."

"Dad," I trailed off. "We are home safe. That means things are okay, right?"

He smiled. "Sometimes, things don't have to make sense, I guess. At least Cheryn seems to want to continue to be friends with you."

"Yeah." It was time to be honest with him. "Dad, you said I can always tell you anything. And we can talk about anything, right?"

"Of course," he said. "Anything."

I nodded. "I know why Mom left."

"Oh?"

"She left because she made a choice. It wasn't the easiest choice, either. It couldn't have been easily made, and I don't think either of us are in the position to understand why. She wanted you to know that nothing you, or Tim, or any of us did, did anything to make up her mind."

"Is that a fact?"

"Yeah," I said. "Choices we make cause consequences, and everyone involved has to work hard to make them into something we can understand."

"That's an interesting argument. Who said that?"

"You did," I replied. "Last winter, you tried to tell me sometime around Valentine's."

He nodded. "You know what, Jessica? Today you surprised me. You're really not the young kid you used to be. I'm impressed."

"You've trusted me to watch Tim all this time," I said. "But I wasn't able to tell you the important things, especially when they mattered."

"You've told me enough," he replied and patted me on the shoulder. "It takes a big girl to stand up for her friends. Even if it means admitting to something illegal."

It sure was nice of Mr. Arlen to pay my fine.

"Michael wrote you a check."

I leaned back in the chair and stared into the glowing coals.

"Not to cover your fines. For the reward money. Paid it straight to you."

I sat up and looked back. "Why?"

Dad smiled. "Because he said you earned it. I left it for you on the kitchen counter. After all, it's time you had a savings account."

"Dad," I said. "I've had a savings account and a credit card for four years."

He chuckled. "There you go again, surprising your old man. Can we agree to be more open with each other? No more secrets?"

"Deal," I replied. "No more secrets." Only one remained, but maybe he didn't have to know any more than that. To give him the full account of Mom's phone message felt unnecessary. I didn't have the heart to tell him about the late-night call, but I felt like he had heard what was. Mom's departure had split the family, and he had suffered enough.

Before going to bed, I found the check Mr. Arlen left me. It was a check for $2,000. The reward money had been $1500, but he must have thought I needed more. I suspected that our fines amounted to at least that much, but I tried not to think about how much Michael and his wife had went through this past week. Instead, I put the check into my top dresser drawer and went straight to bed. It was the end of a very long day, and I was glad to rest.

Monday July 13th, 2009
Friday Harbor Herald

BREAKING NEWS. Rachel Arlen has been found safe and sound. To the surprise and relief of many Friday Harbor citizens, the teenager was located as part of an ongoing experiment at Jaquim Labs, located just north of downtown. Police are pleased to announce that no actual scientific or medical tests were performed on Arlen, citing that the teen voluntarily signed up for a study that was feloniously filed and advertised. Accord-ingly, the reward money has been delivered to the assisting party, and the teen has since returned home, physically and mentally fit despite the ordeal. The teenager, as a minor, was legally unable to sign any contract without parental consent. In accordance, Dr. Louise Gardiola was charged with unlawful imprisonment, conspiracy to commit robbery, and subjectification of a minor with intent to study or medically commit acts of a scientific nature. Accordingly, she has resigned her position as head of the laboratory complex. She will be formally charged today in San Juan County District Court and is expected to plead guilty. The Arlen family requests privacy during this time of celebration and happiness.

Police are looking for Jason Trom, former security guard at Jaquim Labs, who is wanted for providing crucial information relating to the case.

Also related to the Arlen case was the filing of burglary and murder charges against Dr. Julian Wilton and Dr. Brooks Bagley. Both doctors, who each hold doctorates of marine biology from the University of Boston, were responsible for the robbery of the Friday Harbor Hardware store, located at 360 Spring St. Stolen aquarium paraphernalia and other missing items were discovered at the Ichthyology Lab at Jaquim Labs. In regards to the murder chargers, both men are being questioned for their involvement in the death of Harrison MacGregor, pilot of the Cessna 425 that crashed Tuesday, July 7th. FAA officials reported evidence of a physical altercation on the plane's flight recorder, and Dr. Wilton was quoted as suggesting the pilot may have been injured prior to the crash. Herald staff will continue to cover this story as more information becomes available. At press time, both men were reportedly being detained in the San Juan County Jail, each held with a million dollars bond.

Police issued a statement that Gary Bridgewater, who was charged in relation to the case yesterday, July 12th, was formally cleared of all charges and has since had the arrest removed from his record. In response, Bridgewater released this statement. "As a celebratory gesture for Rachel coming home, 10% off all fresh juices this week. Salute!"

In an unrelated story, Dr. Gregory Pruitt has made a statement to Herald staff that he has completed his investigation regarding his bent 7-iron. "I regret to inform the citizens of Friday Harbor that I was personally responsible for the bending of my seven iron, which was damaged on the 14th fairway upon my right knee. I deeply regret disrupting the community and making my own problems seem worse than those of other, more important matters." Dr. Pruitt later went into detail about his upcoming vacation to Scotland to "better prepare himself for the rigors of retirement." One Herald reporter later contacted the doctor's office to discover a recorded message, stating "All appointments for the remainder of the month are cancelled" and referred callers to the office of Dr. Janice Huntington. Herald staff would like to recommend Dr. Megan Tothson of Roche Harbor for local medical needs, as we at the Herald are unable to determine why a general practitioner would refer his patients to a dentist. Dr. Huntington declined to comment on the matter.

A softly falling rain kept the air cool that Monday morning. That didn't deter Cheryn from making an appearance, however. In the cool humid air of the dawn, she sat on the bench in the bay singing the melody of a song that resembled Mom's favorite song to play on the piano, Bette Midler's "The Rose."

Umbrella in hand, I headed out to the end of the dock to find Cheryn brushing her hair.

"Hey," I said.

Cheryn giggled as she hummed to herself.

"What's so funny?"

"Humans really do respond to siren song."

"You think so?"

Cheryn nodded. "Every time I sing, you come."

Even though the bench was wet, I sat. "Maybe I just wanted to see you."

"Did the police ever find that security guard?"

I shook my head.

"That's too bad." Cheryn continued to brush her hair. "You had a campfire last night?"

"Yes, but nobody came."

"I'd have come, if I hadn't been so tired. I still owe you a bag of marshmallows."

My smirk earned a smile from her.

"No," I said, "You don't owe me anything."

"I promised you a wish once, but you already know that I can't deliver on that promise. It's not fair for me to lie to you."

"Cheryn, you've already done more for me than any little wish could."

She looked up from her work. "So have you."

We sat together in silence for a while, but didn't talk about much else. Eventually, we both decided to meet up again soon. I had to work later, after all.

At a quarter to nine, I headed down Turn Point Road and made my way to work.

I didn't make it.

Outside of town, just above the bluff near Jepson's shipyard, someone in a grey truck with a matching topper blocked the road and rolled down the window. There, holding a pistol and pointing it directly at me, was Jason Trom. The pistol had a pearl handle, though I only had eyes for the hole at the end of the barrel.

"Don't move, Jessica Summers."

My feet instinctively slammed on my bike's brakes and I put up my hands.

"Dammit, I said don't move."

So I didn't move again.

He quickly pushed the door open and jumped out, leaving the engine running. "Get in the back if you want to live."

I wasn't in any position to argue, so I dismounted the bike and walked toward the cab with it at my side.

"Leave the bike on the side of the road."

I did so. Although he knew someone would see it, I made no effort to hide it.

"Go on now, get in the back."

He hadn't said where exactly, so I approached the door to the cab.

Trom waved the gun toward the covered pickup bed. "Back there, come on now."

I made my way to the back as directed. He then closed it and locked the hatch. A moment later, the truck began to move, and along with it the contents of his truck, which ranged from old pop cans and rusty nails. As far as I could remember, the police hadn't charged him with anything yesterday. Yet, I was clearly his prisoner.

He drove back towards Barnacle Point, before stopping and pulling south onto the field toward Jackson Beach. As the truck didn't have the best of shocks, it made for a bumpy ride. I was fortunate enough to be able to cover my head from the bumps.

On the far side of the field, Trom turned onto a road, possibly Pear Point Road, and then made a quick left turn onto the point. The truck stopped and settled with a groan and a shudder as he killed the engine. A moment or two later he unlocked the back.

"Out. Move."

He had brought me to a warehouse on the end of the point where a speedboat was docked. I hadn't seen where he got it, but he handed me what appeared to be a live grenade that had a rope tied through the ring. Was he crazy?

"Wrap the rope around your wrists."

"I don't want to pull the pin."

"If you're competent, you won't," He raised the gun. "Do it careful-like or we'll both blow sky high."

I began to do so. "You should have stayed around yesterday."

"Shut it."

"They didn't charge you with anything."

"Shut it!"

I continued to wrap the rope in silence. He then lowered the gun and wrapped the strands of rope tighter. They were situated in a way so that if I tried to pull the rope loose, it would pull the ring of the grenade and set it off. Now, I have zero experience with grenades beyond movies or CSI, but I knew enough not to mess with the ring.

"Walk." He motioned toward the speedboat, putting the gun in a concealed holster.

To say I wasn't afraid was an understatement. I was shaking, but thankfully the rope had enough give to allow for a light amount of movement. He must've planned for this, knowing how dangerous it was to work with live grenades. I knew he had spent time in the military, after all.

"Into the boat."

Down the dock I went, into the speedboat, climbing over the back.

"Go up to the front."

I continued past the helm as directed and sat next to a large net that was similar to the one Cheryn had given me a week ago. It could have been one of Bridgewater's.

He pulled on a short loop of rope that was holding the boat along the dock before jumping in and putting the key in the ignition. Trom then started the engine, closed the windshield door between the twin helms, and engaged the drive gear.

"Don't try to be a hero."

"Where are we going?" I asked.

"Shut up already." He threw on a life jacket loosely and accelerated. We were moving. "We're going to place you're probably familiar with. The same place I found a mermaid."

Great, I thought to myself. *And you think I can help you find another one?*

"That green girl was my ticket off this island. And because of you, I'm stuck here. No, that's not acceptable, Jessica Summers. You'll help me or else."

Since I was hardly in a position to argue, I could only nod slowly as my eyes drifted toward the live grenade sitting in my lap.

Twenty minutes later, I was still shaking as I continued to hold the grenade gingerly. During the ride I had taken an opportunity to look over the item he had given me. I realized that the rope looped only through the ring held the pin. Nothing else was connected to the grenade. If I wanted to, I could drop the grenade and go over the edge. There was a problem, though. There was no way for me to know if shrapnel could go through the steel boat. It didn't seem likely, but I did not want to chance it. And if I were to toss the grenade into the water, what then?

Knowing the surrounding waters from my many canoe cruises, I was certain that Trom had brought us to Hicks Bay, along the south shore of Shaw Island. Parks Bay was along the far side of the ridge to the northwest. Cheryn couldn't be anywhere nearby.

Trom shut off the engine and dropped an anchor. "Okay, we're here. Tell me how to find your mermaid friends."

"I'm sorry, I don't know."

He pulled out the gun again. "You found one. You're the expert."

"No, I never found one, Mr. Trom," I said calmly. "One found me."

"You're lying."

"I swear I'm not."

"Lucky for you I've done this before." He reached into a wooden box behind him that had a burlap bag over the lid. From within he removed an explosive device that resembled a stick of dynamite. "It wasn't easy, but after a few of my boom sticks she practically begged me to bring her aboard." He ripped the wick and tossed it into the open channel, where it sank. "Of course, I had more nets that day, and it was low tide."

A moment later, a six-foot plume of water broke the surface, sending a shockwave into the surrounding waters. I thought I saw a fish turn belly-up a moment later. Fortunately, nothing penetrated the boat, and we were still floating.

"That's—" I stopped myself. He was a loose cannon. I didn't dare say what I felt. Madman. Fish killer. Inhumane. I could've chosen any of them and been correct.

"Underwater flares are less lethal," Trom said as he retrieved a second stick. "I've been making modifications for months, especially since I saw her, last January, out near that flat rock in the bay, sunning herself in the warm sun. It took me all year to come up with something workable that wouldn't outright kill her," he said before pulling the cap and tossing the stick into the water. Another plume of water erupted later.

I winced. Mr. Trom had gone crazy. Absolutely crazy. I didn't dare turn away from him to check if anything had died as a result.

"Hunting was a hell of lot easier during the fireworks," he replied. "But then, I question Dr. Gardiola's qualifications. She couldn't determine that the creature had hearing damage." He opened the windshield door and grabbed the large net before heading back to his side of the boat. With a skilled spin, he threw it off the starboard side toward the shore, putting the lead from the net over the arm of the throttle. "It only took two charges to get her attention."

"Of course it did," I said quietly. Nobody would want to hang around with explosives going off, no matter who they are. Except maybe the deranged man I shared the boat with.

Trom took a third flare from his box and ripped the cap before tossing the flare as far as he could into the channel. Even though I couldn't duck and cover without letting go of the grenade in my hand, I hunched down anyways. Another plume of water erupted as the flare exploded. The resulting shockwave caused the boat to rock slightly.

"Those fishing nets of Bridgewater's sure made it easy, I must say," Trom said as he continued to scan the water for any sign of activity. "She went right for them. Practically begged me to take her into the boat."

Surely that had been an exaggeration, but I ignored his comments as my mind began to race. Grenades and flares like these were terrible things, but remembering one of my science classes, I recalled that the shockwaves, especially underwater, were the real dangers. Since the human body was comprised mostly of water, a shockwave underwater would be worse than the shrapnel itself. The body had air cavities, and surely mermaids were similarly constructed. No wonder Mariana feared us.

"You're not in any hurry, are you?" Trom collected another flare. "Because I'll admit I've got no way of knowing if one of your friends are here. My fish finder can't tell the difference between the explosions and other, more solid objects."

Mariana had a grotto nearby, certainly, but I had not asked where. If she had lived anywhere close to Cheryn's, it could likely be here along this side of Shaw Island. Of course, Cheryn had said others lived here long ago, but had left. Then again, this was the spot where Mariana was caught. Surely she wouldn't return here, with so many bad memories?

"I'd hate to use another flare. My diving days are behind me, and the last time I did this, there was a lot more time."

Sound often travelled very far underwater, due to the consistency of sound travelling through a medium. Denser liquids often vibrated less, and thus sound travelled further. It reminded me of how Cheryn spoke differently underwater. As my mind continued to work, I began to wonder if Cheryn had heard the explosions herself. There were fireworks going on at the time. Perhaps nobody but Mariana and Trom were around to hear the underwater explosions.

"At least there aren't any tourists here today," Trom said as he prepared another flare. "They make fishing difficult." This one he threw off the stern. It exploded near the surface, sending both water and shrapnel into the air.

"How do you know you haven't already killed her?" I asked. It was a horrible thought, but certainly a real possibility. "You want to capture one, not kill one, right?"

He seemed to agree. "Very well. No more flares, for the moment. How's your arm? Shaking? Numb?"

"Fine," I said. It was the truth. "I'm in no hurry to get blown up either."

"Of course you're not," he said with a sly grin. "You're a young woman with her future ahead of her. So too is your friend Naomi. Sad that she had to be a part of this too."

"Then why hurt her? If you hurt me, you hurt her." Maybe sympathy would work.

He chuckled. "Nice try. If I hurt you, I hurt you."

So much for sympathy. Or logic. Maybe gambling on leaving the grenade in the bottom of the boat was my best option after all. Then again, how far did sound travel above the air?

"What about setting off explosives during the day?"

Trom shook his head, confident in his scepticism. "These things sound just like fireworks. People set them off even after the Fourth, sometimes all month."

I thought I heard a soft pop in the water. I looked toward the distant shore, instantly regretting having done so.

"You hear something?" He turned on an electronic fish finder mounted on the helm. "Something must be nearby."

"Provided it survived the shockwave," I said.

"Shut it." He scanned the device, listening for any sign of activity on the water's surface.

As I gazed toward the east shoreline of Hicks Bay, I saw red hair emerge from the water behind Trom. Cheryn surfaced, just to her eyes, before disappearing a moment later.

Trom quickly looked up. When he turned, he didn't see anything and went back to the scanner. "Where are you?"

"Cheryn told me that nobody can catch her," I said. "Naomi tried, even inside of a swimming pool. She wasn't able to catch her."

"Quiet," Trom muttered.

As he continued to monitor the fish finder, I saw Cheryn surface again. This time, she surfaced to her shoulders. She pointed down into the water, looking directly at me.

I gave a quick nod.

Trom quickly spun around again, and Cheryn vanished as quickly as she had before. "Dammit, this is your last warning." He turned and reached for the lead to the net.

This was the moment. If I understood Cheryn's idea, she wanted me to dive into the water. I couldn't tell if she knew I had a grenade in my hand or not. Then again, I had trusted her when we drove off of Mr. Bridgewater's dock head first into the harbor. I had trusted her when she appeared on my dock that first day over a week ago. I trusted her implicitly. If I dove over the edge, I had to believe she would pull me safe of the area. This was a steel bottomed boat, and I had to believe that it could contain the shrapnel from the grenade. Although I found myself shaking more than ever, there was no better option.

I stood up on the seat, and with a twist of my wrists, the grenade dropped into the bottom of the boat. Then, I leaned back and fell head first into the water off of the port side.

"No!" He fumbled for the gun and fired into the air, the bullet grazing my arm.

Below, I was sinking into the water. My eyes were open, but the water was not perfectly clear. However, I felt the tug along the back of my shirt, and soon Cheryn was pulling me to safety. Even when the grenade went off, she didn't stop. A second explosion burst at the surface.

"I have you," she said. "Hold your breath for as long as you can."

The green tunnel continued for another moment. I held my breath. She had protected me again, and perhaps I now owed her more than a bag of marshmallows. I owed her my life.

Just as I began to feel the darkness creep into my sight, Cheryn brought me to the surface. While we had traveled to the south side of the channel in the shadow of Turn Island, Trom's boat was visible, perhaps a mile away. The gas tank had exploded and the boat was on fire.

"Did he get off the boat?" I asked.

"Why were you out here, anyway? Especially with that

security guard?"

I told her. As I described the episode, I thought for sure she'd laugh at the absurdity.

"Really?" Cheryn didn't laugh at all, allowing me to relax. "I see, so Mariana either would be forced to flee into the nets or into—" She hesitated. "Gosh, Jess, you're lucky to be alive. Hey!" She checked my arm, where a hole had been burned into the fabric.

"He shot me?" I checked my arm. "Did he shoot me?"

"Almost," Cheryn said. "Had he aimed any closer, yes, he would have."

"Incredible." I couldn't imagine my luck. Or for that matter, Cheryn's. "Cheryn, why did you come over here?"

She looked toward the flaming boat. "Should I go back and get him too?"

"No," I grabbed her shoulder. "He had more grenades, more flares—"

Suddenly, the remaining flares and grenades began to go off as they caught fire and exploded. The blasts within the box of flares sounded like fireworks, until a final explosion caused the boat to break apart. By now there wasn't much left, and whatever remained of the boat began to sink, engine and helm included. Eventually the explosions stopped as any leftover devices became waterlogged and sank harmlessly.

"Cheryn, why did you come out here?" I asked again.

"I heard the explosions and kept my distance," Cheryn said with a smile. "I suppose I was hoping for more fireworks, but these weren't as pretty. Maybe because it's daytime?"

"No," I smiled. "These are nothing like those kinds of fireworks."

"Suppose it doesn't matter," Cheryn said as she turned away from the wreck. "Fireworks only come a few times each year, after all. Here, hold still," Cheryn said as she used her knife to cut my wrists free. "Is that better?"

I nodded.

"Good." She looked past me with a giggle. "Ahh, now that's interesting."

"What?" I turned to see Jason Trom struggling for air as he surfaced beneath a collection of ropes that had once been fishing nets. Tangled hopelessly within, he had no hope of escape.

"Well, it's up to you, Jess. Do I release him?"

A small part of me realized that sooner or later he'd have to be released. But then, a much larger voice in my heart screamed to let little dogs lie. Although my Girl Scout den leader would have certainly given me a few choice words about doing the right thing, I shook my head. He had just strapped me to a live grenade. Not only that, the area wasn't safe.

"Either way," she replied as she returned the knife to the sheath, which was strapped to a leather belt around the hem of her blouse. "Using those explosives suggests a rather unbalanced individual, wouldn't you say?"

"You sound like a psychiatrist," I said.

Cheryn smiled. "Someone threw out a bunch of those books once. Would you like to borrow them? They're very interesting."

"No thank you." I glanced back to Mr. Thom, who was still floundering in the water. "Cheryn, does Mariana have a grotto here? Have you seen her since yesterday?"

"She lives further north of here, near a place called Skull Rock."

I thought a moment. "Is that near Orcas Island?"

She shrugged. "Don't know." Suddenly, she looked toward the channel. "I'd better go."

"Wait, what?" I turned to look behind me. A smaller Coast Guard boat with blinking lights was approaching. "That's just a patrol boat."

Cheryn held onto my hands and pulled me backward, kicking with her tail so I could feel the current below my shoes as we backed further toward the shore. Apparently, she didn't want them to see me just yet either. Perhaps she didn't want to leave the water with any boaters.

Now that we were out of view from the patrol boat, Cheryn surfaced again. "Should I go and help them?"

"No," I said. "I don't think you'll have to."

We waited as the patrol boat approached the wreck. Two divers leapt off the boat wearing flippers and scuba gear. Another sailor began looking through a pair of binoculars. She was scanning the water for other survivors.

"Over here!" Cheryn pulled me closer to the shore, behind a low hanging tree that draped over the surrounding water. "Stay low."

"Cheryn," I said. "I have to go back there."

"Why? Jess, won't they find you?"

"Exactly," I said. "If I don't and they take Trom into custody—"

"The security guard?"

"Yes," I nodded. "If they just pick him up, he won't be charged for kidnapping."

Cheryn nodded and helped me swim. "Go quickly!" She then went under.

There was no time. I began to swim as fast as I could, and called to the crew. "Hey! Help! Over here!"

Suddenly I felt something push me from below. Cheryn was giving me a boost, holding onto my feet as I swam. I stopped kicking my feet and used only my arms.

"Ahoy there!" The female sailor aboard the patrol boat threw out a life ring on a rope. I swam as close to it as I could, and when I couldn't feel Cheryn pushing me any longer, I grabbed hold. The sailor pulled me in, and soon I was able to climb up using a ladder along the back.

"I'm Lieutenant Janet Simmons of the US Coast Guard," she said. "Our crew detected an explosion. Were you on a boat near here?"

"Yes, but not as a passenger. May I explain?"

By the time I had explained my kidnapping, the divers had recovered Jason Trom and brought him on board the Response-class cruiser. Apparently, the crew was based out of Anacortes and had been patrolling the channel. Perhaps they hadn't heard the underwater explosions, but they certainly head those final blasts. I was thankful they had been nearby.

Trom had been shaken up from the explosion, and though he might have suffered a ruptured ear drum he was otherwise largely intact. Honestly, he fared much better than I imagined. As soon as the crew heard my explanation of the situation, they gave him a pair of handcuffs.

I sat in the cabin below the cockpit, wearing a towel over my wet clothes as the crew convened with Friday Harbor Police and set sail for the courthouse. They must've known that Officer Roberts and Deputy Hammond were looking for Mr. Trom. Friday Harbor may be on an island, but that doesn't mean we were completely isolated.

Something else dug at me, however. I knew that Cheryn was okay, but even though she had said Mariana's grotto was far from here, I wanted to know what happened with her. Despite this feeling of unease, I couldn't share anything with the Coast Guard crew. Cheryn had given up so much the day before, to draw her back into my own conflict would destroy that work.

Ten minutes later, the Coast Guard anchored in Friday Harbor and delivered Jason Trom to the police. Once I was released to the police, they resumed their patrol and went back to recover the remains of Trom's speedboat. I made sure to thank Lieutenant Simmons for their assistance.

Dad arrived halfway through my meeting with the police. Along the way, he picked up my bike on the side of the road. Lucky me. He was obviously shaken up at hearing what had occurred, and overwhelmed to see I was safe and sound. My ordeal had not been nearly as involved as Rachel's, but I was certain I'd make the paper this time.

Before we left, I made sure the police knew that Trom had been the one to kidnap Mariana.

Deputy Hammond nodded when I told him.

"Huh," he said, as is his usual way. "Makes sense someone would have found a way."

"He used underwater flares," I said. "During the fireworks, nobody would have known."

"Clever," Hammond said. "Fellow must've been pretty desperate. He then gave her to the lab for study, and the case got interesting from there."

"Yes sir," I said with a nod. "And off the record, sir, Cheryn helped me today also."

"Huh," Hammond said. "It's nice to have friends in low places." Though he had been taking notes, he hesitated. "What did Miss Harvin do to assist?"

"Pulled me from the speedboat before the grenade I had been holding went off."

Hammond nodded. "This sounds like an official report. Are you sure you want me to put Cheryn into it? I feel like we discussed this already."

I hesitated. This was the same discussion, to be true.

Suddenly, I heard a commotion in the front office. Was that Kelsey?

"Officer Jepson! There's someone disturbing the local wildlife!"

"Is that Kelsey?" I asked Deputy Hammond.

We went into the main office of the station to see Kelsey leaning over the desk. "I heard explosions, bombs, or dynamite or something. Is someone fishing with dynamite? This is a wildlife preserve! Who would do such a thing to the local maritime population?"

Kelsey, you may have just redeemed yourself. I turned to Deputy Hammond. "I think we have our angle."

He nodded. "Huh."

Tuesday July 14th, 2009
Friday Harbor Herald

BREAKING NEWS. The second of two kidnapping cases this month occurred Monday when a second teenager, Jessica Summers, 16, was kidnapped and held against her will by Jason Trom, former security guard at Jaquim Labs who only resigned his post yesterday. According to Miss Summers, who was later rescued by a crew from the United States Coast Guard, Trom was disturbing local wildlife by using live grenades and underwater flares. He admitted to local police to have captured her, believing she would assist him in searching for the rare Green Sturgeon, a local legend. While the crew of the Coast Guard cutter declined to comment before returning to patrol, area witnesses could not determine if Trom was actually fishing for the fabled sturgeon, or more common pollock or trout. As an unbiased reporter of the news, it is not the policy of the Herald to speculate in open investigations.

According to the police report, Trom was taken into custody following the destruction of his speedboat, which occurred when his arsenal malfunctioned. Coast Guard crews recovered the passengers moments later, when the news of the kidnapping broke and Summers was rescued. The whole span of the incident was reported to have been over in less than two hours.

Herald staff attempted to question Trom, but were denied an official interview. Trom did make this statement as he was escorted into custody by police, however. "There are more things in the bay than you might think, and I'll find them all! Mark my words!" According to one local witness, if there was anything in our local waters beyond what has been previously recorded, certainly the researchers at the University of Washington's Camp Caution would have found it by now.

According to Gary Bridgewater, supervisor of the Saturday Square Juice Bar, Summers has been released to her family and is reported to be unharmed.

"Jessica is a resilient young woman," Bridgewater said in a phone interview, "and continues to surprise us all. Although she may have missed a day of work, I can hardly discipline her for something that was not her fault."

In other news, Dr. Eric Jennings has been appointed interim director of Jaquim Labs. His first act was to restore the jobs of researchers employed by the lab's Scuba Training department who were sent home July 6th. All workers were excited to re-turn to their jobs, and report that any specimens in the lab have been determined to be safe and unharmed. CORRECTION: On Tuesday, July 6th, the Herald reported that the Ichthyology division of Jaquim Labs had been sent home, having overlooked the Scuba Training division who had been sent home the day before, July 5th, without pay. The closing of the division was only for the day, and the Ichthyology staff returned to their jobs the same day the story was published, whereas the Scuba Trainers were sent home indefinitely. All employees are now working at their jobs again. The Herald regrets the error.

Herald staff would like to remind its readers that the final day for entries in the writing contest is tomorrow by midnight. Contestants must submit up to 40 lines of poetry or 5,000 words of either fiction or essay. Be sure to mention which por-tion of the contest you are entering. Good luck to all who participate.

The Herald is pleased to announce Gina Prince of Sidney, B.C. came in first place in Monday's Paddlethon Regatta, follow-ed closely by Robert Manning of Anacortes, Was. Third place went to local kayak enthusiast Harold Jens. Race officials con-sulted video and GPS data to determine that Prince narrowly defeated Manning by a mere fifteen hundredths of a second. For her efforts, Prince received a $100 gift card to Vinny's Ristorante along with the grand prize of a new Moken kayak. The second-place prize was a crock pot. Mr. Manning reported that it will make a fine addition to his man cave. The Herald sends a hearty congratulations to all participants.

Although I had missed work Monday, Mr. Bridgewater for-gave the incident. He didn't give me my wages, but receiving an excused absence was better than nothing. After all, I spent most of the morning and the afternoon at the police station. At least Miss Jackson managed the place, and thankfully the crowd was light.

Most of the day Tuesday was spent at home. Dad set me up with his lawyer, who helped me ensure that the proper disser-tations and documents were filed for the kidnapping charges. At the same time, we returned to the police station after lunch to sign a few more documents. Finally, half past four, it seemed like life was beginning to quiet down again. As we left downtown, the tourists continued to come by the boatload, and everything seemed normal again.

Cheryn came by that Tuesday evening, and she brought Mariana along. Though she was still shy, Mariana was pleased to see me. As a token of her gratitude, she gave me a large peri-winkle blue pearl as a gift for helping her return home. She did not stay for long, however, and soon it was just Cheryn and me visiting again.

"I'm not sure if she still trusts humans yet," Cheryn said. "Give her time."

"Of course," I said. "I will. But Cheryn, can I ask you some-thing?"

She nodded.

"She said you both had an argument. What was it?"

Cheryn smiled. "She didn't want me to sit on your dock anymore. She was afraid that I'd get into trouble. Then, Mariana didn't expect me to make friends."

"That's all?" I felt a little disappointed. "I mean, I had expect-ed some major disagreement." Given everything I had gone through with Cheryn, it was nice to know that drama didn't happen among mermaids as frequently as it did on land.

She smirked. "To be honest, Jessica, I felt right away that this place was fairly safe. Even still, I didn't make contact with you until that day when the water tasted different."

"Does the water taste cleaner again?"

She shook her head again. "Smokier. If anything, it came from the residue of the underwater flares that Trom had used in capturing Mariana that very night. Other times when there have been fireworks fired off nearby, the taste of smoke has stayed above the water. This time was different, and that's why I began to get curious."

"I asked you this earlier, and I'm still wondering. Why did you come to my dock?"

Cheryn gave a shrug as she gazed into the starry night sky. "I guess I liked the music you played all those years ago. Why did you stop playing?"

I couldn't give her an answer. Why? Because I didn't know myself.

"Maybe you needed an audience," she said with a smile. "You should play the piano again sometime, but only if you want to."

I nodded. "I will."

"Don't worry too much about Mariana," Cheryn said. "She already looks healthier from being home again, and she'll warm up to you. She needs friends too."

~  ~

That night, the weather was foggy and cool much like it had been when I first met Cheryn. Dad and Tim had gone into town for ice cream, and although it sounded fun, I declined. I was too caught up in my own thoughts. Meeting Cheryn, then Mariana, and everything about Rachel that had happened stuck with me. But soon, I had sat down at the piano and began to play. My first song might've been *Moonlight Sonata* by Beethoven. Next, I tried to play "The Rose." I made a lot of mistakes. Maybe it was time to take lessons.

Dad brought me back a strawberry sundae, my favorite. Although the sundae had melted slightly from the ride home, the dessert really hit the spot. While my mother had always told me never to rely on sweets to cheer up, this time it did the trick.

Before going to sleep that night, I sat at my desk and stared out the window. Everything that had happened was remarkable, but somehow, I still felt that I hadn't succeeded in telling everyone that I had met a mermaid in a manner that wouldn't get me laughed out of school. Taking my pencil in hand, I began to write down everything that had happened since July 4th. Somehow, seeing everything on the page in front me finally convinced me that those events had not only happened and were real, but could become real to those who read them.

As I continued to write, the words became blurry and my hands attempted to give up, but I had to get every word out. Towards the end, I must've fallen asleep. The following morning I'd wake with a wicked pain in my neck and drool splattered across the final page.

Sunday July 19th, 2009
Friday Harbor Herald

We at the Herald are pleased to announce the results of our sixth annual writing contest. There were twenty-four total entries. Eleven entries were submitted for poetry, while eight entries were fiction with the remaining six composed of creative non-fiction essays. All the awards were given out at a special ceremony at The Happy Clam diner last night, Saturday the 18th. After a night filled with seafood, salmon and salad, our youth winners were celebrated and announced as follows.

Courtney Christensen, a Junior from Friday Harbor High School, received the Poetry prize with her 26-line poem "Flowers in the Starry Sky."

Paul Engfer, a Freshman from Friday Harbor High, won the Fiction prize with his piece entitled "Patriotism on the Horizon."

Sofia Bakken, a Sophomore college student currently enrolled at UW Anacortes, won the Essay prize with her essay "How Fireworks and Funnel Cakes Saved My Beagle."

For their efforts, each winning author received a gift card to Amazon for $100 along with a certificate to commemorate their efforts. In addition, their story will be published in today's paper. All prizes were furnished by Herald staff. A heartfelt thank you goes out to those of you who entered. Readers are encouraged to visit our webpage to view all entries submitted.

Today is half price hot dog day at The Happy Clam. Mention this writing contest to receive a free medium malt with the purchase of an any meal basket.

For the better part of the week I worked on my essay before turning it in at the last moment. Perhaps writing down an account of my adventure with Cheryn hadn't been the best idea, but Dad encouraged sharing my story about the mermaids in San Juan Channel. Even though I had convinced one member of the Ichthyology Division that mermaids existed, it seemed the word of Douglas Rovan would convince few others. I had least one admirer, but again, even though fathers loved their daughters dearly, rarely did that affect pop culture or public opinion. In the end, the story would add to the local flavor without ruining Cheryn's efforts to remain hidden.

In the meantime, we had the rest of the summer to concern ourselves with. School was four weeks away, and we were free to enjoy it again. Cheryn was reading the essay as Naomi shared a new batch of blueberry muffins as the three of us gathered along the dock as the final rays of sunset overtook the sky. Cheryn and I sat on the bench while Naomi sat on the edge of the dock just in front of us.

"You didn't win the contest?" Naomi asked as she placed her own copy on the dock. "How could they not select yours? That's impossible."

"They didn't like that I submitted it as an essay," I replied. "Apparently the judging board thought it should be fiction."

Cheryn folded the essay closed after reading the final page. "I love the title."

Naomi held it up and read the title quietly. "My Adventure with Cheryn." She gave a nod. "The title certainly delivers what it advertises. What do you like about it the most?"

"I don't know, it has a nice ring to it," Cheryn smirked. "I'm sorry you didn't win, Jess."

"I'm okay with it," I replied. "After all, the world's not yet ready to believe that mermaids are real and living nearby."

Cheryn nodded. "Agreed."

From the deck on the back of my house, Dad gave a yell. "Jess! Martin and John are here. Should I bring out the marshmallows?"

"Guess it's time to start a fire," I said.

Naomi stood up. "Leave it to me."

"Jess, it's taken almost two weeks for you to introduce me to some mores," Cheryn said.

"S'mores," I said with a smile.

"S'mores," she corrected herself. "Will tonight finally be the night?"

"Oh yes," I said. "And I promise, the wait will be worth it."

Twenty minutes later, John delivered Cheryn to a bean bag cushion he had brought specially for her. It was made of a waterproof canvas, and as the material was sapphire blue in color, the seat matched her scales perfectly. That way, anyone cruising along the channel wouldn't notice her tailfin as easily as they might otherwise. Martin had brought something special for Cheryn as well, delivering it inside of a basket wrapped with a ribbon and a towel.

"So many gifts tonight," Cheryn said as she unwrapped the towel. Inside the basket was a black beret, exactly her size. "This is wonderful! Thank you so much."

"I thought you needed something beside the sun hat," Martin said. "For meetings."

Cheryn put the beret on, finding it was a perfect fit that actually accented her red hair. "When I wear this in the air, I won't have to brush the hair out of my face all the time!"

"You're very welcome," Martin said before sitting across from her.

Naomi handed out several skewers with a pair of marshmallows mounted in place. "Does anyone have any objections, or shall we begin?"

"No objections," Martin said.

"Ready," John said.

"Absolutely ready," Cheryn said.

"Excellent." I smiled and addressed the group. "Welcome to tonight's meeting of the Red Shoe Adventure Club."

Friday, July 4th, 2010
Friday Harbor Herald

    Tonight's patriotic festivities will be held at Saturday Square, across from the Saturday Square Juice Bar. Ferry service will be suspended from 5 PM until midnight. Westbound passengers should take note that the Seath will not depart for Sidney, B.C. until that time, should any passengers require travel after an evening of fireworks, frankfurters, and firecracker cotton candy. Eastbound passengers, please take note that the Chelan will not depart for Anacortes, Was. until the following morning at 6:45 a.m. July 5th.

    The Friday Harbor Festival begins at 1 p.m. with a parade lead by the Friday Harbor Marching Sailors, followed by the Main Street Fair and our annual blueberry pie eating contest. All entries for the baking contest must be received by 12 noon. Applications for the triathlon must be received by 10 a.m. There is no fee to participate in either event.

    Be sure to attend this year's annual presentation of "Pig War Picnic" presented by volunteers from the local Kiwanis club. The curtain drops at 3:00 p.m. on the grounds of the San Juan Historical Museum, weather permitting. Visitors of all ages are welcome. Donations of food and gently used clothing are encouraged. Proceeds will benefit the local chapter and are greatly appreciated.

    Don't forget about our seventh annual writing contest, open to all writers, containing an essay about your favorite moment of this year's celebration. We welcome all kinds of stories, poems, or essays that show our town festival in its best light. Contest entries 5,000 words or less for fiction or essay or poems amounting to less than 40 lines must be submitted by July 15th. Please include your name, age, and a short bio separate from the entry that shows your patriotism. Please be sure your entry is added to the correct contest. Remember, this contest is closed to Friday Harbor Herald staff members and their families. All rules, judging criteria, and age categories can be found on the newspaper website. Submit your contest entry today and get the most out of your July 4th Celebration!

    A special message from Mayor Goldwater: Prior to tonight's fireworks, all street lights and exterior lighting around the downtown district will be dimmed. Local businesses and docked boats are encouraged to dim any interior or exterior lights while the show is underway. Firework patrons are encouraged to bring flashlights, but refrain their use during the show unless there is an emergency. All street lighting will return to normal levels following the finale. Remember to keep track of your loved ones. Celebrate safely and enjoy your day!

After a full day of excitement at Saturday Square, I returned home to find that I would not be watching the fireworks alone. Dad and Tim watched from the deck. John, Martin, and their folks formed a line of chairs in front of the deck, along with Rachel and Naomi's parents.

Out on the dock, however, the prime seats were reserved. Rachel and Naomi each brought a chair to the end, sitting so that if they leaned back, they could see the entire sky. John and Martin sat in the canoe, which remained tightly fixed to the dock with ropes on both ends. Mariana also joined the group, opting to sit along the edge of the dock right in front. The best seats, of course, belonged to Cheryn and me. We sat side by side atop the bench. All of us gazed up toward the stars as the glow from the downtown lights faded to black.

Our eyes grew wide as the first firework kissed the night sky. We were in for the greatest adventure of the year.

Afterward

When I first wrote about the San Juan Islands, I had yet to set foot in Friday Harbor. The reality of the place is incredible; there is beauty similar to that of the north woods mixed with a taste of oceanside sea air on a landscape of shadowed islands across foggy waters. The entire region is a wonder from any angle. It is a place where stories happen every day.

For many years, I have been working on a story idea where a group of kids assemble over a campfire telling stories to each other. I'll admit it's an old-fashioned idea in a modern age of smartphones, the Internet, and social media. But even in times like these, the old standbys continue to remain relevant. Growing up in Minnesota, I always imagined that the social campfire was a rite of passage. When you were listening to that ghost story, tale of that abandoned barn, or that fated walk through the woods, you were the sole audience of a director who had carefully choreographed a drama, comedy, or factual adventure that captured your interest explicitly. Nothing else mattered. The smoldering marshmallow on that stick of oak, the mosquito dancing around your ankles, the cool breeze coming off of the lake. You sat and listened to that story, letting it surround you. As the story unfolded, your world developed and changed into something more exciting. By the time the fireflies went to sleep and the stars were high above, you had not only listened to that story in its entirety, but lived it and even digested it.

As I continued to write stories and become more and more entranced by the siren song of the mermaid and her own unique set of legends, I began to embellish that original idea. "Hey, what would make a mermaid want to come to a camp-fire?" The questions continued. Why would she choose to go ashore, and what would she hope to find there? What would interest her other than marshmallows and chocolate? The idea stuck with me for a long time, and while I was able to formulate a few drafts, I had yet to find the right combination of settings, characters, and plot that felt complete.

Finally, I was in my final semester at Hamline University when I needed two more credits to graduate. The prospect of paying full price for another semester was daunting, and paying out of pocket for a summer class was equally as unlikely. The solution? Independent study. Go write a novel and discuss the writing process of a longer work compared to a short story. Motivation secured, the time came to tell Cheryn's story.

So, I needed to find a setting for this proposed work. I wanted it to take place in America, in a location where the characters could have access to the open ocean, and located on an island in order to keep the action contained to a small, managable setting. Most importantly, the location had to be large and modern enough to increase the potential cast of characters without becoming too overwhelming or complex. I've always enjoyed the splendor of the Pacific Northwest because of its similarity to Northern Minnesota and its lake culture, and with all its other amenities. Without question, Friday Harbor became the winning setting.

Fiction, even when created with a fantasy element, has to be researched and factual if it is to be accepted as believable by readers. Most of my initial research regarding the setting was performed on the Internet, where I discovered that the city had a high school, a library, a courthouse, and—ironically—a research camp. Friday Harbor had most everything I needed to construct my story—except for a few key features.

There needed to be a place large enough to host a small traveling amusement park. Hence, Saturday Square. The location I chose for this fictional square is set near the ferry station, north of the roundabout at the base of Spring and Front Streets. Saturday Square would feature a juice bar, a newspaper stand, and a small kiosk for whale watching tours, much like the waterfront does in real life. The difference was that the square itself could also be an attraction, changing itself as needed for various city functions, festivals, and seasonal celebrations. As this story occurs around the Fourth of July, a kidnapping had to occur near the Tilt-A-Whirl. Why? Because 'Tilt-A-Whirl' is fun sounding, specific place that invokes certain memories. Given the space of the ferry, a truck transporting a traveling carnival, presumably, could fit inside the loading area, ride to Friday Harbor, and open for business on the island. (That research was actually performed on board the Washington State Ferry System.) Much like the city commons in East Coast towns or the central park of a midwestern suburb, Saturday Square would be the center for holiday activities, and in this story, ground zero for a kidnapping.

As Friday Harbor is a city centered around the ferry and the waterfront, Jessica Summers is a young woman who knows her way around that space. She knows it as well as she does her backyard, and has to know her hometown in order to accomplish Cheryn's mission. For the purposes of the story, Jess had to live in a spot where she could see both the ferry, downtown Friday Harbor, the Marina, and the open channel, all with easy access to the water and a dock to enjoy them equally. Thus, her home is somewhere on Turn Point, overlooking Brown Island and the channel beyond. (Note that I did not actually search for her house or model her home off of an existing home for the novel, out of respect for residents in the area. This is also true of other character's homes.)

Without a clear view of the downtown area, Cheryn would never have wanted to visit Jessica there. Cheryn is a unique character among mermaid characters, for she does things that most mermaids would never do. She aspires to be an acrobat when she lives underwater, she doesn't always hide from others that are different than her, and she never hesitates to make an acquaintance when her very nature might suggest a solitary or secretive life.

Another aspect of the city that needed to be addressed for the purposes of the story was that of the local paper. Regrettably, I could not find any printed copies of the local paper when I visited Friday Harbor. I have found that there is a local paper—the San Juan Journal—but in my research, I discovered it is easier to find online. But for the purposes of my story, the Friday Harbor Herald made for a necessary plot point and, while a paper of that scope might only be printed weekly, needed to be printed daily for the updates in the chapters and the progress of Rachel Arlen's case. For this to fit the illusion into the story, it is implied that the paper could be printed or posted online.

The airport on San Juan Island is large enough for small prop jets and charter planes, which I've discovered come and go quite frequently. I was unable to turn over any research that confirmed plane crashes have occurred, however. For story purposes, there was little need to make any fictional alterations to this space.

The only remaining setting required was the research facility where Cheryn believed a fellow mermaid was being studied. While I did not have time to properly explore the American Camp or the University of Washington Camp Caution facility during my visit, their very existence confirmed that marine biology research occurs on San Juan Island. I envisioned the Jaquim Labs facility just north of the Camp Caution site, nestled behind the trees from the harbor and large enough to host a scuba training facility but small enough to remain hidden from the harbor. Hence, the building is only two stories tall. Of course, there is no facility of its kind in the real Friday Harbor. But if there was, what kinds of research would occur there? The waters of the Strait of Juan DeFuca are a wildlife preserve, and certainly the researchers there would monitor the waters for invasive species, plant life and the like. Thus, Douglas Rovan's job of a researcher at an ichthyology lab was created to give Naomi a reason to go to the facility, and an insider's guide toward locating Mariana.

Because this proposed facility would be small and space inside would be limited, it seemed impractical that any re-searchers would consider performing autopsies or vivisections on site. Hence, I flew in the team from Boston—who were talk-ing about their subject a little too loudly when their plane was scheduled to land—and would have taken Mariana from Friday Harbor to study her, had Jess and her friends not intervened.

Finally, I decided to be mum about the location of Kelsey's home and her mother's shop. I have a hard time imagining that anything illegal would have ever occurred in a shop like the Karma Korner, and have a respect for any entrepreneurial spirit who might run a shop like it. Kelsey herself, however, is, I'll admit, a bit of a stereotype. But her character is not without merit, for her motivations are real to her. She, like me, would love to believe that mermaids are real and populating the waters near her home. Suppose it's possible that a few others might share the same dream.

Most stories about mermaids set a goal of the mermaid wanting to become human. For Cheryn, that doesn't motivate her because for her to be human is neither realistic or necess-ary. She's content being who and what she is, something that many stories fail to address. I consider this an important life lesson, because at some point in our lives we begin to realize we may not ever have enough money to afford a luxury sports car, the opportunity to experience the Northern Lights or a full solar eclipse, or to walk on the moon. Our childhood dreams might never come true, and in the end, we learn to be content with what we have. To clarify, though, we should never stop dream-ing. To live without dreams is to never know what we are capable of.

After finally visiting the city of Friday Harbor in the summer of 2017, I was pleasantly surprised to discover that this was indeed the place to set Cheryn's story. Although this body of work is Cheryn's story, I chose to let the reader see it through

Jess's eyes. The islands have a mythical quality that, I suspect, a mermaid would love to call home. Its climate is warm enough, even in the wintertime, so that the waters don't freeze over like they do in Minnesota and other inland waterways. And, most importantly, the islands are incredibly beautiful, even when the fog rolls in.

When I boarded the ferry from Anacortes to Friday Harbor, the morning fog was so thick and grey that I couldn't see twenty feet past the railing. But halfway through the ride, the fog began to lift as the islands gradually revealed themselves. The damp clouds hung heavy and low, making the islands appear to hover in the mists. It was then I knew that Friday Harbor was the perfect place to set this novel.

Upon reaching Friday Harbor itself, the fog had lifted and a blue sky emerged. Spring Street is full of many interesting storefronts, filled with all kinds of useful items that tourists and locals alike would want or need. The Spring Street Deli, in particular, makes the best sandwich around. Clearly, the internet cannot prepare a traveler for the incredible place that Friday Harbor actually is. It only took me a few moments to realize how appropriate and correct a fit the place was for this story.

In the end, Friday Harbor impressed me in a way the internet could never hope to. Thus, I hope that the folks living on San Juan Island can forgive me for kidnapping one of their own, even if Rachel Arlen is but a character and might not have or ever lived there. I also hope they can forgive this tourist for blocking Turn Point Road on the afternoon that I visited, stopping to take pictures while locals were trying to go about their day. I enjoyed my time on the island, was awestruck by its size and beauty, and hope to visit again soon.

Before I wrap this up, let me challenge you to find places on the map that aren't New York, aren't Hollywood, and aren't Orlando. Places like Friday Harbor, which might seem off the beaten path and ordinary. It's places like these where real people live, and live genuinely, where the interesting stories occur. Even if you're only passing through a place like that for the day, stop and go into a shop on Main Street. Ask about the local restaurants. Try a locally made craft. Explore a local landmark. Skip the drive thru and get out of your car for a few hours. You might be surprised what you find.

Real stories are never scripted, and rarely happen on the well-traveled routes. Find your own, personal adventure, and never stop exploring.